CWA0471000

My Romantic Tangle

Middlemarch Shifters 13

Shelley Munro

My Romantic Tangle

Copyright © 2023 by Shelley Munro

Print ISBN: 978-1-99-106316-8
Digital ISBN: 978-0-9941433-1-0

Editor: Mary Moran

Cover: Kim Killion, The Killion Group

Munro Press, New Zealand.

First Munro Press electronic publication January 2017

First Munro Press print publication February 2023

For Paul

INTRODUCTION

ONE PLUS ONE EQUALS three.

Tiger shifter Hari Daya takes one look at Ambar Patel's photo and is smitten. Further research heightens his fascination. An arranged marriage would work, except the lady isn't buying and tells him to take a hike.

Ambar is already involved with human Jake Quinn. Casual pleasure and lovin' works best for her since she dreams of traveling the world and delving into new experiences. The frisson of heat and desire she feels for Hari is unacceptable. There will be no tiger mate for her.

Jake Quinn has no idea either his lover or his new friend are shifters, but there sure as hell is something weird going on in his head. As much as he enjoys sex with Ambar, he's thinking about Hari too. Suddenly there's kissing and togetherness way past his comfort zone. The slide into sinful pleasure with both Hari and Ambar is easy—it's the relationship dynamics that give them headaches and make them wonder if they're making a huge mistake.

CHAPTER ONE

HARI DAYA'S BREATH EASED out in a soundless whistle when he caught his first glimpse of Ambar Patel. His feline part froze, attention fixed on his prey.

No doubt about it—he wanted her.

One glance at her striking exotic looks, the nubile curves, and he knew he'd been right to stealthily liberate her file from his cousin and travel halfway around the world to locate her.

While she looked attractive in the photo he'd carried with him for the last six months, the flat black-and-white portrait didn't capture her essence. It didn't show the teasing sparkle of her eyes or the luster of her long, black hair. It did nothing to showcase her easy manner with the customers who shopped for groceries at the Patel Store or the sensuous way she moved despite her height and robust frame.

His.

A rush of air escaped him, the accompanying rumble sounding like a purr of contentment. After a quick glance in both directions to see if anyone was watching, he lifted his nose and opened his mouth, dragging the breath across his receptors to test the early morning air for scent.

Yeah, she was all tiger.

Satisfaction throbbed in him, even though Hari knew winning her wouldn't be easy. Marriage brokers arranged matches in the local Indian community in London where he'd spent most of his life. It was a way to ensure wealth stayed in the family, for prestige to remain intact, but one look at Ambar told him everything. He wanted her in his bed and in his life.

And he'd do anything to get her there.

The idea of a stealthy hunt didn't bother him. Seduction—his feline rather liked the idea. Another purr erupted along with a pleased grin. He had plenty of money and had no need of a dowry to sweeten his bank account. No impediment there.

He'd placed the official things in motion already, applying and receiving the necessary documentation to start a new life in New Zealand. With his computer skills, it wasn't difficult to obtain work, and he'd covered that angle quickly, signing a contract for freelance design work he could take care of while he set up base in Middlemarch.

City born and bred, the countryside captured his heart—the endless green and open spaces. The mountains and the crisp, exhaust-free air. It was easy to see why the Patels had moved from Auckland to the South Island of New Zealand. The sense of freedom sang through him, enticing his feline to run and play. Other cats lived in the area—he could smell them along with the Patels' distinctive tiger scent. On one level that pleased him, but it made him realize he shouldn't dally outside on the street, spying on Ambar Patel like a voyeur. Six months had passed, and he had to make sure no one else had claimed her first.

Time to make his move.

Straightening, Hari switched his laptop bag from one hand to the other and strode toward the store, sighing when Ambar moved out of sight. Impatiently, he waited for a mother and daughter to leave. He pushed the door open, setting off a bell. The tinkle faded seconds after the door closed behind him. The faint strains of off-key humming drifted from behind the scenes, making him smile.

He marched up to the counter, unaccountably nervous because this meeting was so important. "Hello?"

Footsteps sounded, and Ambar came into sight again. He felt his lips curve in the beginnings of a smile and opened his mouth to speak. Nothing came out.

Aghast, he snapped his mouth shut so he didn't look like the village idiot. That would be a first and a terrible impression on the woman he wanted to spend the rest of his life making happy.

Swallowing, he tried again. "Hi, I'm Hari Daya." He stuck out his hand and waited for her to take it, desperate to touch even in an innocent way. His breath eased out with a whoosh when she clasped his hand. Soft and feminine, the touch left him with sex on his mind. He couldn't wait to experience her fingers wandering his naked body.

"It's nice to meet you, Hari." Her welcoming smile faded while he stood there like a fool. "I'd like my hand back now." She tugged to emphasize her point.

"Sorry." Damn, this wasn't going the way he'd intended. He released her hand, his heart beating a fraction faster. Who knew he'd turn into an idiot the minute he stepped into her proximity? He wiped his clammy palms on his jeans-clad thighs. A first, that's for sure. He continued to stare, imprinting her image in his mind so he could recall it later. Belatedly, he noticed the pucker of her forehead, a cute wrinkle between her golden-brown eyes.

"I'm here to marry you," he blurted. "I need to speak to your brother."

For an instant she stared at him, her mouth dropping open. Then her teeth clacked together, her lips pursing in a firm line. Pure fire erupted in her eyes. "Out!" The thrust of her finger indicated the direction.

"Huh?"

Before he could say another word, she was around the counter and shoving on his shoulders, pushing him to the door.

Hari was so surprised and distracted by her touch he didn't put up a fight. She propelled him outside.

"We're closed," she snapped at the elderly man about to enter. Then she slammed the door and shot the bolt, turning the *Open* sign to show *Closed*, every line of her body indicating fury.

"What was that about?" the elderly man asked.

"I have no idea," Hari said, irritation building inside him. Anger at himself. At her. He hadn't handled that well. It's true he wasn't exactly pretty to look at—not like his cousin. The scar he'd received during a childhood squabble zigzagged down the left side of his face. But he had a nice smile. Other women told him that, and he took care of himself. Damn. What the hell should he do now? Surely his scar didn't bother her? Some women couldn't get past it, and over the years he'd become used to people staring. It didn't bother him, not as much as it had during his teen years. "I suppose they'll open again later?"

The elderly man didn't seem particularly perturbed. "No doubt young Rohan will come along soon."

He wandered off, leaving Hari wondering what to do next. A glance up the street showed a café. The number of vehicles parked outside attested to the fact it was open and the food half-decent. His stomach grumbled and that decided him. A cup of coffee and something to eat would do a lot to settle his nerves while he pondered his next move.

Hari pushed the door of Storm in a Teacup open and stepped inside. He ordered a coffee and a cooked breakfast at the counter before checking for a table. All full. That would be right, considering the way his morning had gone already.

The woman behind the counter noticed his dilemma. Feline, he determined after an unobtrusive sniff. "See the guy with brown hair sitting alone at the table in the far corner? That's Jake. He won't mind sharing. Just head over and introduce yourself."

"Thanks." At least not all the natives were hostile. He navigated past a child's stuffed toy and an ornately carved walking stick leaning against the corner of a table before stopping where the woman had indicated. "Hi, I'm Hari Daya. The woman at the counter said you wouldn't mind if I shared your table."

"Jake Quinn," the man said, his easy grin putting Hari at ease. Jake registered the scar on Hari's face, but his behavior didn't change. "Take a seat."

"Is the café always this busy?" Hari asked, glancing at the full tables.

"Pretty much," Jake said. "Emily Mitchell owns the place and does the cooking. Most of the employees are family."

Human, Hari thought. He sensed curious eyes on him and caught the faint scent of feline. At least they didn't attack first and ask questions later. In some regions, they didn't welcome strangers, either feline or human. A little research on Middlemarch had reassured him nothing untoward would occur after his arrival unless he invited trouble.

Most of the shifters living in the community were black leopard, although he understood there were lions and tigers now that the Patels had moved to the area. All the felines lived in secrecy, participating in community activities without their human neighbors suspecting a thing.

"What brings you to Middlemarch?" Jake asked.

"Some of my friends said it was a great town." Hari didn't want to say too much and mention the Patels. Small town gossip was the last thing he needed. "I'm actually looking for somewhere to stay for a few months while I do some freelance design work." And try to court Ambar Patel, he added silently.

Jake glanced at Hari's laptop bag. "Computer design?"

Hari nodded, far more comfortable talking about his work than his reasons for arriving in Middlemarch. "I'm designing websites for a firm in Auckland. Sometimes I do sites for large companies and other times it's for a small business or someone who is self-employed. Last month I designed a website for an erotic romance author." He paused to gauge the other man's interest before he continued. "I like the variety, and the job gives me plenty of time to work on the game I'm designing."

"A game? Can you tell me more or is it top secret?" Jake's blue eyes sparkled with enthusiasm and genuine interest. He didn't avert his gaze from Hari's scar or show distaste, instead treating him like any other new acquaintance. Jake's casual manner put Hari at ease.

"It's a fantasy game about a horse race on a foreign planet. The players have to catch a hell-horse and train it to race. They have to navigate the local customs and the aliens on the planet, face the weird hell-horses and all sorts of dangers before they get to race their horse. It's a race to the death and the hell-horses eat each other. The first over the finish line or the last one standing is the winner."

"Sounds gruesome. Gamers will love it. What are you calling the game? Do you need someone to test it for you?"

"I'm calling it *House of the Cat* because one of the main characters is a feline shifter." Hari paused to study Jake and saw he was serious. Interest sparked to life in him, one Hari would have described as sexual if Jake had been a member of the opposite sex. Embarrassed by the weird thought, he rushed to speak. "Actually, someone to help me test the game would be great. I have to find somewhere to live, but once I'm set up, I'll get in touch." Hari pulled out his wallet and handed Jake one of the business cards he'd designed and printed the previous evening. They displayed his email address and his new cell phone number.

"I can do better than that. I live on a farm. My father and I used to run it together, but he had a mild heart attack and decided to turn it over to me. You can stay with me. I have to admit the money would come in handy and I could use the company. You're not a smoker, are you?"

"No, I don't smoke. What about women?" Hari asked.

Jake blinked. "What about them?"

"Now that you're living alone do you have drunken parties and women visiting all nights of the week? I don't mind a party now and then, and I don't begrudge a man feminine company, but after flatting with my cousin and his friends and suffering through nonstop parties, I don't want to try to work with that sort of distraction again."

"You don't expect me to live like a monk?"

"Hell no," Hari said. "A happy medium works for me."

Jake chuckled. "Works for me too. Why don't you visit later today and check out the place? Most days I'm working on the farm and you won't see much of me until the evening."

A different woman arrived with their breakfasts and set the plates in front of them. "Is that everything?"

"Thanks, Isabella," Jake said. "This is Hari. He's moving to Middlemarch. Hari, this is Isabella Mitchell. Unfortunately, she's married. I keep asking her to run off with me, but she persists in saying no."

"Pleased to meet you." He winked at Jake. "Maybe I'll have more success."

Isabella snorted. "Please! It took me a long time to catch Leo. I'm not throwing my fish back."

"I'm not sure Leo would appreciate being compared to a fish." Jake smirked up at her, and for the second time today Hari felt pleased with his decision to move to Middlemarch. A woman. A new friend who liked gaming. For once things were working out for him.

"We won't tell Leo," Hari promised.

"I might tell him." Isabella shook her head, but it was easy to see the humor lurking just out of sight. "Enjoy your breakfast." She left to answer the summons of a bell.

"So what do you say?" Jake slathered butter over a slice of whole grain toast. "You'd have your own bedroom and en suite."

"How much will you charge me?"

Jake frowned. "How about two hundred a week plus you pay a share of the groceries and power? Does that sound reasonable?"

More than reasonable. It sounded on the cheap side to Hari, not that he was about to argue. "Sounds great. When can I come and check it out?"

"Could you come with me after we're done here?"

"Works for me." It would give him time to make sure Rohan was at the store for him to speak with in person and

11

maybe Ambar as well.

Things moved quickly after their breakfast. Hari viewed the room at Jake's and agreed to his terms. He unpacked his rental car, made himself at home and headed back down the winding gravel road to the township of Middlemarch. It was time to meet Rohan Patel and discuss his marriage to Ambar.

"ROHAN. ROHAN!" AMBAR STOMPED into the house she shared with her brother and his mate Kiran. The scent of freshly brewed coffee made her turn in the direction of the kitchen. She burst through the doorway and glared at them both before focusing on Rohan.

"I asked you to do one thing. One thing! And did you do it? Oh no." She threw up her hands in disgust, her scowl intensifying.

Kiran took one look at her face and stood. "Maybe I should go."

"Sit," Ambar ordered. "Rohan, you didn't cancel the marriage broker."

"I did so." Rohan met her gaze without a hint of deceit. "I cancelled the contract with the marriage broker and told him his services were no longer required."

"Then why did a man turn up in the store this morning and tell me he'd come to marry me?"

"What man? Where is he?"

Ambar glowered at both men. "I pushed him out of the store, slammed the door in his face and hightailed it straight here." She twisted the golden band on her right hand, the ring she'd inherited from her mother and wore to remind herself of her desire to live an independent life. While men were lots of fun, she didn't need one to survive. She did not need a mate to complete her life.

"Why didn't you bring him here? Or ask him to wait at the store and call me so we could sort it out?"

"I'm not marrying him, and you can't make me." She wrenched on the gold band again, trying not to think about him. Hari.

"Rohan doesn't intend to force you to marry anyone," Kiran said, handing her a mug of coffee. His unruffled manner went a long way to restoring her calm.

"I can't believe you closed the store," Rohan complained. "How are we going to grow our business with you shutting shop at the slightest provocation?"

"Provocation? You call this provocation?" Ambar snapped, the fragile hold on her temper fraying again. "I supported you and Kiran. I expect you to tell this...this man to leave Middlemarch and never come back. I told him, but I expect he'll only listen to a male."

Rohan pushed back his chair and stood, circling the table to stand at her side. For a moment Ambar wanted to deck him until she registered the concern on his face. All the fight drained from her. Deep down, she didn't think he'd arrange a marriage for her. He knew she valued her independence, but he didn't know of her desire to travel. She hadn't confided her list of dream destinations to anyone.

"Finish your coffee and we'll go back to the store

together."

"But what if he's gone?"

Kiran chuckled. "Isn't that what you want?"

"He was actually quite nice," Ambar said, recalling his tentative manner. "He had an awful scar on his face. I'd hate for him to think I acted like a boor because I couldn't bear to look at him. I think he was nervous."

"Where was he from? Did he say?" Rohan asked.

"I didn't give him a chance." Ambar frowned, trying to recall his face in detail. Apart from the scar, she didn't remember much. "He wasn't from India. He sounded English to me."

Rohan took a sip of coffee. "I wonder if Dad used a broker over in England as well as the one in India. There's a large Indian community in Manchester and a smaller one in London. I didn't find anything in the paperwork in the office. Did he ask to speak with me?"

"Of course he did. I was consigned to the little woman box straightaway," Ambar snapped, her top lip curling in disdain.

"Why didn't you just tell him to piss off?" Kiran sipped his coffee, studying her carefully like one of his animal patients. "Why did you flick your tail and run away? You know a male tiger's typical response is to chase."

She winged him a glare. "I did *not* flick my tail. I'm not interested in another man. You know I'm dating Jake."

Rohan's brows rose and his lips quivered as if he was trying not to laugh. "But you did run away."

The hot air whooshed out of her at the challenge. Heck, they were right. Why hadn't she told him to take a hike? She thought back and focused on everything she remembered about the man. His scar. His height—about four inches taller than her—and his English accent. She thought a bit harder and it hit her. His scent. He'd smelled familiar, and when she'd heard the tinkle of the doorbell, she'd thought it was Jake. She'd always liked the way Jake smelled. It was one of the first things that had attracted her to him, and from there things had advanced until they shared a bed on a regular basis.

Sin.

A smile curved her lips at the thought of Jake's muscular and very naked body moving against hers. She did love to sin with Jake, even if her parents were rolling in their graves with horror, shame filling them at the antics of their once virginal daughter.

Yeah, Hari had smelled much like Jake. Male chocolate, she thought with a satisfied smirk. Weird. She'd never come across anyone whose smell captivated her in the same manner.

Ambar nodded. "You're right. I did run away. I panicked when he said he'd come to marry me. I don't want to get married."

"What about Jake?"

"Jake is happy as he is—single. Besides, he's too busy with the farm. Sometimes we go for a week without seeing each other."

"Fuck buddies," Kiran said with a grin at Rohan.

Rohan growled deep in his throat and both Kiran and Ambar laughed. They'd had this discussion before. Rohan said their parents wouldn't approve, and Ambar always countered that he could talk, living openly with another male.

"I'll talk with him," she said, knowing she owed it to the man. "I'd hate him to think I ran off because I didn't like the way he looked. I actually shoved him out of the store."

Kiran's lips twitched. "Shoved?"

"I think I got away with it because I took him by surprise. He didn't put up a fight. If he'd wanted to, he could have pushed back."

"Which says a lot about him," Kiran said. "The men I knew wouldn't have put up with a woman shoving them around."

Ambar stuck out her chest. "I'm not an ordinary woman." The tilt of her chin dared them to say otherwise.

"I'll come with you for moral support," Rohan said. "Besides, if he's from the old school he'll insist on discussing the matter with me. Are you done with your coffee?"

"I'd better go," Kiran said. "Gavin and I are doing rounds this morning."

"Anything interesting?" Ambar asked. Kiran worked with Gavin Finley, the local vet and feline doctor.

"Time will tell." Kiran stood to stack his dirty dishes in the dishwasher.

"Okay, let's get this done," Ambar said, impatient now to get her life back on an even keel.

"You might have scared him off," Rohan said as they left their house to walk to the store.

"You didn't see the expression on his face." Now that Ambar had realized she'd memorized his scent, she wanted

16

to see him again. It was purely scientific interest of course. "Did you want me to do the orders this morning?"

"If you want." Rohan pulled the keys to the rear door from his pocket and unlocked it, standing aside to let Ambar enter.

The phone rang as they stepped inside and someone thumped on the front door.

"I'll get the phone," Ambar said. If that was Hari pounding on the door, she'd let Rohan deal with him first. Suddenly, she felt unsure. She hated the idea of marriage and commitment to a mate. Instead, she wanted to experience life and enjoy some of the normal things other girls her age took for granted, things she'd missed while living with her ultra-strict parents.

Their antiquated desires for an arranged marriage shouldn't stir uncertainties in her the way they did. While she'd loved them, respected them, it didn't mean their way was the right way.

Ambar grabbed the phone just as the faint tinkle of the front door indicated Rohan had opened for business. "Patel Store," she said. "Yes, we can have your order ready for you. Two o'clock. Sure. Let me grab a pen and paper. Okay, I'm ready." Ambar took the order, suggesting a couple of specials to the customer. She checked through the stock orders and faxed them to the warehouse before she left the office. Taking a deep breath, she rounded the corner to find Rohan serving a customer.

Hari Daya wasn't waiting for her, and to her annoyance, she experienced a blip of disappointment, although she couldn't for the life of her understand why.

The morning passed with a steady stream of customers. Hari still didn't come. Chagrin replaced her trepidation. Wasn't she good enough to fight for? Why was he giving up so easily? Awareness of the contradictory nature of her thoughts brought irritation. The man couldn't be bothered to face her again before he left. Too bad. What did she care when marriage was the last thing on her mind?

She had the gorgeous Jake to fill her sexual needs, plenty of friends and a good relationship with Rohan and Kiran.

Okay. Hari wasn't coming to visit again. She was over it.

The clock on the wall above the counter clicked over to midday. "I might make a sandwich and a cup of tea before I enter the invoices into the computer," she said. "Do you want one?"

"Please."

Humming under her breath, Ambar headed for the tiny kitchen area and made sandwiches and a pot of tea. During the months since their arrival in Middlemarch they'd fallen into a routine that worked for both of them. When Rohan had first mentioned the idea of relocating to the country, she'd balked. He'd talked her around, pointing out the advantages of other felines and open spaces, and the big one—their own business with their names above the door instead of their parents'. She was glad she'd agreed to the move.

"Rohan, lunch is ready. I'm heading to the office."

"Thanks."

Ambar switched the radio on low, humming along and occasionally bursting into song. According to Kiran, her singing voice sounded like a frog on a bad day, but that didn't stop her enjoyment as she ate her sandwich and started work.

The tinkle of the doorbell continued throughout the afternoon. A lot of tourists popped in to grab drinks and small items to tuck into their backpacks before they tackled the Otago Rail Trail, and now that the locals realized their prices were reasonable, they had a steadily increasing trade. During the first few weeks of opening, a large number of single males had dropped in for their groceries. That continued despite the fact she and Jake were together, albeit in a casual manner.

Thoughts of Jake led her to thoughts of sex, and excitement tugged at her. They had a date tonight. Maybe she'd suggest they stay in and watch a movie, get busy on the couch. A smile curled across her lips. She did love to get busy with Jake.

Another customer arrived. Cocking her head to listen, she heard the rumble of masculine voices. Foreboding cinched her stomach tight.

Rohan stuck his head around the corner. "Got a minute?"

"Sure." A tremor went through her hand and she clenched her fingers to a fist as she pushed up from her seat and went to join Rohan.

She smelled him seconds before she saw him.

Hari Daya.

Her steps slowed while she took in his appearance. He had short black hair with a slight wave to it and skin a fraction darker than hers. She and Rohan had inherited fair skins that told of English ancestors and she guessed Hari's family tree held similar blood. Tall and fit in appearance, he looked good. True, the scar on his face wasn't pretty, but he had nice eyes—brown with light golden flecks. For the right woman, he'd make a good husband.

"I'm sorry I was so rude earlier," she said, extending her hand in greeting. Unbidden, an astonishing thought popped into her head. What would he look like naked?

Hari took her hand, and she had to fight not to jerk from his grasp. A series of tingles swept up her arm, reinforced by the naked image in her mind that refused to budge. Immediately, her nipples tightened, pulling to hard peaks and brushing against the cups of her silky bra with each of her startled breaths. She knew without a downward glance her nipples broadcasted her unexpected arousal loud and clear. With a gasp, she yanked her hand free, aware of the heat collecting in her face.

"It's all right," Hari said, his English accent curiously seductive to her ear. "Rohan told me he'd canceled the contract with the marriage bureau."

Realizing she was still staring, Ambar moved away to stand by Rohan. She caught the touch of amusement in his eyes and glared at him.

"It was our parents' idea," Ambar blurted, wishing he didn't smell so good...like...like catnip.

Hari inclined his head. "Parents often think they know what's best for us. At least it gave us a chance to meet." He smiled, and Ambar found herself staring again. A smile transformed his face, making her forget the scar. "Thanks for talking with me." He glanced at Rohan. "Great to meet you." With another nod, he left the store.

"That wasn't as bad as I thought it might be." Rohan's smirk announced brotherly teasing ahead.

"Yeah, I'll go and finish entering the statements." Ambar left without giving Rohan a chance to torment her. What the hell had happened in there? If she'd met him in a bar or at a party, she would have shown interest without a qualm. The moment she'd touched him again she wanted to get to know him better, wanted to touch more than his hand. It had been his scent at first then he'd smiled.

Groaning softly, Ambar dropped onto a chair. She closed her eyes and her parents' faces popped to mind. They bore approval and were nodding with encouragement. They would've supported a match with Hari. She knew it without a doubt.

Guilt assailed her, bringing another groan. She was doing the right thing, sending him away. If she'd agreed to go ahead with an arranged marriage her life wouldn't be her own. She'd have to move wherever her husband ordered, away from Rohan and Kiran and her friends. After following commands for the majority of her life, she refused to give that much power to a man.

Besides, once she'd saved enough money, she intended to travel, start ticking places and experiences off her list. While that might mean she'd leave her family and friends one day, at least she'd do it on her terms.

No, this was better. Despite the glimmer of attraction toward him, she'd live the life she and Rohan had always wanted with freedom. Her own choices. No arranged marriage for her.

The rest of the afternoon passed in a daze, her concentration shot. Her mind kept returning to Hari, which was plain wrong since she was with Jake. She liked Jake. They had fun together. A smile curled across her lips. Jake was hot and the sex between them incredible. Each time with Jake, she thought the pleasure couldn't improve, yet it did.

The store closed and both she and Rohan left for home. The phone rang not long after they stepped indoors.

"It's for you, Ambar," Rohan shouted from the kitchen. "Jake."

She picked up the extension, a grin on her face. "Hi." She couldn't wait to see him.

"I'm running late. I had problems with a couple of ewes and had to call the vet," Jake said the moment she answered the phone. He sounded exhausted.

"We don't need to go out tonight. Why don't I come to your place? I'll bring a casserole for dinner and we can watch a movie or something."

He hesitated, and Ambar could almost see the frown on his forehead. "Are you sure? We can still go out."

"I'm positive." Some quality time with Jake would push Hari right out of her head and reinforce exactly what she wanted—freedom to make her own decisions.

AN UNFAMILIAR CAR SAT outside Jake's house when Ambar arrived. Surely Jake didn't have visitors now when he was so tired?

22

She grabbed the casserole dish from the passenger seat, and after a brief knock, she opened the front door and entered the house. The scent of food drifted to her. Exotic spices. A curry of some sort.

Ambar burst into the kitchen. "Jake, I thought I was making—" She came to an abrupt halt and blinked, trying to clear the naked image that sprang to mind the second she saw him. "You! What are you doing here?"

"I live here," Hari said.

"But you...you...said you were leaving." Good grief. She was stuttering. Ambar swallowed. "You said you were leaving Middlemarch." Fate was laughing her arse off right now.

"I never said that." Hari turned away to stir something in a pot. "Jake said you were coming around. He's in the shower. Do you want a drink? There's a bottle of white wine in the fridge."

"Wine? Ah sure. Okay. I'll get it." Ambar set the casserole on the counter and grabbed a wineglass from the cupboard. "Do you want one?"

"I'll take a beer, thanks."

Hari didn't seem surprised to see her. Did he realize she and Jake were together? Lovers? He didn't seem uncomfortable with the fact. It made her feel better about sending him away despite the dash of pique sprinkling her relief. Even now her skin tingled because of him and she didn't like it one bit. Pressing her lips together, she handed him a can of beer. "I'll go and see how long Jake will be."

Ambar hurried down the passage to the bathroom, trying to tell herself she wasn't fleeing. She knocked on the

23

door and stuck her head into the bathroom. "Jake?"

"Hey!" He grinned at her and wrapped a towel around his waist.

Her gaze ran across his chest and the faint trail of hair that ran beneath the towel. Her agitation faded, replaced by frank appreciation. "Don't dress on my account."

"I wouldn't want to scare my new roomie."

"Hari is staying?" Ambar had no idea what was going on here. Confusion. Yep, her new middle name. "Here?"

"Hari wanted to stay in Middlemarch. He said he knew people here and intended to stay longer. I can use the company and the money, so it works out for both of us."

Ambar nodded, but all she could think was that Jake didn't know the truth. He didn't know Hari had traveled from the other end of the world to marry her. Anger flared to life, and she lifted her chin. If Hari wanted to play games, let him. She refused to change her mind about marrying him. She ignored the frisson of excitement she'd felt the second time they met, the way she couldn't push either him or his enticing scent from her mind.

None of that mattered. Her life would progress without an arranged marriage, without Hari Daya.

Oh yeah. Let the games begin.

CHAPTER TWO

"I'll let you get dressed," Ambar said.

"You don't have to leave." The glow in Jake's blue eyes gave her a fair idea of what he had in mind.

"Later." To take the sting off her abruptness, she moved closer, curling her fingers into his biceps and kissed him. A hum of pleasure hit her as their lips touched, followed by a dose of his addictive scent—the one she found so pleasing yet so difficult to describe. It contained a hint of soap, the muskiness of man and an indefinable something she could never express in words. Hari's scent held the same unknown quantity.

It pleased her feline so much she had the urge to shift to tiger and wallow in the deliciousness of it. Now wouldn't that scare the crap out of Jake? She snorted inwardly, feeling snippy because inappropriate thoughts of Hari were spoiling this intimate moment with her hottie.

When she pulled back, he grinned at her. "Are you sure

we can't head straight to the bedroom?"

"I'm starving," Ambar protested. "You'll have to feed me first." Her stomach rumbled to back up her words.

"You're always hungry. You should have an arse the size of a bus."

There was a moment of startled silence where Ambar fought to keep her twitching lips still. She would not laugh. *She would not*.

Instead, she managed a sniff. "I have a fast metabolism."

She, Kiran and Rohan had discussed telling Jake about her tiger status. They'd decided as long as the relationship remained casual, Jake didn't need to know the truth. If the situation changed and talk of marriage emerged, obviously Jake would have to learn about her feline self.

That would never happen.

Jake eyed her warily. "Sorry. That wasn't very nice."

A laugh exploded from Ambar. "Probably on par with me saying you have a small dick."

Jake winced. "Ouch."

"Don't worry," she cooed. "We both know it's not true."

"I need to spank your arse."

"Ooh, fun and games. Maybe later tonight."

"It's a date." Jake leaned over to nuzzle her neck, scoring his teeth over the fleshy part where shoulder and neck met. He'd done it before and she'd liked it, but this time she groaned out loud at the intense flash of pleasure emanating from the traditional marking site for feline shifters. Grasping his shoulders, she clung, tilting her head to give him better access. Her breasts felt heavy, her nipples tightening again. With her excellent sense of smell, she knew her pussy was moist and ready for Jake's possession.

A brisk knock on the door jerked Ambar from the sensual spell.

"Dinner is ready," Hari called through the door.

"Go," Jake said in his husky voice. "I'll be out in a couple of minutes."

Ambar left, her trembling legs getting her to the kitchen somehow.

"I didn't realize you and Jake were together." Hari's watchful eyes took in her pink cheeks and the flare of his nostrils told her he could smell her arousal. A glow lit his eyes and she took a hasty step back, putting the island counter between them. It wasn't that she was afraid he'd grab her. No, so far he'd acted like a gentleman.

The problem was her.

Each time they were in the same room, her thoughts drifted into inappropriate territory. Naked...she shook her head sharply, hoping to jog the vision away.

"Jake and I have been together for almost six months."

Hari nodded, his scarred face remaining expressionless. Ambar wanted to shake a reaction from him. If it were her, she'd be pissed, irked and everything in between, yet Iceman here didn't react at all.

"Do you want me to do anything to help?" Maybe if she concentrated on something else the edgy sensation she experienced with him would disappear.

Hari jerked his head in the direction of the table. "Set the table for me?"

"Sure." Ambar moved to the cutlery drawer, pleased to have something to do. There was something wrong with a woman who lusted after two different men in the space of five minutes. "That smells good. What is it?"

"Chicken korma and rice."

"Do you like cooking?"

"I find it relaxing, and it helps me think through any problems I'm having with work."

Curiosity bloomed in Ambar. "What sort of work do you do?"

"I'm a designer. Mainly websites, but sometimes I design book covers or help with online advertising campaigns."

"Hari's designing a game as well," Jake said, entering the kitchen.

The vague suspicions inside Ambar transformed into alarm. "How long are you staying in Middlemarch?"

Hari shrugged. "I'm not sure. I like what I've seen of the town and surrounding countryside. I can work anywhere. It might as well be Middlemarch."

Ambar's eyes narrowed. "So you're staying here indefinitely?"

Jake padded past her on bare feet to grab a beer from the fridge. "Stop interrogating him. If Hari's cooking tastes as good as it smells, he can stay as long as he likes."

Hari winked and handed her a plate of curry and rice. Ambar opened her mouth to blast him, cast a quick, frustrated look at Jake and pressed her lips together.

It was the weirdest thing sitting at the kitchen table with the two men. Despite her unease, Hari and Jake conversed easily and laughed often. Neither of them ignored her—in fact, they went out of their way to include her, but she still found it strange eating dinner with her lover and an

ex-prospective husband. Then there was the flirting stuff...
Nah, it was her imagination. Hari's arrival had upset her,
making her imagine sexual things.

"This is delicious," Jake said. "I don't suppose there's
more?"

"I made plenty." Hari started to rise but Ambar waved
him back.

"I'll get it. Do you want another drink?"

"Another beer would be great," Jake said.

"Hari?"

"Please."

Still bemused with the situation, Ambar served the two
men with seconds and drinks. Jake expected her to stay
the night. Heck, she wanted to stay the night, but it was
gonna feel weird because Hari's feline senses would let him
overhear and smell...everything.

Eek! A wave of heat suffused her face. She met Hari's
gaze and watched his eyes narrow. He glanced at Jake
and back at her before shoveling in another mouthful of
curry. His careful expression told her Hari guessed both
her thoughts and unease.

Ambar returned to her seat and finished her dinner
in silence, listening to the two men talking. Who knew
that a website designer and a farmer would have so
much in common? And why hadn't she known Jake
was so interested in computers? She knew he'd argued
with his father for a long time about modernizing their
methods. Since he'd taken over the farm, he'd spent many
evenings working to set up everything on his computer.
His accounts and stock records, he'd told her.

The night moved on with the three of them doing the dishes and cleaning the kitchen together before watching a movie. They shared the large brown couch because that was the best vantage spot. Ambar sat between the two men to watch the adventure flick containing lots of car chases and shooting.

She couldn't have repeated the plot even if someone offered her a monetary incentive, not with the body heat of both men searing her sides, their scent winding through her with every uneasy breath she dragged into her lungs. The warmth seeped deep to her bones, making her heart race and her pussy pulse with awareness. Worse, she could smell her arousal and knew if she could, then her problem wouldn't be a mystery to Hari.

Damn feline senses.

She started to fidget.

"You okay?" Jake caught her hand and laced their fingers together.

"Yes." A lie. She knew it, and judging by Hari's quick glance, he knew it too. She almost cried with relief when Jake put his arm around her shoulders and drew her closer. She sank against his muscular chest and continued to stare at the action on the screen, still not taking in a thing because of her frenzied thoughts. Maybe she should go home after all?

Hari shifted his weight a fraction, bringing their legs into contact again. She stirred then stopped. If she moved her leg or scuttled home to safety, Hari would win. He'd think his opinion or presence mattered to her. He knew about her and Jake. Let him deal with it.

The decision eased her angst and allowed her to relax. It was time to show Hari she meant what she said. She was with Jake, and the weird attraction she was feeling for Hari was nothing more than feminine appreciation for a sexy male.

Hari watched the movie and wondered why he'd ever thought someone as beautiful as Ambar wouldn't have a man in her life. He'd been bigheaded to think she'd be his for the taking. Although he'd researched Ambar and her family, he hadn't realized her parents had died. For a while, he'd thought about pretending to be his cousin and making inquiries, but he'd tossed the idea aside once he realized the parents would do the arranging and take care of the correspondence. He couldn't do that because his parents were long dead and his aunt and uncle would've asked questions, probably expecting him to step aside for his cousin.

Watching Ambar cuddle with Jake was killing him. Not that he could go with instinct and attack his competitor. The man was human, and this situation wasn't Jake's fault. He didn't know what Ambar meant to Hari.

How could he?

Besides, if he got physical and staked a claim, Ambar would twitch her pretty tail and sashay away. Her brother had made it very clear Ambar would choose her own mate and that he'd support his sister in any decision she made regarding her future.

Hari closed his eyes while his mind scrambled for a way

out of this mess. Bottom line—he wanted Ambar. Her lack of virginity didn't matter. That would be hypocritical considering he'd had sex before. It was the future that mattered.

Ambar's scent filled his lungs along with the more masculine scent of Jake. What the hell? That was bizarre. He risked a glance at Ambar before letting his gaze drift to Jake. He liked the human. They'd dropped into an easy friendship almost straightaway, and he needed to stay with Jake so he could plan his next move with Ambar.

The movie trailed to an end. Thank god he'd seen it before and would be able to discuss the plot with some intelligence.

Jake yawned loudly. "I'm off to bed. I need to get up early in the morning to muster the cattle for drenching." He stood and held out his hand to Ambar. "Coming?"

"Sure." Ambar's obvious discomfort gave Hari hope. If she didn't care, she wouldn't feel so awkward.

"See you in the morning," Jake said.

"Goodnight." Hari struggled to restrain a growl as he watched them disappear from sight. Fuck, this was gonna hurt, hearing them have sex, because he had no doubt they would. If he'd been in Jake's position, he'd want to make love to Ambar at every opportunity. He'd want to have children with her. A sharp growl escaped this time. Jake better not be thinking about offspring. That *would* send Hari over the edge.

In the distance, he heard the murmur of voices, the faint rattle as a pump kicked in and water flowed from a tap. Hari groaned because the next thing he heard was the rustle of clothing. He slapped his hands over his ears, leapt to his feet and headed to the kitchen.

A drink. Damn, he needed a drink. It was the only way he'd get through the night.

"Hey." Jake stepped close to Ambar and brushed a lock of dark hair from her face. "I'm glad you're here." It had been a rough day, and the earlier phone call from the bank manager hadn't helped his piece of mind. *Arsehole*. At least he'd been able to tell the pompous city man he'd taken in a boarder to help with the cash flow situation.

"You're so beautiful." Earlier, he'd noticed the frank appraisal in Hari's eyes. Strangely it hadn't pissed him off. His new roomie had winked at him when Ambar wasn't looking, and he'd grinned back.

A male-bonding moment.

The offer to Hari had been an impulsive one, but he thought it might work. They'd already discovered similar likes, and it felt as if they'd known each other for years. Besides, since his parents had left, he'd gone days without seeing anyone because he started work early and continued until dark. Returning home to an empty house after a hard day sucked. Hari cooked and apparently enjoyed it. While Jake knew his way around a kitchen, most nights he was so bloody tired a sandwich sufficed for dinner.

A full belly and a beautiful woman to share his bed.

He was a lucky man.

Ambar laughed, the sultry sound making his balls

tighten with anticipation. "I'm not beautiful."

"You are to me. You're bold and confident." He unfastened the top button of her shirt and ran the pad of his finger around the exposed V of skin. "Sexy. I like the way you laugh and smile. The way you smell. The way you tilt your head when you're listening to me."

A grin lit her golden eyes. "Maybe I like some things about you." She yanked on his shirt and slid her hands beneath the cotton to stroke his lower back. He shivered, remembering the first time they'd made love. Ambar had been a virgin. He'd struggled to go slow and make it good for her, part of him terrified yet so turned-on he had difficulty holding back.

In the past, he'd gone for experience, the sort of woman who knew the score and wouldn't get clingy. Ambar had shoved aside his reservations when he'd told her she wasn't the kind of woman he usually took to bed. Ambar had told him about her parents, how she and Rohan had escaped arranged marriages when their parents died in a car accident. Marriage wasn't for her, she'd told him. She wanted to enjoy herself, make friends and have fun.

Part of him had suspected a trap, making him wary. His fears hadn't materialized. They saw each other two or three times a week, and this worked for both of them. She didn't interrogate him, demand his presence or act clingy when they were with his friends at the pub.

Hell, he hadn't thought about another woman for months, which was unusual for him. Normally, he drifted from woman to woman because they started to bore him with their demands, inevitably becoming too possessive.

"You have good hair." An impish glint brought out her exotic beauty, made his breath catch. "What sort of shampoo do you use?"

He growled, and she giggled as she lowered her hands to grab his butt. Leaning forward, he kissed her, stifling her merriment when their lips touched. She always tasted so good and he loved the way she smelled, sort of spicy and feminine. Like nothing he'd smelled before, it was a mixture of the outdoors and green forests. He burrowed his fingers into her hair, tugging out the jeweled clip restraining the long strands. He held her head in place, lightly massaging her scalp because he knew she enjoyed this.

Sexy and enticing. A groan built in his throat as he struggled to go slow. He nibbled her bottom lip, nipping it lightly before taking possession of her mouth and stamping his will on her. She murmured a soft surrender and pressed closer, her hands coasting up to grip his shoulders.

Lust slammed him, his cock filling as their tongues twined. Unable to help himself, he freed one hand and cupped her backside, rubbing against her, grinding his cock against her belly, savoring the growing urgency, the pleasure. God, he wanted to rip off her clothes and fuck her. A hard and unrestrained joining. He craved the hot, wet slide into her clinging warmth.

"Clothes off." He growled the command, his earlier fatigue fading. His fingers worked rapidly, unfastening the rest of the buttons on her shirt. He peeled it down her arms, ripping off a button in his urgency. She laughed at his haste, unperturbed while he stripped her to bra and panties.

"In a hurry, lover?"

"You have no idea." He scooped her off her feet and tossed her on his bed.

"My hero." She fluttered her long eyelashes at him. "Not many guys could throw me around like that." She made herself comfortable, regarding him with a sassy smile. Brimming with confidence, she didn't stress about her body and constantly ask him for reassurance. Self-belief in a woman made him hot.

"Who are you letting throw you around?" Yeah, maybe she wasn't beautiful in the traditional sense, but people noticed her when she entered a room. His friends liked her and were waiting for him to turn her loose so they could pounce. Jake didn't think that would happen for a long time. Hell, once she discovered his financial troubles, she'd probably give him the flick.

"Just you. I'm not interested in numbers."

"Good to know." He watched her face the entire time, fascinated by the clear desire. She didn't hide. She didn't play games.

Oh yeah. Time for action. His shirt flew through the air. He unzipped his jeans and tugged them off, removing his boxer-briefs at the same time. Naked, he paused, loving her avid gaze running across his body. His dick lifted under her scrutiny. The slow lick of her tongue over her full bottom lip reminded him of how it felt when she took his cock inside her sexy mouth. The visuals weren't too bad either.

"Are you going to stare at me all night? I thought you

were in a hurry?"

"I am." He prowled closer without taking his eyes off her. Looming over her, he grinned, although he suspected it didn't look pretty. Probably predatory. He traced a forefinger along the lacy edges of her bra.

She stirred restlessly, trying to hold him in place when he lifted his hand. "Take off my bra. Touch me."

"Nothing I'd like better." He'd thought he wanted to hurry, but now she lay in front of him, he decided this was better—slow seduction. He pinched her nipple before lowering his head and taking both nipple and bra into his mouth. Using his teeth and tongue, he teased her until she writhed against him with needy cries. When he lifted his head, a damp circle showed on the silky fabric.

"Tease." Her lips formed a mock pout, in direct contrast to her laughing features.

"It makes you hot." Hell, it made him hot. Ambar made sex fun, giving him pleasure and trusting him to return the favor. She didn't keep score. If he were the marrying type of guy, Ambar would be the one.

A part of him knew keeping her was selfish, but his days and nights wouldn't be the same without her. No color. There'd be no excitement, just days and days of hard, grinding work on the farm.

He forced suddenly stiff lips to a smile. "When you're hot, you go off like a firecracker. It's much better for both of us."

"If I didn't know better, I'd say you read the ladies' magazines. You know about foreplay."

"Smart-arse."

She chuckled, the husky sound driving lust deep into his balls. He lifted her bra cup up and away from her breast, taking her taut peach-colored nipple into his mouth. He drew on it hard, just the way she liked, and closed his eyes. Shutting off his sight allowed him to concentrate on his other senses, the small sounds of enjoyment she made deep in her throat. Sort of purring noises like a cat issued when a person stroked its fur. And her scent—it intensified with her arousal. His fingers mapped her silky skin as he released her nipple and started to explore the rest of her body. He followed the scented skin down her rib cage and paused to ring her navel with his tongue, the faint tug of her hands in his hair telling him she wanted him to hurry.

Good idea, but then this would be over too soon. He wanted to prolong the buildup, lengthen the pleasure and drive them both crazy. A trail of kisses led him lower, over her hipbone to the edge of the lacy panties.

His eyes flicked open and registered the color. "They don't match."

"Tell the fashion police."

"Will they disbar you?"

"Probably," Ambar said with a laugh. "The matching bra and panties are in the wash. We've been busy this week and I haven't had a chance to do the laundry."

"Rohan and Kiran don't make you do the washing?"

"Hell no. We take turns with the chores. We've been busy this week. The guys are probably going commando, but they haven't complained yet. It was a challenge to find something clean."

"I'll take them off for you. That way no one will know."

"Good idea," she said with a sigh. She lifted her hips, and he tugged her blue panties down her long legs. When he glanced up at her, he noticed she'd freed her black bra and cast it aside. "I've heard the fashion police like tying people up—the ones they catch in misdemeanors."

"Yeah." He grinned at the idea and filed it away for later use. "I might have to snitch."

"You'd tattle?"

"I could report your misdemeanors. I bet they're busy. They'd let me administer your punishment."

"Hmmm." Her eyes narrowed, and if he weren't mistaken a glint of interest showed as well. Yeah, he'd consider the tying-up thing for the near future.

He ran a finger across her upper thigh and glanced up in a silent order to part her legs. He inhaled and traced a finger over the pouty folds of her pussy, taking in the delicate flush suffusing her face. Damn, she was pretty. Leaning closer, he tasted her. God, he loved going down on her. She was doing that sexy rumbling sound deep in her throat. He lapped her juices then slowly pushed a finger inside her.

Heat. It burned his finger, the sensation of warmth echoing in his cock. He wanted to burrow into her core and never leave. Ambar made his worries disperse and gave him peace. His tongue curled around her clit, gently teasing the distended nub until she couldn't contain her whimpers, the jerk of her hips. He added another finger, pumping slowly while he built the intensity, layer upon layer. Her hips gyrated, her purrs coming harder and faster.

"Jake," she whispered, her vaginal walls clamping down hard on his fingers as she came.

The ripples were still pulsing through her when he lifted his head and reached over to grab a condom from the nightstand. With trembling hands, he rolled on the latex, lined up and surged inside her clinging flesh.

Their mouths met in a gentle kiss that gradually morphed into needy. Desperate. He crushed her mouth under his, invading and retreating in hard, even strokes. Good. It felt so damn good whenever he was inside her. Ambar made him forget his problems.

"Hell, Ambar. You're amazing." The bed creaked with the force of his thrust.

"You always say that."

He grunted, having trouble thinking. It was much better concentrating on the sensations rippling through his body. "I'll have to go for different next time."

"Bite me," she said suddenly. "Mark me so I can look at it later and remember doing this with you."

He stopped, fully embedded, and his brows rose as he looked at her. "A love bite?"

"Yes, please."

"Anywhere I want?"

"As long as it won't show at work."

He'd marked women before during sex, but Ambar's request was different. He felt his cock throb the second he registered her demand. There was nothing he'd like better, to know she carried a souvenir of him when they parted. He dropped a slow kiss on her mouth, his tongue surging inside.

Her hands snaked around his neck, and she clung, arching her body against him and throwing herself into the kiss. Everything she did was with enthusiasm, and that was an incredible turn-on. When he lifted his head, her eyes glowed with gold flecks and her skin bore a delicate flush while his cock bathed in liquid heat. He rocked into her, a small teasing thrust that dragged against her flesh.

"Faster," she demanded, her fingernails digging into his shoulders with painful intensity. The sensual ache served to drive his need for her higher.

"Soon." The idea of marking her skin held enormous appeal. Where? That was the question. His gaze roved her breasts with their peach-tipped nipples, her upper chest and higher to her neck. Decision made. Jake swooped, sucking on the soft pad of skin partway between neck and shoulder.

She gasped the second he started sucking, hips jerking hard enough to send a frisson of pleasure right through him. When he lifted his head, she breathed hard, the red mark very obvious against her golden skin.

"There," he said, eyeing the mark with satisfaction. "That should do the trick."

Ambar said nothing, merely remained still with her eyes closed. It made him worry.

"Ambar?"

A slow smile curved across her lips and her eyes flicked open. They glittered, the corners of her eyes narrowed and surprisingly catlike. "That felt fantastic. Fuck me now."

"Good idea." Jake didn't know what had happened, but somehow the sexual tension between them had ratcheted sharply upward. He thrust into her with hard, digging strokes, relishing the friction, the searing fervor between them. The fact she was robust and didn't freak when he used his strength was an incredible turn-on.

Instead, she clung to him, buried her head in his neck and used her sharp teeth on him, leaving her own mark.

A groan escaped him when he felt her teeth on his upper chest. He thrust once more and exploded, groaning loudly as he came. A couple more slow thrusts were enough to make Ambar climax again, and he savored the pulse of her pussy clasping his cock and massaging him through the final pulses of his orgasm. Sighing, he withdrew and dealt with the condom. Once finished, he rolled to his side, dragging her against his chest.

Exhaustion caught up with him and he drifted off to sleep with Ambar clasped possessively in his arms.

Ambar sensed the second Jake dropped off to sleep. Typical male. Her lips curved in a grin until she remembered she'd almost bitten him and mated with him in the heat of the moment. She'd wanted him as she'd never wanted another man. The feel of Jake thrusting into her, his mouth sucking at her neck had even driven Hari from her mind.

Bad. It was a bad idea for her to suggest biting.

The last thing she needed was a mate. Heck, she'd scarcely avoided an arranged marriage, so why would she want to do something stupid like biting Jake—a human? Not that she had anything against humans, but having to explain the mating process and her tiger shifter status raised a new set of problems.

Her mind chased 'round and 'round. Even though she enjoyed spending time with Jake, sleeping with him, she didn't want a serious relationship. She wanted to play, to experience life, and enjoy everything she could squeeze from it.

Jake was her first lover. It didn't mean he had to be her last one, no matter what her parents might say. *It didn't.*

Confusion clouded her thoughts as she recalled the excitement she'd felt when he'd sucked on the mating site—the fleshy part where her shoulder and neck met. Surely, she shouldn't have felt so excited or tempted if they weren't prospective mates?

Carefully, she turned in Jake's arms, not wanting to wake him when he was so tired. Jake didn't want a serious relationship. He'd made that clear right at the start of their involvement before they'd slept together.

The faint pad of footsteps in the passage outside Jake's bedroom jerked her from her stewing thoughts.

Hari. Another problem.

When she and Jake had first retired tonight, she'd felt self-conscious, knowing Hari would hear more than she was comfortable with him knowing. That had disappeared once she and Jake had started kissing and touching, but hearing Hari prowl the house brought it back again.

This was weird. She should have told Jake about Hari traveling from England with the expectation of marrying her. But Hari hadn't told the truth either.

Sighing softly, she closed her eyes and counted imaginary sheep. They transformed into tigers, beautiful tigers that smelled of honey and spices and seductive male musk. She wanted to follow, tried to pursue, but they flicked their sexy tails and left her in the dust.

Soft lips and roving hands woke her.

"What's the time?" she mumbled, cuddling closer and enjoying Jake's warmth.

"Almost time for me to get up."

She felt the distinct prod of his cock against her belly. "Almost?"

"Yeah. About ten minutes before the alarm goes off."

"We'd better make use of that time then." Ambar burrowed under the blankets, reaching for his cock.

"You don't have to do that."

"I want to. I like the way you taste."

"But what about you?" The bed covers muffled Jake's voice.

"I'm not useless. I can get myself off easily enough if I want."

"Is that right? Some men might worry about all that self-sufficiency." Laughter threaded through his words.

"You're not most men," Ambar retorted, knowing her words were true. Jake was a special man. She fingered the mark he'd made on her neck. It didn't hurt yet touching it sent a sensual jolt through her. "Let me start your morning off the right way."

She wouldn't think about Hari in a nearby room. Her sharp hearing caught the sound of footsteps in the kitchen, the running of water and the clink of a pot. Her mouth tightened as she hesitated. She'd told Hari she wasn't interested in a relationship with him, and no matter how good he smelled she refused to change her mind.

Moving closer, she caressed Jake's cock and ran her fingers over the smooth shaft. She wrapped her lips around the tip and licked and sucked until he groaned, letting his taste wash over her and reveling in his soft groan of appreciation. His hands crept beneath the covers to hold her head in place. She lapped at the slit, gathering a drop of fluid with her tongue. Aware of the timeline and the ticking clock, Ambar upped her pace, taking him deep and sucking hard. He trembled, groaned and jerked his hips. He thrust with care, using her mouth, taking his pleasure. His scent intensified, surrounding her in the enclosed space, making her head swim and her body surge with unremitting need. Unbidden, her feline pushed to the surface, sharp claws protruding from her fingertips.

Holy crap.

Jake yelped. "Watch those teeth, babe."

Ambar froze, muttering an apology around Jake's cock. Double holy crap. Her canine teeth had popped into prominence. She could feel the faint ache in her gums, her feline pushing her body to complete the shift to tiger. Ambar placed her left hand on the mattress and curled her claws into the fabric, focusing on remaining in human form. Tension simmered inside her as she wondered what to do next. She could hardly stop, not when she'd offered in the first place. One thing was clear—she needed to get him off quick so she could leave, or at least get away from Jake before he saw her claws and teeth. And would he notice her tongue had become rougher than usual?

Using a combination of hands and her mouth, she worked harder to get him off, relieved when he started to rock his hips, pushing his shaft deeper into her mouth. Her usual enjoyment in Jake and his sexy body had faded with

45

the attempted takeover of her feline.

On automatic, she moved her head faster and mentally urged him to hurry. He was close—she knew it. Even as the thought entered her mind, he gave a raw, guttural cry and climaxed in her mouth. Ambar swallowed automatically and carefully licked him clean, trying to act as usual even though her mind screamed at her to get the hell out of his presence.

"Babe, that is a brilliant way to start the morning." He dragged her from beneath the covers and hugged her tight, running his hands through her long hair. Ambar turned her face into his chest, concentrating on holding her human form. He dropped a kiss on her shoulder then sighed. "I'd better get moving. I have a long day in front of me. Is it okay if I take the shower first?"

Normally, she'd insist on sharing the shower. Not today. "You go ahead. I might laze here." The stupid canines made her words emerge with a strange lisp. Thankfully, Jake didn't seem to notice.

The moment he left the bedroom, Amber jumped from the bed and scrambled into her clothes. She couldn't seem to get her nails and teeth to return back to normal. Still barefoot, she hurried down the passage, the scent of coffee becoming stronger as she neared the kitchen.

"Good morning," Hari said without turning away from the stove. "You timed that well. The scrambled eggs are almost ready. I've made extra."

"Hari," Ambar said urgently.

Something in her voice must have alerted Hari to her alarm. He removed the eggs from the heat and turned to face her. She bared her teeth and held up her hands to show him her fingernails. The beginnings of black claws protruded above her fingernails.

"They won't go back." One whiff of Hari's scent and her body went on high alert. She battled an inappropriate urge to rub against him and, in desperation, moved to the other side of the kitchen. Panic filled her as she fought the change to tiger. "What do I do?"

"Has it happened before?" Hari moved closer, concern in his brown eyes.

"Never. Don't come any closer," she blurted finally in desperation. She was running out of room to retreat, and his scent was driving her crazy. Worst of all, she was a hairsbreadth away from jumping him. Her sharp claws dug into her palms until the faint scent of blood drifted up to her.

"I'm not gonna bite," Hari said, his English accent holding a trace of irritation.

Ambar rolled her eyes. Men were so slow, so dense sometimes. She decided to spell it out for him, halting her flight. Instead, she prowled across the kitchen to him, letting her need blaze across her face. "It's you I'm worried about."

47

CHAPTER THREE

"GET A GRIP," HARI snapped, holding up his hands in a halt motion. He spoke to himself more than Ambar. He had to stop, to rein in his desire for her. "You don't want me. You're with Jake." He thought quickly, part of him cursing the way he was guarding the other man's interests. "What's the most embarrassing thing that's ever happened to you? Quick. Tell me."

"The elastic snapping on my panties when I was at school," Ambar said without hesitation. "I had to take them off and go without. It was a windy day."

Hell. That wasn't a good visual to sear into his brain. "Picture your human form and recall how you felt when it happened, your embarrassment." He would not think about her bare ass. No matter how much he wished otherwise, Ambar had made her choice and it wasn't him. "An embarrassing moment always works for me when I want to lose an erection. According to my cousins, it does

48

the job for them as well. This isn't much different from an unruly erection."

"You've got that right," she said, her words distorted because of her teeth.

Hari watched her for a moment longer, noted the mismatched shirt buttons, the color in her cheeks, and her kiss-swollen lips before he returned to the scrambled eggs. He'd heard her and Jake last night and it had almost killed him. No wonder he was so bloody tired.

Right now he wanted to touch her so bad his hands trembled, the wooden spoon tapping the edge of the saucepan in a rhythmic manner even though he tried to hold it steady.

Jake's arrival added a buffer and made Hari concentrate on cooking, but his senses kept working, scents and sounds causing his feline to writhe beneath his skin. "Are you ready for breakfast?" He should keep Jake talking until Ambar controlled her tiger. Hell, he could do with a spot of control himself.

Jake glanced at the clock on the wall. "I should get moving. I need to muster some cattle."

"By yourself?" Hari asked, grabbing some bread and putting it into the toaster.

"Yes, just me and the dogs."

"I don't have anything pressing to do today. If I help, will that leave you time to have breakfast? It's ready now." Hari competently dished up the scrambled eggs and handed Jake a plate.

"You?" Ambar said in disbelief. "You're from the city."

"So?" Hari pulled a face at her, set two more plates onto

49

the table, grabbed some toast and the coffeepot. "I have a brain. I can follow instructions."

Jake collected coffee mugs from the cupboard and slid onto a chair. "You'd really like to help?"

"Yes." Hari poured coffee for them all, noting Ambar's teeth and fingers appeared normal again. "I need to think about the website I'm designing. A change of scenery will give me a chance to think."

"That would be great," Jake said. "I'd appreciate the help."

The expression on Ambar's face told Hari she didn't welcome his offer. Too bad. He'd thought over his situation during his sleepless night and decided to go ahead with his plan to stay. Despite being with Jake, Ambar was aware of him. While he wouldn't do anything underhanded, he didn't intend to walk away either. It wasn't as if he had anywhere else he needed to be. That reminded him, he'd better check in with his uncle and aunt and let them know he was in New Zealand. They were the only family he had left and would expect him to contact them. He didn't need to give them specifics regarding his whereabouts.

Jake asked Ambar about her plans for the day, and Hari listened attentively, thirsty for knowledge of the woman he wanted to mate.

"I'm working in the store most of the day."

"Don't you need to do laundry?"

Ambar snorted, her golden-brown eyes gleaming with humor. "Yeah, you're probably right."

A private joke. Harry tried not to feel left out and

failed. He stared at his scrambled eggs, fighting to keep a frustrated growl trapped in his throat. The color bled from his knuckles as he gripped his knife and fork.

"Hari, do you have any boots?" Jake asked.

The air hissed through his lips, and he forced himself to relax. "Just a pair of runners."

"There are spare pairs of boots in the laundry. Check to see if any of them fit you." Jake stood and grabbed his plate and coffee mug. With efficient moves, he opened the dishwasher to stack his dirty dishes inside. "I have to get the dogs. Meet you outside." After bending to kiss Ambar goodbye, he left them alone, his cheery whistle audible long after he'd disappeared.

Ambar glared at him. "Why do you have to stay here?"

"My nearest relatives are my uncle and aunt in London. I don't have any better place to go. Besides, what do you care? You're with Jake."

Her mouth firmed and she stood, anger evident in the flash of her eyes. She stacked her breakfast dishes in the dishwasher and slammed the door shut hard enough to make him wince. "I'll finish here," she said in a tight voice. "You don't want to hold up Jake."

"See you later."

"Not if I see you first."

Hari grinned and strolled off, whistling a tune similar to Jake's. His presence bothered her and that gave him hope.

JAKE HADN'T REALIZED HOW lonely his days had become

until he took Hari with him to muster stock. Hari asked constant questions, and Jake found himself telling the other man about the things he hoped to achieve with his cattle-breeding program and his present problems with cash flow.

"Maybe you need an investor," Hari said. "Or perhaps you need to diversify."

"When my father oversaw the farm, I tried to persuade him to grow a crop of some sort. See the river down there? Part of our land goes down to the water and the land is suitable for growing crops. He refused. Said he'd never planted crops before and didn't see the need to start now."

"Some people are resistant to change. So why haven't you grown a crop this year?"

"I don't have the money. I had to mortgage everything so I could buy out my father."

"He made you pay?"

Jake shrugged. "He needed money to buy a house in Dunedin and to do the travel he and my mother wanted to do in the future. I don't begrudge my parents the money. They've both worked hard." But he hadn't expected he'd need to go so far into debt either. The stress was eating him alive. The only time he forgot was when he was with Ambar.

"Are you serious about Ambar?"

Jake shot him a quick look. "Why?"

"Just curious."

Jake grinned. "She's great, isn't she? There used to be lots of women, but since meeting Ambar, I've been a strictly one-woman man. Neither of us wants anything serious. We're happy as we are." Although this morning had been weird. He'd noticed the vibes between Hari and Ambar despite the hundred things whirring through his mind. Jake loved spending time with Ambar, and he'd hit it off with Hari. He'd hate it if he couldn't see them at the same time.

Hari read the tension in Jake's body language and knew he had to do something to alleviate suspicion. The last thing he wanted was for Jake to chuck him out of the house.

For some reason, Hari's cousin popped into his mind. His mouth opened before his brain engaged. "So what do you do about sex out here in the country?" It was the sort of thing his cousin would say. Personally, he preferred a more subtle approach.

Jake shot him a quick look across the cab of his vehicle. "You've noticed the predominance of males."

"Not really. I just presumed things would be more difficult in a small town with everyone knowing each other."

Jake shrugged, and to his horror, Hari realized he'd become aware of the other man. His proximity. His scent—soap layered with the man and the lingering aroma of Ambar and tiger. The sexual awareness blindsided him, shocking him to the core. Bloody hell. He wasn't gay, wasn't attracted to other men. Confusion made him swallow and admit that the weird recognition he'd experienced the previous day still lingered. Something about Jake pushed his sexual buttons. He swallowed again. Nah, it had to be something to do with Ambar's scent lingering on Jake's skin. He refused to entertain other ideas. Men...nah, it'd never happen.

Jake spoke, thankfully unaware of Hari's inner turmoil. "There's always been a shortage of women in Middlemarch. The women tend to stay in Dunedin or move farther afield once they finish university. The men return to the land."

"Do you regret coming back?" Curiosity burned Hari. Despite his dismay at the weird attraction to Jake, he wanted to learn more about him. A bloody slippery slope, for sure. He cursed inwardly. No matter. Yeah, no way would he act on the appeal of the other man. They could remain friends, even if Jake had access to Ambar and the inside track, so to speak.

"Financial problems aside, I love working outdoors. I like the freedom, the wide-open spaces and the fresh air. I enjoyed university, but the city smothered me."

As a feline, Hari understood the trapped feeling. It was his need for the outdoors that had made up his mind to move to New Zealand. Here in the country he could shift and run—once he learned the safe places. Ambar would know. "I never felt at home in London. Too many people."

"The town puts on a yearly dance to attract women. A train load arrives from Dunedin," Jake said. "I've never met anyone at the dance I wanted to spend more than a night with." He grinned and added, "If you want a woman around here you have to move fast. The Mitchells have snapped up all the good ones. Only Joe and Sly are single these days. You'll meet them at some stage. I went to university with them. Man, those were some fun times."

"So if I want sex with anything other than my own hand I need to go to Dunedin?"

Jake chuckled and pulled up by a gate. "That's about the size of it. I'm lucky with Ambar. Neither one of us wants anything serious, but we enjoy spending time together. It's working well. Hell, I've never been with one woman for such a long stretch."

And judging by what Hari had heard last night, they wouldn't part any time soon. Just his bloody luck. Underhanded tactics…no. He discarded the thought once again. That wasn't his style. If he won Ambar, he wanted to know he'd done it fair and square.

Hari climbed from the vehicle and waited while Jake released his three dogs. After their initial sniff of him earlier this morning, the dogs kept a healthy distance. He made a mental note to ask Ambar how they behaved with her.

Hari followed Jake through the gate into the paddock. Some of his inner tension dispersed on taking in his surroundings. A fresh breeze blew over a rise, ruffling his hair and bringing a green, herby hit of plants and trees. Towering piles of schist lay like a giant's building blocks, providing shelter for the Hereford cattle they intended to muster today. Overhead a hawk soared lazily. Hari watched until the bird disappeared behind a stand of pines.

"I can see why you like it here."

"Yeah. It's beautiful. I even like it during the winter, despite the cold and the snow."

"Do you get snow in the town itself?"

"Mostly we get snow on the surrounding hills and that's it. I'm going to send the dogs over to the right. I'll head that way too since that's mostly where the cattle graze. Can you go to the left and look for stragglers? There's a gate in the direction I'm heading. You'll see it as soon as you climb over the brow of the hill. I want the cattle in the yards, which are just through the gate."

"Okay," Hari said, and with a brief wave, he walked in the direction Jake had indicated. Once he was out of sight, he raised his head and opened his mouth to inhale. The air rushed across his receptors, dragging in the scent of cattle. Hari took off at a jog, relishing the pull of muscles. He couldn't shift right now, not without knowing the protocol of the local shifters, but this was the next best thing. Hari spotted the first group of cattle, and with a whoop, he increased his speed, angling his approach to send them down the hill. The animals froze when they saw him racing toward them—then with startled moos they bolted toward the gate. Job well done.

Hari scented again and hunted out more cattle. By the time he had them all, he'd built up a healthy sweat.

The clouds cleared and the sun came out. Hari whipped his T-shirt over his head and used it to wipe the sweat off his forehead and chest.

With a final scent, he decided he had the stragglers and jogged toward the massed animals, gently nudging the stubborn red beasts forward. Once over the brow of the hill, he saw a bigger herd. A swift glance at his watch told him almost two hours had passed. He watched Jake open the gate into the next paddock and use his dogs to direct the cattle. Jake raced ahead to clear the way into the yards.

Hari trotted after the cattle, subtly herding them to the

gateway. He picked up a few more along the way and realized he hadn't enjoyed himself so much for ages. If Jake didn't mind, maybe he'd tag along in the mornings and work on his web design during the afternoon. It wasn't as if he was desperate for money since he'd done well in the past.

Down at the yards, Jake whistled the dogs and glanced back up the hill. He heard a loud whoop and watched Hari charge after a cow. Shit, he was fast. He outran the cow and sent it charging back to the gate. Grinning, Jake turned back to the cattle already milling around inside the yard. He opened the race and counted them as they moved through to the far pen. Hari seemed to have everything under control with the herd moving steadily. Jake grabbed the drench and drenching gun from the small storage shed near the race and started work. At this rate they'd be done by early afternoon, and he could catch up on some of the other chores he'd let slip due to lack of time. He set to work, running cattle into the race, drenching them and sorting the ones he needed to sell before refilling the race. Hari pitched in and impressed Jake with his willingness to help. For a city boy, he didn't mind getting his hands dirty. Two hours later, they'd finished. Jake let some of the cattle back into their original paddock, and the thirty head he'd decided to sell he put into a smaller one, handy to the yards.

"How do you feel about a swim?" he asked.

Hari wiped the sweat off his forehead with a brawny

forearm. "Sounds bloody good to me."

Jake grinned. "Let's go."

They ambled to his vehicle, neither in a hurry since they'd completed their task. Hari waited while Jake organized the dogs before climbing into the passenger seat.

"That was fun. Would it be okay if I help you in the mornings? I'd need to work during the afternoons, but it would be great to get outdoors for part of the day."

Jake stared, wondering if he was hearing things. The man wanted to help him? Hell, his assistance this morning had been a godsend. A job that would have taken him most of the day on his own had ended up taking half a day. "I can't afford to pay you."

"I'm not asking you to," Hari said, his mouth tightening as if Jake had insulted him. "I enjoyed myself this morning. No problem, I won't force myself on you."

"No, fuck! You surprised me. I'd love your help, as much as you want to give me."

Hari gave a stiff nod, and the icy atmosphere lightened a fraction.

Relief suffused Jake. He'd taken an instant liking to Hari and enjoyed his company. The last thing he wanted was to drive him away. Deep in thought, Jake started his vehicle and backed away from the gate.

"There's a swimming hole at the river."

Hari nodded. "Sounds good."

Silence fell between them. It was uncomfortable, but not in the way Jake would have ever considered. Hell, it was fuckin' weird. He shot a swift glance at Hari, took in his scar, his golden skin and black hair. He hadn't shaved this morning and light stubble shaded his jaw.

"How did you get that scar?"

"I had an argument with a cat."

"A cat?" It wasn't the answer Jake had expected, but now that he studied the scar up close he could see two fainter lines either side.

"Yeah, the cat was a real tiger," Hari said, his tone wry.

"So you don't like cats?"

Hari grinned, a wide-open smile that jogged Jake back to discomfort. It was hard to decipher exactly what made him uneasy. He hated to label it as sexual...

"I like cats well enough." Hari's husky drawl did nothing to alleviate Jake's uneasiness. Yeah, a swim sounded like a plan. He'd douse himself with cold water. That should do the trick.

Jake took a left turn down a rutted gravel road and pulled up near a line of willow trees.

"This is it. I'll let the dogs go so they swim and get a drink." He turned to grab an old blanket he kept tucked behind his seat.

"Great spot," Hari said, opening his door and climbing out.

"I often finish a day here with a swim."

Hari turned to him, weird golden sparks glinting in his eyes. "I bet Ambar likes it here."

Weird, the change must be a trick of the light. "I haven't brought Ambar down here yet. We're probably going to regret it. It's gonna be bloody cold."

"I don't care," Hari said. "Where do we swim?"

"There's a pool to the right. It's usually deep. Don't dive

from the bank. I haven't checked it for hidden snags since last month."

The dogs ran past, giving Hari a wide berth before wading into the water. Weird. His dogs were normally all over everyone, apart from Ambar. They weren't keen on her either. Did he have racist dogs? The thought would have made him laugh if the reactions of his dogs hadn't been so peculiar.

Hari reached the pool before him. He removed his footwear and whipped off his shirt and jeans before Jake had time to blink. His boxers were next then he waded into the water, glancing back over his shoulder at Jake with a wide grin on his face.

Jake blinked, a mass of feelings bombarding him all at once. He took in Hari's strong, muscular body and the rear view when he turned away. For a city guy who sat in front of computers, he had some serious muscles going on. Jake frowned. An all-over tan. A zing of anticipation swept his body, and to his horror, his cock started to stir. Jake shuddered, dropping the blanket on the stones and sand before rapidly stripping. Normally he swam in his boxers. He guessed it would be more comfortable driving home in dry clothes. Feeling a bit like a Victorian maiden, Jake swept off his boxers before his hesitation got to him. He waded into the water and swore.

"Fuck, that's cold." At least his burgeoning erection had shrunk.

"Sissy," Hari taunted. "Anyone would think you were the city boy." Hari's gaze skimmed his body, and Jake's heart stuttered. He froze, heat suffusing him. Hari smirked and splashed him. The cool water did nothing to stop the second wave of heat that shot straight to his cock. Mortified, Jake dived under the water and put some distance between them when all he wanted to do was touch.

"AMBAR. AMBAR! WHAT IS wrong with you today?" Rohan demanded, a note of exasperation coloring his voice. "Concentrate."

"Sorry, I have a lot on my mind."

Her brother scanned her face and snorted. "That's what too much sex will do to you."

"You would know," Ambar replied sweetly.

"Yeah, but I don't let it screw with customer orders. Don't you remember anything our parents taught us? The golden rule."

Ambar wrinkled her nose at her brother. "Good customer service is king. I think that one did get through to me after about the twentieth time. I try to forget the other stuff about marrying a good man and preferably one from India."

"What's the problem?"

Ambar sobered, thinking about Jake. Immediately thoughts of Hari slipped into her mind, the two men now intertwined. She felt heat slide across her cheeks and knew her brother would notice.

"It's sex." His blunt words seemed to echo through the store, which was thankfully customer free.

"Oh yeah," she said. "But I'm not sure telling you about my problems is a good idea."

Rohan reached for a packet of cereal and placed it in a cardboard box before adding a jar of strawberry jam. He ticked both items off the order sitting on the desk. "Telling you I was gay wasn't easy. It can't be worse than that."

Ambar checked yogurt and bacon off her list, putting them inside the special insulated box. "You wanna bet?"

Rohan stopped work to study her. "I don't care what you tell me, Ambar. You're my sister and nothing will make me turn my back on you. Okay?"

An ache sprang to life inside her chest, and she blinked to keep tears at bay. She was so lucky to have a brother like Rohan. And Kiran, Rohan's mate was like a second brother. They teased her, shouted at her at times, but they always had her back. While her parents might have been strict, she'd really scored when it came to brothers.

She started talking before she chickened out. "I like Jake a lot. We're good friends and the sex is hot. Last night while we were...ah...I asked him to bite me," she said hurriedly, concentrating on the next item on the list because she was too frightened to check her brother's reaction. "And worse, for the first time, I wanted to bite him back," she added, miserable yet part of her elated too.

Commonsense said the urge to bite Jake meant he was her mate, yet why did she suddenly want to get up and close with Hari as well? And why hadn't she wanted to mate with Jake before?

The long silence made her stomach quiver with unaccustomed nerves. The loud tick of the clock out by the cash register underscored Rohan's silence. Swallowing, she raised her head to study his expression.

"Did he mate with you?"

"No, he didn't break the skin. But I wanted him to so bad, and then this morning, we... I couldn't get control of my feline. My teeth and claws wouldn't melt away. I had to get Hari to help me."

"And did he help?"

Why wasn't Rohan saying anything useful? Nosy questions weren't helpful. "Yes, he helped." She glared at him defiantly. "But that's not the worst thing. I wanted to jump Hari as well. Either Hari or Jake would have worked for me this morning. I wanted to bite them both." Tears started to thread through her words. "Rohan, what the hell is wrong with me? How the heck can I go from not wanting to mate with anyone one day and the next I want to bite both Jake and Hari and drag them off to bed?"

CHAPTER FOUR

HARI GRINNED AT JAKE, taking care to crouch in the water so his erection didn't show. He wanted to fuck the other man. He didn't care that Jake was male with the same equipment as him. His feline wanted him. His feline wanted Ambar. Preferably both at the same time.

A threesome? A tiny growl squeezed past his lips at the notion, his feline really getting into the idea now that Hari had pictured it.

Damn, didn't that beat all? It was something he'd never considered. In the past he'd confined himself to one lover and he'd been picky. While he'd been sexually active at university, he'd never let himself think or act too far beyond so-called normal perimeters.

He needed to think about this. Decide how to act.

"How far does the pool extend? Do you want to race?" Maybe if he could get his mind off sex, his erection would fade. The cold water wasn't helping deflate the problem. Thinking of embarrassing situations wasn't working, although if he put his mind to it, he could create a new one right now.

Hari caught the gleam of anticipation in Jake's blue eyes and knew he'd chosen the right path. If fate meant him to pursue both Jake and Ambar, things would fall into place. There was no point stressing about something that might not happen.

"See the flax bush on the riverbank?"

"I see it," Hari said.

"The water is shallow there. I'll race you to the flax bush and back. And you should probably know I won lots of awards for swimming at university. I toyed with training for competitive swimming."

A chuckle escaped Hari. "Bring it on." He took pleasure in the faint blush that darkened Jake's cheeks. He took half a step toward the other man before acknowledging the impulse. He halted abruptly. "You say start."

Jake might have been a champion swimmer, but as a tiger, he loved the water.

"Go!" Jake hollered, his shout disturbing two ducks floating on a tranquil stretch of water to their left. They quacked and took off in a flurry of feathers.

Laughing, Hari dived smoothly beneath the water. When he surfaced, he stroked rapidly, his kicking feet propelling him through the water. For a while, they were neck and neck. They turned upon reaching the flax bush, the burn of exertion pleasing his feline. Hari pulled ahead, reaching the finish line first.

"Yes!" He leapt into the air, pumping his fist in the air.

He went back under the water and came up grinning to find Jake staring at him with a strange expression on his face. Hari thought he caught a flicker of anger. Maybe he wasn't a good loser?

"Are you pissed at me?" Hari didn't believe in tiptoeing around problems. He thought about his attraction to Jake and grimaced—most of the time anyway.

"No," Jake said hurriedly, looking away. "Good race. You're fast."

Hari forced a smile when he wanted to obey the urge to move closer and run his fingers across the other man's muscular chest, testing the light covering of hair for texture. "I've had enough." His muscles tensed as he fought his instinct to close the distance between them. "I'm gonna get out and dry off."

He had to get away from Jake before he did something to shock the hell out of both of them, like touching Jake. A sharp bark of laughter escaped him. Actually touching was the least of his problems. Suddenly he understood why Ambar had been in such a panic this morning. Wading from the water, he tried not to think about Jake or wonder if the other man was watching his butt.

Hari stalked to the blanket and spread it out with a flick of his wrists, briskly running his hands over his body to wipe off the worst of the water before dropping onto the ground. Shit. Bloody erection. At least his claws weren't showing too much. He could make out a faint line of black beneath his nails, but they weren't jutting above the tip.

Gritting his teeth, Hari lay back on the blanket, closing his eyes while he listened to the sounds of the water and Jake swimming. It did nothing to relax either him or his cock. Then he heard splashing sounds to indicate Jake's approach. A shot of heat rushed through him, and he almost moaned aloud. Jake couldn't miss his arousal. He turned on to his side to hide. Although he knew he shouldn't, Hari watched Jake approach through narrowed eyes. The man was bulkier than him, in his prime with broad shoulders tapering down to slim hips and long, muscular legs. His chest had a light covering of hair that arrowed downward to his groin. Hari swallowed, unused to the surge of lust that hit him when he caught sight of Jake's cock.

But even more interesting was the fact Jake had a hard-on the same as him. Judging by the expression on Jake's face, he was having a problem with his body behaving in such an unruly manner.

On impulse Hari sat up and grinned at Jake. Something told him openness was best.

"What's wrong with the water around here?" He gestured at his dick. "I thought that cold was meant to make things subside, not make them worse."

Jake let out a spluttered laugh and sat on the far side of the blanket with a body's length between them. "It's never happened before."

"You ever had sex with a man?"

"Hell no," Jake spluttered and shot a quick glance in Hari's direction before looking away. Jake's gaze was like a stroke of fingers along his cock, and Hari felt the resulting rush of blood as he lengthened.

"Me neither," Hari said, shifting uneasily.

"Maybe we should change the subject."

"Good idea," Hari said, although he didn't think that would help matters. There was something weird going on and it seemed Jake was the catalyst. Or maybe he was the catalyst. Whatever. The fact remained that he wanted both Ambar and Jake.

"Tell me what you're going to work on this afternoon," Jake said.

Good plan. Stick their heads in the sand and pretend nothing was happening.

"I'm juggling two contracts right now. A romance author wants me to design a website for her, and I'm doing some work for a new business that sells kitchen equipment via the internet."

"How did you get started with romance authors?"

Hari grinned. "A friend of a friend writes erotic romance for an e-publisher and needed a website. Word of mouth is a wonderful thing."

"My mother used to read them."

Hari's grin widened as he recalled the books he'd read in the name of research before he designed his first author website. "Somehow I don't think they're the books your mother used to read. Maybe that's where I got the idea," he mused, thinking out loud about the shenanigans of the three lovers in the last one he'd read.

"What idea?"

Hari's cock gave a jerk. "Never mind." His gaze drifted to Jake without permission. "I think I'm dry enough." A suit of armor might make a difference even if it was only of fabric. He jumped to his feet and rapidly dressed. Part of him was relieved when Jake started to dress as well.

"What sort of design are you doing for the kitchen equipment place? Hari?"

Hari realized he'd been staring at Jake's backside and frowned, a flash of heat flooding his face. God, he was mooning like a teenage girl with a crush. "They said they wanted something fresh and vibrant. I was thinking of some sort of play on citrus fruits, using lemon, lime and orange as the primary colors on the site."

"Will it be graphic heavy?"

"Not if I do it right," Hari said. "I know some people still have slow access—"

"What the fuck is wrong with me?" Jake snarled, cutting in on Hari's reply.

"What do you mean?"

"I mean that all day I've been aware of you. Sexually aware." Jake swallowed, refusing to meet his gaze.

Hari was impressed. Most guys he knew would run a mile before they even thought about voicing the subject. "I feel the same, and it's scaring the crap out of me. Maybe I should leave or at least move out."

"Hell no," Jake snapped. "That's stupid. We're adults. We can deal with this."

"How?" Quite frankly, trying to ignore Jake wasn't working too well for him.

"Hell if I know." Jake pulled on his boots and stomped to his vehicle. He whistled the dogs, and Hari finished dressing before following.

He climbed into the cab and waited for Jake to join him, body tense and blood pounding through his veins.

69

He curled his fingers into his thighs, unsurprised to feel the bite of claws. He'd never had a problem with control before, not even as a teenager undergoing change for the first time.

Jake opened the door and slid behind the wheel. He glanced at Hari and their gazes caught. Before he knew how it happened, Hari leaned toward Jake, and the other man did the same. Their lips touched. They both froze. One of them groaned. Hari didn't know if it was him or Jake. All he knew was that one little touch of lips wasn't nearly enough. His hand snaked out to curl around Jake's nape. He savored the brush of springy hair beneath his palm before the real sensation hit. Soft lips. The abrasive touch of stubble. The nip of teeth as they experimented to find the perfect angle.

Hari opened his mouth and Jake's tongue darted inside to taste. A moan rumbled from deep in Hari's chest and his cock tightened to the point of pain. All he wanted to do was get closer.

He wanted skin, a flat surface. Yeah, all of that.

Jake groaned against his lips, and Hari pulled back. They stared at each other for a long moment.

"Well." Brilliant conversation, it wasn't. Hari simply wasn't capable of witty dialogue when his world had turned upside down twice in one week. First Ambar and now Jake.

Jake stared at him for a fraction longer. He swallowed audibly before looking away to start the vehicle. "We're not gonna do that again, right?"

"I DON'T UNDERSTAND WHY you had to travel halfway around the world," Aunt Gita said in a muffled voice.

Hari could imagine her stirring one of her curries with her wooden spoon, the phone tucked between her right shoulder and ear. The thought brought a pang of homesickness, but it soon passed. While he might return to England for a holiday or business trip, this was his home now. With Jake and Ambar. A sense of rightness and warmth filled him, and he knew he'd made the right decision to move to New Zealand despite the newness of his situation.

"I needed to move on, Aunt," he said in a soothing voice. The last thing he wanted to do was upset her. "I'll still fly back to visit, but there are too many memories there for me. I miss my parents."

"I know you do, Hari. You're a good boy. A good influence on Sanjay. I wish the boy would settle down with a good Indian girl instead of parading around all those white girls."

"Some of those white girls are very nice," Hari protested. "Does color matter if they make Sanjay happy?"

"I'm too old to teach someone how to cook a traditional dinner," Aunt Gita snapped back, although laughter colored her words. She paused and Hari heard the tap of a spoon against a metal pot. "I'm afraid Sanjay will get into trouble. You were such a good influence on him."

"I need to live my own life," Hari said, not willing to voice the truth. His cousin Sanjay was a spoiled,

71

self-centered twit who was full of arrogance. "I've always wanted to travel."

"Well, you can't travel much farther than New Zealand," his aunt retorted.

"I rang to give you my phone number and email address."

"Let me get a pen."

Hari waited while his aunt searched. He smiled, hearing her muttering under her breath. In his mind's eye he could see the pristine kitchen, smell the tang of spices and see the pot of fresh coriander his aunt liked to keep on the window ledge.

"I'm ready."

Hari gave her the details and said goodbye, promising to send his aunt an email with some photos of where he was living. He hung up with a sigh. Time to get to work. At least Jake had left after dropping Hari off at the house. He might have a chance of concentrating now.

Without conscious thought, his mind went back to their kiss. It had been unexpected yet spectacular. A case where reality surpassed anything he might have imagined.

"Bloody weird." He shook his head as he powered up his laptop.

It had been an experiment. That's all. No matter how great the kiss had felt, how right it had seemed, Jake wasn't interested. He'd fled, making it clear he didn't want to repeat the kiss or come anywhere near Hari.

Hari couldn't make up his mind how he felt about Jake's reaction—whether he should be pissed or relieved.

He'd kissed Hari.

Hari had kissed him back.

Did that mean he was queer?

Fuck.

Jake mended the fence on automatic pilot, pounding staples into the fence posts with his hammer.

Bang. Bang. Bang.

Mind in turmoil, he wondered if he should ask Hari to leave. His breath hissed past his lips at the idea. No! He didn't want Hari to move out.

So what the hell did he want? That was the question.

Even though they hadn't known each other long, Jake felt at ease with Hari. It was as if Hari had always been part of his life. With Hari around, his loneliness had eased. But he wasn't bloody queer.

Bang. Bang. Bang.

Sex with Ambar was the best ever. Nah, he definitely wasn't gay. But he couldn't stop thinking about what might be with Hari, what could happen if they went beyond a kiss. Not that he knew exactly what beyond would mean or feel like. Maybe similar to anal sex with Ambar. But receiving...

A shiver ran the length of his body, rocking his sense of self. It went against everything he'd ever thought, and yet the kiss with Hari had felt good. It had felt right.

With the fence repairs finished, Jake moved on to his next job, fixing a hole in the hay shed so the remaining hay didn't get wet and rot. Next came the problem with the water trough.

Five hours passed as Jake powered through lots of small jobs he'd put off due to lack of time. Now, with his stomach so empty it was practically gnawing his backbone, he admitted he was procrastinating and terrified to return home.

"Idiot," he said, disgusted with himself.

Decision made, Jake collected his tools and slung them on the back of his vehicle.

By the time he pulled up at his house, the sun had set and daylight was rapidly receding, blotting out the scenery with darkness. It was with trepidation that he opened his front door and stepped inside. He toed off his boots, peeled off his socks and walked to the kitchen in bare feet.

The welcoming scent of dinner floated out to meet him, bringing a sense of home and warmth that hadn't been present before. At least not since his parents had left. Hari's face drifted into his mind. God, he needed a drink.

He headed straight for the fridge and pulled out a beer. The tab made a satisfying hiss when he opened the can. The crisp tang of hops slid across his taste buds as he turned to survey the kitchen.

Hari wasn't there.

Jake swallowed another mouthful of beer and went in search of Hari. He saw him the moment he entered the lounge. Hari had cleared off the table and set up his laptop there. He had papers spread across most of the surface and a pair of rimless glasses perched on his nose. Jake's first impression was of a sexy professor until he took in the tight white T-shirt and the faded jeans that hugged Hari's thighs and hips as he leaned over some of the pages he'd arranged on the tabletop.

One look and he felt his body respond. Confusion rioted through him, and he crushed the can in his right hand, cursing when beer shot out the top.

Hari didn't even jump. He merely turned around and smiled, as if he'd known Jake was standing there all the time. "You ready for dinner?"

"I need a shower."

"Ten minutes?"

Jake nodded. Although he was pleased Hari was behaving normally, a part of him experienced pique because Jake couldn't forget the kiss as easily as Hari apparently had. Jake returned his crushed beer can to the kitchen before heading for the shower. Perhaps a cold shower would do the trick.

After his shower, Jake strode back to the kitchen. "Did Ambar ring?"

"Yeah, while you were in the shower. She said she's not coming over tonight. They have a lot of orders to fill and she wanted to catch up with the laundry."

Jake nodded. "I'll give her a call later." His stomach grumbled loudly. "You don't have to cook for me."

"I like cooking. It helps me unwind. Besides, I do quite a bit of thinking while I cook."

"That could be dangerous." Hell, it sounded like he was flirting. Change the subject. His stomach rumbled again, providing him with a great subject starter. "What's for dinner?"

"I found a beef roast in the freezer. I've done vegetables."

Hari expertly carved the meat as he spoke. "Take a seat. I'll bring it over for you."

"You don't have to wait on me."

"I'm not." Hari set a plate of food in front of him and took the seat opposite. Their legs collided under the table and Jake jumped, unaccountably nervous.

"I'm not gonna bite." Hari's expression said he'd thought about it though.

Jake swallowed, averting his gaze to concentrate on his meal. It was better than anything his mother had ever served them. "This is great." He started eating, a moan of pleasure escaping as the meat practically melted on his tongue.

A grin lit up Hari's face. "Better than sex, huh?"

"Cut it out."

"Scared?"

"Confused," Jake countered. "Eat your dinner."

"Yes, sir."

Jake glared at Hari, trying not to laugh when he noticed the suspicious quirk of Hari's mouth. "Cut it out." Unbidden Jake's mouth curled up into a grin. "How did work go?"

"Good. I've almost finished the author site. I'll show you after we've finished eating. I could do with some input on the kitchen site design."

Once they started to talk about work, Jake relaxed enough to enjoy his meal and the conversation.

"You want another beer?"

Jake thought about it and decided something stronger might be in order. "I have some bourbon. I'll grab it after we've finished dinner."

"Sounds good."

They cleaned the kitchen together, working as a team. As the evening progressed, Jake started to feel more and more on edge. A casual touch here. The rumble of Hari's husky voice. His laugh. They added up to trouble.

Every minute seemed to ratchet up the tension in Jake until he wanted to touch Hari so bad his hands shook. Yeah he needed that bourbon now. He strode to the pantry and located the bottle right at the back.

Straightening from his crouch, he found a bottle of cola and two glasses from the cupboard. He poured a measure into each glass and added soda before carrying both glasses to the lounge.

"Thanks. So, what do you think?"

A loaded question if ever he'd heard one. He played rugby for god's sake—the ultimate in masculine sports. But all he could think about was kissing Hari.

"Jake? The website?"

"Ah yeah." He sucked in a deep breath and wished he hadn't. There was too much of Hari in it. He focused on the laptop screen and the striking website design. It was exotic and oozed sex in a totally classy way with the silhouettes of an entwined couple sprawled across the opening page. His mind leaped ahead to the bedroom and the things a couple could do. Suddenly his cock was hard enough to do the business, trying to burst from his jeans. He gulped his drink, desperate to control the urge to run his fingers down Hari's back and nuzzle his neck, to kiss the soft skin behind his ear, right where his scar started.

"What do you think?"

Jake shook himself free of the sensual spell and cleared his throat. He didn't think he should repeat his exact thoughts. He coughed again, took another sip of his drink, draining the glass dry. "It's great. Very sensual. Ambar would say it was hot."

Mention of Ambar should have stopped the sexual surge inside him or at least redirected it or slowed the thing down. That didn't happen.

"I think the author will be pleased."

"Yeah." Jake nodded and wondered about getting another drink. Or even better, he should head to bed and keep out of trouble. A snort escaped at that, his mind and body battling about what he should do next. A drink. "Show me the other site. Bring it up while I get another drink."

Hari sent him a long look that made his bare toes curl into the carpet. Without taking his gaze off Jake, Hari picked up his glass and swallowed the remains in one go. "You can fill mine as well."

Jake took the glass, suppressing a shudder when their fingers touched. For a moment he thought Hari would say something, but he remained silent. Jake stalked into the kitchen, his body pulsing with sexual energy. Still confused but no longer surprised by the awareness between them, he topped up their glasses. This time he poured a larger measure of bourbon and less soda.

Taking another deep and hopefully fortifying breath, Jake sauntered back to the lounge with the two drinks. While he'd been in the kitchen Hari had set up the laptop on the glass-topped coffee table and was busy plugging in two gaming controls.

"Feel like testing out my game?"

"Yeah." Just the thing to keep him focused on something other than Hari. Jake settled on the couch so he could see the screen. Unfortunately, he hadn't realized how close they'd need to sit. Their thighs brushed. Jake made a sound of distress and jerked from Hari's touch.

"Steady. I'm not gonna jump you."

Yeah, but that was the problem. After their earlier kiss, Jake wasn't sure he could stop himself from jumping Hari. Of course he could do it the easy way and walk away...

Jake considered the alternative yet again and discarded it. Something inside him refused to act the outraged virgin, refused to turn his back and walk away.

"Let's play," Jake growled. "Any instructions or things I should know about first?"

Hari chuckled. "I want you to start with the same knowledge as a beginner. That way I can make sure I've set everything up in an instinctive manner."

"You have inside knowledge."

"Your point being?" Hari's evil grin held a hint of challenge.

"All right, smart-arse. Game on." Jake picked up the control and peered more closely at the screen, trying to focus on the game instead of the man seated way too close to him.

"Wanna bet on who will win?"

Jake looked at Hari then and became enmeshed in his stare. Was it his imagination or did Hari's eyes flash gold?

Jake blinked. Nah, it was simple. He was going nuts. Maybe he should have gone out tonight and dropped in to see Ambar.

"You keep drifting off," Hari said, his voice husky.

"Sorry. I'm tired."

"We can do this another night."

"Nah, it's okay. We'll play for an hour and then I'll hit the mattress."

Hari's eyes flickered again. Definitely gold.

"Your eyes are funny. Must be a trick of the light."

"Stop changing the subject. Do you want to bet or not?"

"What did you have in mind?"

Hari's brows rose, his mouth curling with sudden amusement, and Jake knew he wasn't going to like what came out of his mouth. "A massage?"

"I was thinking something more hands off." Jake fought to repel the visuals slipping through his mind.

"You're no fun." Hari fluttered his lashes at him. *Fluttered them.*

Jake felt his mouth drop open and punched Hari in the arm. "Knock it off. I told you to stop flirting with me."

"Is it working?"

Jake picked up his drink and knocked back most of it. "We'll make the bet for a new bottle of bourbon. I'll get us another drink." He leapt to his feet and went to the kitchen, returning minutes later. "Let's play."

Hari nodded, pushed a button and the screen burst to life. Sound roared from the speakers he'd set up earlier.

Jake concentrated on the screen, tried not to let Hari distract him. "Are there levels to work through?"

"Yes. You have to collect crew and a ship before you can buy your hell-horse."

"Yeah!" Jake cheered when he managed to avoid a pirate attack and stole their ship while they were distracted. An hour passed quickly and the level of his drink steadily declined. He yawned and grinned sheepishly at Hari. "Maybe I should call it a night. It's getting late."

"It's okay. We've highlighted a few areas I need to tweak." Hari clicked a few buttons and shut down the laptop before picking up his drink and leaning back. Their legs still touched.

Part of Jake wanted to move, yet he stayed exactly where he was, too comfortable to move. "I should go to bed."

CHAPTER FIVE

HARI STARED AT JAKE. All evening need had sizzled through him. *Hunger*. If Hari hadn't been a tiger shifter, he might have thought he was going mad. Shifters were more fluid in their ideas of love, so while the idea of Jake wasn't exactly what he'd had in mind, he was willing to follow his feline's dictates. And right now, his feline wanted body contact.

Leaning over, he took the empty glass out of Jake's hands and set it aside.

"Are you gonna kiss me again?"

"The thought had crossed my mind," Hari said. "Mostly because I want to see if this afternoon was a one-off."

"No." Jake shook his head.

"No, you don't want me to kiss you? Or no, it wasn't a one-off?"

Jake swallowed, his confusion clear. He didn't know what the hell was happening to him and signaled uneasiness with every subtle move of his big body.

Hari would have laughed, but the primitive hunger flooding him called for action. Without giving it another thought, he leaned in and pinned Jake against the couch. He registered the wall of muscle against his chest, hard instead of soft. It didn't matter. One of them groaned and craving exploded in him. Hari closed the last bit of distance between their mouths and settled in to tease and tempt the other man with his kiss. It was soft, a little tentative even though his feline stirred uneasily, pushing for hard and fast. Raw desire yanked his stomach tight.

"Open your mouth for me, love. That's right." Hari smoothed his hands over Jake's face, his fingers skating over the dark stubble shading his jaw, the endearment coming easily. God, this afternoon hadn't been an aberration.

If anything, their kiss seemed better.

Jake moaned, his hands creeping up to grip Hari's shoulders. The firm pressure of Jake's hands anchored Hari and told him Jake wanted this too. Hari's nostrils flared, cataloging Jake's scent. It reminded him of the fresh outdoors, mouthwatering and tempting.

He licked Jake's bottom lip, tasting him and the bourbon he'd been drinking. Then he started kissing Jake in earnest, caressing his starkly male lips, twining their tongues, fucking his mouth until his groin throbbed with the desire to come. Only the need to breathe made him ease back a fraction.

Jake stared at him through startled blue eyes, his lips swollen and red from their kisses. "I like kissing you."

Tiredness and the bourbon slurred his words. His eyes drifted shut and he cuddled into Hari like a sleepy kitten.

Smiling, Hari wrapped an arm around him, the closeness feeling exactly right.

Hari heard a car and tensed until he recognized the quick cadence of Ambar's steps and her scent. Good. He was glad she'd come. They needed to talk, probably alone without Jake around. They needed a plan. He only hoped she wouldn't try to send him back to England again. That wasn't going to happen. Not now that he had a reason to stay. A sudden smile bloomed. Two reasons.

He pressed a kiss to the top of Jake's head, a sense of satisfaction filling him despite the painful pressure of his cock against the fly of his jeans.

A sharp gasp jerked his head up. Ambar stood in the doorway, her hand pressed to her mouth. They stared at each other for a long moment before she turned and fled.

Hari scowled when he heard the shriek of tires as they fought for purchase. Hell, he hadn't seen that coming. From what he knew of her to date, he'd thought she'd march inside and demand to know what the fuck they were doing. Instead she'd run like a wimpy girl.

Part of him was disappointed. He glanced at his watch, saw it was late and decided there was no point chasing after her at this time of the night. Tomorrow would be soon enough.

"Hey, sleeping beauty." Hari shook Jake awake. The man did look beautiful in a purely masculine way, certainly better-looking than Hari with his scar. He shook Jake a little harder and watched his eyes flicker open. Soft blue eyes. Beautiful blue eyes.

Confusion clouded them for an instant before he closed them again.

Smiling, Hari pulled away enough to tug Jake to his feet. He half carried and dragged Jake to his bedroom, shouldering open the door and directing him to the bed. They fell to the bed in a tangle of limbs. Hari thought about leaving then gave in to temptation and settled back beside Jake. Even though they were still fully clothed, he fell asleep with a smile on his face.

AMBAR DIDN'T REMEMBER RUNNING to her car and speeding back to Middlemarch. Her hands gripped the steering wheel, her mind in turmoil. What the hell was Hari up to and Jake...as the old cliché went, it took two to tango.

They were doing a mighty close dance. Way too intimate for her liking.

Her foot pressed the accelerator until her car sped along the gravel road, furious tears running down her cheeks. She swiped them away with the back of one hand to clear her vision.

"Stupid!" she snarled, anger making her grip the wheel so hard the color bled from her knuckles, hurt a piercing ache in her chest. "Why didn't you storm into the room and demand answers? Ask them what the hell they were doing?"

Yeah, why hadn't she ripped them a new one? They

both deserved it. She wasn't sure who she was furious with more—Jake or Hari.

Even worse, it had all happened so quickly. She and Jake had made love this morning, so what the heck had occurred during the day to change things? Another flood of tears ran down her face.

Panic—that's why. She'd taken one look and instinct had taken over. Terror still rippled through her, making her breathing sound labored and choppy. Her pulse raced and her clammy palms stuck to the steering wheel. As she turned off the gravel onto the main road, she slowed for safety reasons and rubbed her eyes again. The last thing she needed was an accident. That really would crown her crappy day.

Five minutes later, she screeched to a stop outside the house she shared with Rohan and Kiran and stormed inside. She stomped straight to their bedroom and pounded her fist on the door.

"Can I come in? I need to talk to you."

"Can't it wait until the morning?" Rohan's growling reply sounded muffled.

She thumped on the door again to emphasize her urgency. The door rattled in its frame.

"Quit that," Kiran ordered in a terse voice. "Just a minute."

Ambar paused a beat and opened the door. "Minute's up," she said, turning on the light.

Jake and Hari. God, she still couldn't believe it. Jake was so...so masculine and he loved sex. It showed with his every touch. He liked having sex with her. She knew it.

Men weren't that good at pretense. Besides, she knew he'd stopped seeing other women. The thought sank in and took on another meaning.

Had he stopped playing the field because he'd discovered a liking for men?

Kiran blinked at her, his mouth set in a grumpy snarl. "Did you have to turn on the light?" He took a closer look at her and concern replaced his tetchy mood. "You've been crying. What's wrong?"

Rohan's face appeared from under the blankets, his lips swollen and his black hair sticking up in a good impersonation of a hedgehog. "We were busy. You couldn't have—" He broke off on catching a glimpse of her tear-stained face. "What is it? What's wrong? I thought you were staying the night at Jake's."

"I was." Ambar sniffed and walked closer to perch on the corner of their big bed. "I walked in on Jake and Hari together."

"Together?" Kiran asked blankly.

Rohan frowned. "Together how?"

"They were wrapped in each other's arms." Ambar bit back a sob as the vision replayed through her mind. No, she hadn't been mistaken.

Rohan frowned. "Maybe it was innocent?"

"I know what Jake looks like after he's been kissing."

"So what did they say when you asked what they were up to?" Kiran asked.

She let out a disgusted sigh. "Nothing. I mean, I didn't ask them anything. I turned into a stupid wimpy girl and ran away in a panic. I was just so shocked. Halfway back

I thought about returning to confront them, but…" she trailed off with a shrug.

Rohan sat up properly. "What will you do?"

Ambar jumped to her feet and started pacing. "I don't know. I have no idea." The more she paced, the more she realized that jealousy simmered inside her. The knowledge brought a frown. "I'm jealous."

"You have feelings for Hari," Rohan said with a chortle.

"I do not," Ambar snapped. "I barely know the man."

"That hasn't stopped Jake," Rohan pointed out with a sly smirk.

Ambar scowled, not liking the truth pointed out to her. "What would you do?" Her gaze went from Rohan to Kiran and back. "Wipe that grin off your face, Rohan, otherwise we're going to fall out."

"You're not allowed to hit Rohan. I like him exactly how he is."

The searing glance the two males shared made Ambar uncomfortable. She paused in her pacing to glare at them. "Not helping."

Rohan sobered but the echo of his hilarity continued to glow in his eyes. "You keep reminding us you're an adult."

"Still not helping," she snapped.

Kiran interrupted before brother and sister started bickering. "This is what you do. Leave it tonight. Work out why you're angry. Is it because Jake's been unfaithful or is it because you're jealous of Hari and Jake together? Once you know the answers, you'll be able to decide what to do. Only you can come to a decision. Neither of us intends to tell you what to do because you *are* an adult." It was a long speech for Kiran and one that made sense.

She was the only one who could decide what to do. "Thanks," she said, making her way to the door.

"Ambar?" Kiran's voice halted her.

"Yes?"

"Don't make us get a lock for that door," he said.

She nodded, acknowledging she'd crossed a boundary she shouldn't have tonight. Not surprising given her emotional turmoil. "I'm sorry. It won't happen again. My thoughts were...are scrambled at the moment." She closed the door and turned for her bedroom. She'd sleep on it and tomorrow she'd confront Hari and Jake and demand answers.

Jake woke slowly, the weight of the body against his back and the arm around his waist bringing warmth. He lay there, luxuriating in the sensation of intimacy. It beat the hell out of waking alone. Sighing because he knew he needed to rise and start his day, he opened his eyes and glanced down at the arm curved around him. The forearm bore dark hairs.

He bolted upright with a cry of shock.

"What? *What?*"

Jake realized several things at once. He was in bed with Hari. They both wore clothes, and Hari woke up a hell of a lot quicker than he did.

"You okay?" Hari reached out to touch him, and Jake flinched away, almost falling off the bed.

89

"What the hell are we doing in bed together?"

"I dragged you to bed last night."

Jake didn't remember much of the previous night. He swallowed, the thickness of his tongue and bad taste in his mouth giving him a big clue as to why he didn't recall his actions.

"That doesn't explain why we're in the same bed." The harsh note of accusation hurt his head. He clamped his mouth shut and even that ached.

"You looked so...tempting I couldn't resist." Hari's hesitation was telling. He'd chosen his words carefully. It was what he didn't say that alarmed Jake most.

"I'm not interested in men!"

"I never said you were."

"You're gay." Jake winced at the condemnation in his voice. He didn't have anything against gay men. He liked Rohan and Kiran well enough. A frown surfaced as another thought occurred. Maybe it was something in the air, but he could think of several gay relationships in Middlemarch. The cop Charlie didn't make much of a secret of his relationship with the vet. His frown intensified because those two men lived with Leticia. And then there was Saul. He lived with another man too, although not in Middlemarch.

"Stop thinking so hard." The whisper-soft demand brought a wash of awareness, the English accent clipped and precise. "It can't be that bad—you're still on the bed with me."

Jake's mouth fell open in shock, and he sprang to his feet, truth beating him over the head. While Hari's presence had scared him, it hadn't occurred to him to put more distance between them. He stared at Hari, taking In his scar, his gold-flecked eyes. His gaze dropped lower to linger on Hari's lips. The memory of kissing those lips swooped in like an avenging angel, the sensations crowding in on him.

He remembered.

They'd kissed. A lot. And he'd liked it.

Confusion scrambled his brain. His hands shook and, to his shock, his cock started to fill, pressing against the fly of his jeans with unrelenting pressure. The urge to touch Hari, to close the distance between them and kiss him again jolted him to action.

"I'm going to take a shower." Escape. He needed to get away from Hari and his enticing scent. Without another word, Jake turned and walked away. In the bathroom, he closed the door and leaned against the hard wood, waiting until his heart ceased its urgent pounding. How did Hari do this to him? Groaning softly, he scrubbed his hands over his face. It was as if an alien inhabited his body, luring him into temptation.

With another groan, Jake started to strip, pausing to open the shower door and turn on the taps so the water heated before he jumped in the shower.

He peeled off the last of his clothes, wincing slightly when the back of his hand knocked his swollen erection. Jake cursed and stepped under the water. Still icy cold, it did nothing to cool the fever pulsing through his veins. How the hell had he landed in this mess?

Jake heard a thump and his head jerked up. The

bathroom door burst open and Hari strode into his view. Unbidden Jake's gaze slid from Hari's face and down his naked body. It should have alarmed him—fuck, his mind was in turmoil, yet his body craved Hari's touch. His eyes widened as Hari prowled nearer. The man was all sleek muscle, unleashed power. Once again, he thought the muscular physique was strange in a man who worked a sedentary job.

The door to the shower opened, and Jake's eyes widened in panic as Hari stepped inside.

"What are you doing?" *Weak. Why wasn't he telling Hari to fuck off? To get the hell out of his house?*

"I'm not going to let you run away from this, from us."

Jake backed into the corner of the shower. "There is no us."

Hari kept moving until Jake had nowhere left to retreat. The heat of Hari's chest against his and the brush of his cock brought a shiver. Jake swallowed, unsure of what to do with his hands. He stood awkwardly, hands fisted at his sides.

They stared at each other until Hari gripped his shoulders and kissed him. Jake melted under the physical contact, still confused, still wary, yet in an odd way, excited. Jake had no idea what he was doing, but he was willing to experiment a little. The muscles of his stomach flexed as Hari drew him under the water. Warm now, it poured over his head and ran over their bodies.

Hari ran his hands down Jake's back until they reached his ass. Jake's heart lurched painfully. He tensed when Hari drew their groins together. Their cocks brushed as they settled against each other. In the past, Jake would have run a mile or punched Hari in the jaw.

Today it was the furthest thing in his mind. His breath puffed out. Involuntarily, his hips jerked, the resulting friction sending an intense burst of heat through him. Jake gasped at the sexual sensation. He sought Hari's gaze and saw he appeared just as startled.

Jake cleared his throat. "You really haven't done this before?"

"Never. I'm working on instinct here."

"We shouldn't."

"Why?" Hari countered, his voice rough with none of his normal elegant accent.

"I'm with Ambar." Jake thought of the pleasure they'd shared in the past. The sex with Ambar was good. Very good, and he didn't understand why he wanted this with Hari when she satisfied him fully.

There was a long pause. The bathroom started to steam up, and he realized he'd forgotten to turn on the ventilation fan.

"Don't worry about it." Hari's eyes blazed a light shade of gold when he looked at Jake. "It will work out."

"But I'm not that guy," Jake said. "I don't sleep around. I don't cheat on my lovers when I'm with them."

Hari nodded. "I know. That's why I know we'll work things out."

Jake knew he should push Hari away. This was sick, besides he was with Ambar. He tried to enforce his will and raised his hands to push Hari away. But unbidden his fingers curled into Hari's muscular biceps and he drew the

SHELLEY MUNRO

other man nearer. Their lips touched, caressed. God, it felt damn good. Jake opened his mouth, craving more. It was yesterday all over again. The thought crept through his mind, rubbing alongside the confusion that had dwelled in him since their very first kiss.

Hari pulled away, far enough for Jake to see his face. Jake thought he might see triumph or maybe smugness at the idea of seducing another man. Instead he saw desire and determination along with a hint of urgency.

Hari kissed his jaw, and instinctively Jake turned his head to give the other man better access, baring his neck. A low growl erupted from Hari, startling Jake a little with its catlike nature. A sharp nip on his lower neck dragged him from his thoughts, his legs buckling under the intense surge of pleasure that took him by surprise. He would have fallen if not for Hari helping him to balance.

"Damn," Hari said, burying his face in Jake's neck.

The water continued to pour over them, the steamy bathroom like a warm haven.

"Are you going to have a panic attack if I touch your cock?"

Jake swallowed. While his body was willing, his mind still protested the situation with Hari. "I don't know."

"Do you want to touch me?"

Something in Hari's face demanded the truth. "Yes."

"Do you want to go first?"

Jake barked out a startled laugh. "What is this? Two kids in the schoolyard?"

Hari grinned. "We've kissed. We're both still alive to tell the tale."

"I'm not gay." Hell, he sounded like a stuck record.

"I never said you were. Go on, touch me. I dare you."

Jake didn't take the time to analyze why, but somehow Hari's challenge made the idea of touching easier. His heart still thudded at a frantic pace and his hand trembled as he curled his fingers around Hari's erection. He used a firm grip, handling Hari the same way he touched himself.

Fascinated, he watched the expression on Hari's face, the deep pleasure before he closed his eyes. Jake pumped his hand, part of him still stunned at the way he was touching another man. The weird thing was that it felt so right and natural.

Jake's cock grew harder with each stroke of his hand on Hari's shaft. A thought occurred and he acted before worry took over. He shifted position, squeezing closer to Hari and gripped both cocks in his hand.

"Aw, hell," Hari muttered.

Oh yeah. A burst of heat struck Jake right away—the naughty, forbidden element doing the rest. Jake gasped as his cock thickened against Hari's. The tight squeeze of his fingers and a brisk pace pushed them both hard and fast. A shudder racked his body while Hari moaned his pleasure. Pressure built in his balls until they lifted high. Heat and pressure rampaged through Jake, and he came in blistering waves against the shower wall.

Hari let out a loud purring sound, his head thrown back as he released in hard spurts. His muscular body quaked, and Jake watched in fascination. He looked so damn hot—masculine and in control with not a shred of weakness in his makeup.

Jake kept stroking until Hari ceased his shudders, easing up on the pressure before releasing his grip.

"I..." Jake trailed off, unsure of what to say and what the hell he thought of jerking off with Hari.

"Don't overthink," Hari warned.

"But I don't understand. How can I want two lovers so much? It's not normal."

Hari reached for the soap and lathered his chest before cleaning Jake. His attentions were matter-of-fact, and Jake stood silently while Hari washed him from chest to groin. Bloody weird. Not only was he letting Hari touch him, he was enjoying it. A few more strokes would have him ready to go again.

"Who decides what is normal? I didn't exactly plan this."

"We can't do this."

"Why not?" Hari watched him intently, waiting for an answer. All Jake could think about was dragging Hari from the shower and starting to experiment in the bedroom.

"What about Ambar? I really like her." Jake paused. "Hell, I'm serious about her. I've never dated one woman for such a long time."

"I don't know," Hari said. "I haven't known Ambar for long, but she seems like a special woman. I was going to help you again this morning, but how about if I stay here and give you time to think? That is assuming you don't want me to pack and leave?"

"No!" Jake stopped abruptly, both embarrassed and perplexed by his certainty. It was one thing he was sure about. He didn't want Hari to leave. "No, I need the

money coming in to keep the bank manager off my back."
A weak excuse and he thought Hari knew it was merely an
excuse to make him stay.

Hari nodded and finished washing himself, rinsing off
the last of the soap. "Do you feel like something for
breakfast?"

"You don't have to cook for me."

"I've told you before. I like cooking."

"I could do with some coffee."

"Your wish is my command," Hari said, and he exited
the shower, grabbing a towel off the rack. He dried himself
and left the bathroom with the towel wrapped around his
waist.

Jake felt the distance between them immediately,
watching Hari until he disappeared from sight. He
switched the shower to cold, but the cooler water did
nothing to dampen the heat rioting through his body.
Resolutely, he gripped his cock and stroked until he came
again. How the hell could he face Ambar knowing he'd
fooled around with Hari? At least she hadn't been around
last night. Seeing him with Hari would be a little hard to
explain.

HARI WAITED UNTIL JAKE left to shift stock before
changing from his jeans into a pair of dress trousers, a
business shirt and a jacket. The idea had come to him
while he'd made toast and coffee for Jake. He needed to
approach Ambar in a formal fashion. His adherence to

the traditional ways would give his request credence—it would make Ambar realize how serious he was about pursuing a relationship with both her and Jake.

Yeah, Hari intended to go courting.

He wasn't sure what he'd do if Ambar refused to speak with him. That could be a problem. He frowned. Probably not the first one he'd face either, even if he did get Ambar to listen.

Stop trying to borrow trouble. Hari grabbed the keys for his rental and strode outside. During the drive to the store, he practiced what he would say to Ambar.

I had the urge to jump Jake so I did. He snorted. Yeah, as if that excuse would work.

I fell in love with Jake. Nope, not true—not yet anyway. His feline had decided he wanted to mate with Jake. Love, that was a different story, although intimacy would build with time—if he stayed in Middlemarch permanently.

Hari pulled up outside the Patels' store. It was closed. His right hand thudded against the steering wheel in frustration. Damn.

Well, he wasn't gonna wait for the store to open. This conversation required privacy, and that's what he intended to have when facing Ambar. Hari climbed from his vehicle, walked to the door and, after glancing left and right to see if anyone was watching, opened his mouth to drag the scent across his receptors. Once he caught the scent, he started to follow the trail. Lucky for him, the previous night had been clear and nothing interfered with the scent trail.

He found himself at the front door of a wooden

bungalow. Red and yellow flowers bloomed in the gardens running either side of the entrance. A surge of nerves hit him while he stood there. Even though he'd planned what he intended to say, now that he'd arrived, he wasn't so sure.

Before he had a chance to knock, the door flew open and he stood face-to-face with the man who must be Rohan's mate.

The other feline growled, long and low, his black hair prickling up into spikes.

"Kiran, what's wrong?"

Kiran stood aside to reveal Hari.

"You," Rohan snarled.

"I've come to talk to Ambar." Hari stood his ground. No way did he intend to back down or show weakness. Instead he'd go with truth. "I want Ambar. Ambar is the reason I came to New Zealand, and from our first meeting I knew my instincts were right."

Rohan glowered at him, baring his teeth. "You've a bloody funny way of showing it."

"I wasn't expecting my reaction to Jake to be so strong."

"Two mates?" Kiran asked, his brows shooting up in surprise.

Rohan continued to stare, not letting up on his glower.

"With respect, I need to discuss this with Ambar," Hari said. "We didn't get a chance to talk last night."

"We all know why," Rohan said.

"I'm not proud of the way Ambar found out. I didn't set out to do it that way." Hari lifted one shoulder in irritation. "I didn't plan on any of this."

Rohan moved closer, only halting when Kiran grasped

his arm.

"We should let Ambar and Hari sort this out," he said.

"He hurt her," Rohan said, his eyes narrowing. "He made Ambar cry."

Hari swallowed on learning she'd wept. The last thing he wanted was to hurt Ambar. From the moment he'd seen her photo, he'd felt an attraction. That hadn't changed, despite their current problems. "I'm sorry I hurt her. All I'm asking is a chance to speak with Ambar."

Rohan stood aside. He hooked a hand behind Kiran's neck and tugged the man to him. They kissed, their interaction making Hari think about Jake and the kiss they'd shared when they'd parted earlier. Lust speared him, ending in a tingling rush at his groin. Ambar had to listen to him. Somehow, he had to make this work between the three of them because he needed Ambar as much as he wanted Jake. Both he and Jake needed Ambar in their lives and in their bed.

He cleared his throat. "Can I go in?"

Rohan lifted his head. "If I hear a single growl coming from Ambar, I'll attack first and ask questions later."

"Noted." Hari hadn't expected anything less.

"And we're running on a schedule here. Ambar and I need to get to the store. Ten minutes."

With a decisive nod, Hari followed the trail, discerning Ambar's slightly sweeter and more familiar scent from the two males who lived in the house with her. He reached a closed door, knocked once and entered without waiting for a summons.

Shit! She'd been crying all right. Her eyes appeared red

and swollen. Hari hesitated, taking half a step back to lean against the door, the truth pounding him in the gut. Seeing them together had upset her badly.

"What are you doing here?" Her voice caught toward the end of her sentence, her anguish twisting Hari's heart. She wore underwear—a turquoise bra and matching panties—and nothing else. With her hair flowing loose around her shoulders, she had never looked more beautiful. A pair of black trousers and a polo shirt sat on the bed, ready for her to don. "I don't want to see you. Or Jake."

"Why did you run? We could have hashed this out last night."

"I didn't want to be a third wheel," she snapped. "You two looked mighty cozy. I didn't think you required my presence."

"Not true." Hari welcomed the flash of fire in her eyes and the bite in her voice because it meant she retained her fight. The sight of them together hadn't dulled every ounce of feeling in her. Her anger meant she cared a little at least. "Jake is my mate."

"Your mate?" All the color faded from her face and she dropped onto her bed. "But I thought..."

"Thought what?" He needed to make her consider the possibilities, think outside what most people considered the norm.

"That Jake and I had a chance together. We were happy." She nailed him with a glare. "Until you came along."

"But you didn't think you and he were mates?"

"Not everyone finds a mate. My parents had an arranged

marriage and it worked for them."

"My parents did too."

"What will your parents think about you hooking up with a male?"

"I don't know. They died in a pileup on the M4 when I was a kid. My aunt and uncle took me in after the accident."

"I'm sorry." Ambar refused to meet his gaze, her fingers plucking at the ruffled bedcovers.

"We don't have much time to talk. I know you need to get to the store." Hari hesitated before deciding upfront and honest would work best. He needed to know if they might have a future together. "Can I kiss you?"

Her eyes widened in horror. "What do you think Jake would say about that? Did you make love last night? No wait!" She held up her hand, color flooding her cheeks. "I don't want to know. I'm damn well not taking Jake's leftovers."

"I'm not leftover anything. Jake and I...we kissed—mainly." Hari recalled the sense of rightness and the pleasure that came with Jake's touch. Knowing she was likely to dodge his request if he didn't take action, Hari crossed the space between them, grasped her hand and tugged her to her feet. He wrapped his arms around her and lowered his head to kiss her.

She fought his touch at first, opening her mouth to cry out. Desperate to prove his point, he used every bit of his expertise, coaxing her to respond. Her taste and scent flowed over him, and his feline writhed beneath his skin. His hands glided over her semi-naked body, reveling in the silky skin and her barely concealed curves.

Ambar moaned, and Hari eased up on the kiss. If she really didn't want this, he wouldn't force himself on her any longer. Despite his tiger genes, he wasn't a savage. His aunt and uncle had reared him better than that.

Ambar's hands crept up behind his head, clutching him to maintain their contact. "Don't stop."

Triumph surged through him as she mashed their lips together. Her teeth nicked his lip and the coppery taste of blood flavored their kiss. But Ambar didn't stop, moaning again. Her hands stroked down his back, coming to rest on his butt, pulling him against her body. His erection lengthened and he knew Ambar would have little doubt about his reaction. It was the same crazy out-of-control sensation he'd experienced with Jake. All he could think was how wonderful it would feel when he didn't have to rein in his lust. Just the thought of sharing a bed with Ambar and Jake sent a shudder the length of his body.

Hari's heart pounded with excitement. Kissing Ambar felt just as good as kissing Jake. Even better, Ambar was on the same page. At least her body was, even if her head wasn't quite with the program.

A growl sounded seconds before the door flew open.

"I told you not to hurt her," Rohan snapped.

"Wait." Kiran hauled his lover to a stop. "She has her hands on his butt. She's not in pain."

Hari shifted a fraction, putting himself between the two men and Ambar, his mouth tingling from her kiss.

She slapped him on the arm. "You don't need to protect me from Rohan."

Rohan glowered at Hari. "I thought you were angry at him and wanted to rip open his guts. Flay the skin from his body. That's what you said at breakfast."

"I am angry at him."

"We're discussing our problems," Hari said.

Kiran nodded. "We can see that. Since you have things in hand, I'd better go to meet Gavin." He didn't attempt to smother his amusement, his lips curling up in the beginnings of a smile.

Ambar's fingers flexed against his butt again before dropping to her sides.

"We need to get to the store." Rohan waited impatiently after Kiran disappeared from sight.

"I'll see you later," Hari said, ignoring Rohan to speak to Ambar. "Come to dinner."

She hesitated, nibbling her bottom lip. "I'll think about it."

Hari didn't want her thinking about it. He wanted action. "Don't run away from this, from us." He pulled out his wallet and extracted a business card. His breath eased out with a whoosh of relief when she accepted the card. "Ring me or, better yet, come out to Jake's to talk." For a long moment, he watched her, aiming for sincerity and attempting to conceal the faint thread of panic that had lodged in his consciousness.

"I'll think about it," she repeated.

With a nod, he left her, pushing past Rohan. As he walked to his car, his mind spun in turmoil. He wanted to try the easy way, let Jake and Ambar decide this was what they wanted. But he would play hardball if that's what it took. He'd fight for what he craved. The physical contact with both Jake and Ambar had told him the truth. They didn't need to know how important this was to him, but they controlled his future.

His chance for a home and family was in their hands.

CHAPTER SIX

AMBAR WORKED ON AUTOMATIC pilot, serving customers, packing orders, and restocking shelves. She knew she replied to the customers, even joked with them, yet she couldn't have repeated a word to Rohan.

"What are you going to do?" Rohan asked when their latest customer left.

"I don't know. Seeing Jake and Hari together last night was a shock. I'm still having trouble getting my head around it."

"But neither man is your mate. I heard Hari say that he and Jake are mates. If that's the case there's nothing you can do."

Rohan's blunt words sent a sharp pain to her temples. All along she'd told herself she didn't want a relationship and definitely nothing serious. After her parents died, she'd decided to step outside the good-girl persona she'd inhabited for all of her life. But the moment she'd seen Jake and Hari together, she'd known she'd lied to herself.

The knowledge had hit her over the head.

"I almost marked Jake yesterday. It was so close, the need so compulsive that it scared me." Ambar shivered, the emotions and the desire to bite and mark her lover coursing through her again.

"What about Hari?"

Ambar swallowed, remembering their kiss. It had been so quick. Not nearly enough to absorb his taste and scent fully. "I don't know," she whispered.

"Kiran and I could always beat them both up."

Ambar gave a startled laugh. "Like that would change things."

"It would make me feel better."

Ambar sobered. "Rohan, what am I gonna do? When I think about the two of them together it tears me apart, and yet I don't think I can walk away either."

"Which one?"

"That's the question."

"Maybe you should stick with the man you know."

"He's not a shifter. He has no idea about us. What happens if it scares him half to death? Besides, if Hari says they're mates I believe him. I don't think he'd lie about something like that."

Rohan glanced at the door when the bell rang, signaling the arrival of a customer. "Would it help if you took the rest of the day off?"

"No, I—" She broke off, changing her mind. "Maybe I could go and talk with Hari. Jake doesn't usually go back to the house for lunch. If I time it right I might manage to get Hari alone."

"Go." Rohan made shooing motions with his hands. "Before I change my mind."

Ambar gave her brother a quick hug and left the store to collect her car from outside their house. She thought of ringing first and discounted the idea. Instead she'd turn up and play things by ear.

The front door opened when she pulled up. Ambar narrowed her eyes at Hari. Tricky tiger genes. The man looked way too good for her peace of mind.

He prowled toward her, graceful yet masculine. Even with the distance between them she couldn't mistake the determination on his face. For a moment she thought he intended to take her into his arms. A rapid step back helped her evade his embrace. She didn't think she'd get through this talk if he touched her.

Her feline stirred restlessly, sensing Hari's presence and wanting his teeth, his touch. His cock.

There! She'd admitted it. She wanted him, but that didn't mean she intended to indulge herself with the masculine treat.

"Don't touch me," she warned him, backing up again.

He cocked his head, a small smile playing on his lips. "Why? You don't trust yourself not to jump me?"

"Of course not." She aimed for scorn and achieved breathless denial that didn't fool either of them.

"Liar, I can smell your arousal from here."

A blush heated her cheeks and she lifted her chin in defiance. "Maybe I met with someone else before I came here."

"Jump from one bed to another? I don't think that's your style."

"You don't know me. You don't know my style." Her hand clenched into a fist, her fingernails digging into her palm. Now he was pissing her off. He had no right, no right at all to act as if he knew her.

"I know more than you think."

"Jake is the one who's trading beds," she said tartly, still burning at his remark about jumping him. He had a bloody cheek accusing her of cheating. She glanced at her car, wondering about leaving. This was a mistake.

"Don't even think about it," he said, an edge to his voice. "You're here now. You might as well come inside."

"I don't even know why I came."

"Because you couldn't walk away. Admit it."

Her mouth firmed. She didn't intend to admit anything.

He offered his hand. She ignored it and stormed into Jake's house without another word, thoughts rioting through her head. The urgency thrumming through her body didn't go unnoticed either. From the moment he'd sauntered outside, her body had softened, her breasts prickling in the beginnings of arousal. If anything, the physical tug she'd started noticing each time they were in the same room had increased.

"Want a cup of tea or a coffee? I think there's some wine too."

"Wine," Ambar said. Something to dull her senses. No. No! She needed all her faculties to do this. "You'd better make that a cup of tea. I haven't eaten much today."

"Tea it is. Come and sit in the kitchen and I'll make you

a sandwich as well."

Ambar followed him, resenting the way he was treating her like a guest. While Hari made a cup of tea and two sandwiches, she paced. Uneasy with her frenzied thoughts and at landing in the middle of a romantic triangle, the urge to run tugged at her, growing with each passing minute. Why not? A run would do her good.

"I'm going to ring Saber Mitchell and ask if I can go for a run on their land. Would you like to come?"

Hari's eyes lit up at the suggestion. "I haven't had a decent run for months. Living in London made it difficult. That's what I like so much about Middlemarch. I don't feel trapped or closed in, even if I don't have the opportunity to shift."

Ambar's stomach somersaulted at the pleasure and anticipation on his face. He'd look the same when he made love. Sexy and masculine. At ease with himself. A vision of him and Jake together, naked on Jake's big bed floated into her mind. She shivered, and when she sneaked a glance at Hari, she caught him watching her with unrestrained desire. Her breath caught. He was a striking man despite his scar. Even after their short acquaintance, she hardly noticed the slash on his cheek now. At their first meeting he'd seemed different, with none of the leashed power and confidence he now displayed. The determination. Oh, and his sexy smile. During their first meeting, his smile hadn't held the same poise.

Ambar found herself grinning back, and only his abrupt steps in her direction jerked her to good sense. "Don't look at me like that," she said, trying for fierce indignation when all her feline wanted to do was rub against him like...like a cat in heat!

Oh hell. That wasn't good. The man had created havoc in her well-ordered plans yet she still wanted him. Poor Jake. He didn't have the slightest idea of the trouble he'd landed in. She'd never considered telling him about her shifter status. Not once.

"I like looking at you. Your photo grabbed my attention from the start. I took one look and knew you were the one."

"Oh please," Ambar said. "What about Jake?"

"Jake is an unexpected treat."

"You make him sound like a special cake. He's a person. You can't mess around with his feelings."

Hari moved swiftly, pinning her against the counter. Ambar froze, inhaling his scent, feeling the shift of his muscles against her. Some of the fight went out of her when she admitted she wanted him.

"This isn't a game. I want you. I want Jake. How this plays out depends on you." He leaned in, his gaze on her mouth.

Her lips started to tingle, and without volition, her tongue darted out to soothe the edgy sensation. She wanted him to kiss her. The acknowledgment banked her anger. "Stop trying to manage me." She gripped his shoulders and shoved.

Hari stepped back, not because of her push but because he'd decided to give her space. His strength was apparent to her now. *Stupid, Ambar.* She shouldn't have taken him at face value. This shifter was like an iceberg with most of his character hiding beneath the surface.

She turned away to ring Saber. Emily answered the phone, and Ambar frowned at her lackluster tone. She hadn't seen Emily at the café for ages. Tomasine said she wasn't well. The attack on Emily had been horrid for all of them. Both Rohan and Kiran harbored guilt at not being able to keep Emily and her unborn baby safe. The resulting miscarriage had upset everyone. Emily definitely wasn't her normal cheerful self.

"Hi, Emily. It's Ambar. How are you?"

Ambar listened politely while Emily said she was fine. It was a lie and they both knew it.

"I wondered if it would be okay for me to go for a run in your back paddock this afternoon. There would be two of us."

"That's fine," Emily said. "Saber won't mind. Just make sure you close all the gates."

Ambar promised they would and hung up, still scowling about Emily. She felt so helpless, knowing there was no way she could make her friend better. Only time would dull her pain.

"Problem?"

"No. It's all right for us to go for a run."

"I look forward to it." A sexy purr colored his polite words, saying way more than Ambar was comfortable with hearing. "I'll go and change into something more casual." The man would attempt seduction. The brazen glint of determination shining in his eyes proved it before he walked away down the passage to his bedroom.

Well, he had his work cut out for him because she was no

pushover. The sharp whip of erotic fear told her otherwise.

Sitting close to Hari during the drive to the Mitchells' land made Ambar fidgety and so sexually aware she actually considered jamming on the brakes and jumping him. Calling herself a fool, she focused on the road and cautiously breathed through her mouth. Breathing either way was a problem since Hari's scent dragged across her receptors. Her feline stalked her mind, eager for the freedom to run. Sharp canines burned in her gums and fingers-turned-to-claws gripped the steering wheel. The more she smelled him, the more strongly her body reacted. Soon the distinct aroma of sexual arousal filled the vehicle and her feline's excited purrs echoed through her mind. Her feline wanted his possession, craved it.

"You want me."

"I don't." A lie and they both knew it.

"When I finally get you naked, I'm going to taste you. I'm going to run my tongue the length of your pussy, gather all your sweet juices to savor." His glance gauged her reaction, his lips forming a shameless smile. "I bet you'll taste delightful."

Ambar froze, her heart thumping hard while her claws dug into the wheel. She could literally feel his tongue feasting on her, and her panties dampened just a little bit more.

"You shouldn't talk like that." Heck, she hadn't even managed a strict headmistress tone. She'd sounded husky and dare she say it, flirty, when she should have come across as indignant or even incensed.

His broad smile told her he'd picked up on that too.

"I can't wait to press my cock to your entrance and thrust inside you. For once, I won't need to worry about tempering my strength. I know you can handle me. Love, think how it will feel with my cock plunging deep inside you."

She was trying desperately not to imagine it, damn it. She belonged to Jake. She was his girl. Temporary girl, she amended hastily in her mind.

"We're here," Ambar said with an edge of desperation. She had to get away from him. He wasn't just a tiger shifter. He was a devil sent to tempt her to sin.

"Where do we leave our stuff?"

Now he acted all businesslike. Talk about confusing her. She hated the off-balance sensation. Maybe if she aimed for matter of fact...

"There are storage boxes on the other side of the shed. This road is a private one so there's never any traffic, but Saber likes us to err on the side of caution." Ambar climbed from her car and took a deep breath to clear her head. The outdoors, the open spaces thrilled her feline, her skin itching with eagerness to shift. Her yearn for freedom and the heady sensation of racing across the land pulled at her control, Hari's presence a dual assault on her willpower.

"I can't wait to see you totally naked. I bet your kitty form is pretty too."

She couldn't suppress her shiver of awareness, her breasts tight and needy for Hari's touch. "Stop trying to seduce me."

"It's working for me." He cupped his groin lightly, a twinkle of pure devilment in his eyes. The golden flecks in them sparkled to life.

So beautiful, they mesmerized her. Oh no. Jolting herself from the spell he'd cast over her with his tricky cat eyes, Ambar turned away with a loud huff and stalked to the gate. She jumped over, landing lightly on her feet. The man would be the death of her. Hari was so different from easygoing Jake, displaying determination and willingness to chase after what he wanted.

When she reached the storage boxes, she hesitated. Normally, stripping off in front of other shifters wasn't a problem for her. This time she froze in a state of indecision, instinctively knowing she had reached the point of no return. She'd have to make a decision whether to let Hari touch her.

Whether she'd cheat on Jake.

Wait. Hadn't Jake already cheated on her? With this very man?

"Strip, love. You know I'm teasing, right? I would never force myself on you."

That wasn't what concerned her. It was her self-control hanging in tatters that disturbed her most.

With trembling fingers, she unbuttoned her shirt. She shrugged it off her shoulders, gaining more confidence when she noticed Hari wasn't even looking. Maybe if she hurried she could shift before he got an eyeful.

She whipped off the last of her clothes and stood to center her mind. Unbidden, her gaze wandered to the right and landed on Hari. Wow. Her mouth dropped open as she studied his formidable assets. While his right shoulder bore a similar scar to that on his face, it didn't detract from his physique. All she wanted to do was run her fingers over his chest to test the muscles flexing beneath his skin. She yearned to sink in her claws and lap his nipples with her tongue until his taste filled her mouth. And that was just for starters.

His lips curled into a sly smirk. "You're looking at me as if you want to eat me for your next meal. Do you want to touch?"

Oh yeah. She wanted to touch all right, but that didn't mean she'd obey the impulse. Ambar ripped her gaze away from the male bounty and closed her eyes to concentrate on her feline. She pictured a tiger in her mind and felt the shift take her. Bones shifted, lengthened. Muscles and sinew reshaped as hair grew rapidly to cover her naked skin. She dropped to all fours, reveling in her enhanced senses—the scents of the distant animals, the green of the flora and Hari.

Part of her wanted to turn to survey him in tiger form. She refrained, instead forcing herself to pad away from the shed. With a flick of her tail, she picked up her pace, moving into a slow lope, leaping across small piles of rock. The air ruffled her fur and happiness soared through her. She heard Hari running behind her and quickened her pace. Males were always faster, but she knew a thing or two, her fitness levels high after participating in regular soccer games with some of the other Middlemarch shifters. She darted left, circling a pile of schist too large to leap over.

Before she cleared the schist, Hari leapt on her. They tumbled together, growling and baring teeth, mock fighting. Both were careful to keep their claws sheathed as they rolled over and over, finally coming to a halt with Hari holding her down, his teeth gripping the back of her neck.

Ambar froze, feeling the prod of his cock. The chase had excited him. She melted inside but growled. Instead of backing off, he mischievously rubbed his chin over the top of her head, playful and a little boisterous. Her growl was a rumble deep in her throat, and they both knew it was mere show with no anger attached. Somehow all the remaining resentment had leached away during their frantic scamper across the tussock, replaced by something else entirely.

Honest desire.

Hari had crashed into her life, creating chaos. If she were in her right mind, she'd send him packing, but she was tired of fighting him and so sick of battling the physical urges constantly rippling through her. A soft sound of submission whispered past her sharp teeth. The tension seeped from her muscles. She was about to sin, except what she felt for Hari didn't seem like a sin. The man was as smooth as the best rich, dark chocolate, and she felt in sudden charity with Jake. Her heart thudded in an erratic manner while she waited for him to make the next move.

Hari rolled off her and circled her until he could see her face. His musky scent filled her every breath along with the hay-like bouquet of the grasses. In the distance, a dog barked and cattle called to each other. Hari stared at her before stepping away and shifting.

Spellbound, she watched his body reform into sexy

human. He crouched beside her, sliding his hand across her head and down her spine. A purr erupted from her and he chuckled, a rich sound that she liked enough to want him to repeat it.

"Shift," he ordered in a voice that didn't brook refusal.

CHAPTER SEVEN

DESPITE BEING MORE THAN a little drunk the previous evening, Jake remembered everything now. The sexual things he'd done with Hari. Heat flushed his face as images flooded his mind. He didn't have the excuse of over-imbibing this morning when he'd repeated the crime. Whistling his dogs, he trudged back to his vehicle with his mind on Hari and how the other man had made him feel—so hot and hungry. When he should have felt disgust, instead there was eagerness to explore more forbidden things with Hari.

Confusion filled him as well because Ambar still figured prominently in his thoughts. God, he'd turned both kinky and greedy. He wanted Hari and Ambar. Alone. Together. He didn't care.

Pleasure-tinged embarrassment punched him when he visualized the three of them together, his cock hardening to a painful erection. After a quick visual sweep of the

119

trees and shadows, he cupped his shaft through his jeans, stroking. Rubbing. It wasn't enough. Biting his bottom lip, he freed the button and zipper of his fly and lifted his cock from his boxer-briefs. A shudder shook him as he imagined Hari kneeling before him, taking the head of his cock into his mouth. He visualized Ambar cupping and massaging his balls. His eyes closed as he sank into his fantasy. The warmth...

He could feel the tight heat of Hari's mouth, the tight suction. Amber's fingers and her nibbling kisses on his flesh. A tongue traced the ridges and whorls of his shaft head, making him wet and progressively harder.

A groan ripped up his throat. The clasp on his cock edged on painful, his languid strokes increasing in speed. Lightheadedness seized him, pressure gripping his balls. Faster and faster his hand slid easily across his flesh, his climax building and building. Another pained cry escaped, his heart pounding as semen exploded from him in an arc and spurted to the ground at his feet.

"Bloody hell." Feeling weak, he leaned against his vehicle before tucking himself back in and zipping up his jeans.

His soft laugh echoed in the stillness, broken only by the wind in the trees. That was a first—whacking off during work hours and thinking about a man while doing it.

Fuck, he had to tell Ambar, even if he'd included her in his fantasy.

Confess.

As much as he liked Ambar, he couldn't continue this way. He refused to lie or cheat behind her back even if it changed their relationship. The thought scared him.

Ambar was the one woman he could imagine in his future. That made this situation all sorts of fucked up because he didn't want to walk away from Hari.

Jake whistled the dogs for a second time, this time fastening them on the back of his vehicle. He might not be gay, but experimentation with Hari hadn't thrown him either, which baffled the hell out of him.

The urge to see Hari beat at him, a need to clear the air and search for explanations. His mind had dwelled on the man all morning, and it wasn't as if he was concentrating worth a damn. He might as well see what Hari was doing.

Jake climbed behind the wheel and backed from under the trees, turning for home.

Halfway down the road, he slammed on the brakes with a curse.

The bull was down. The prize bull his father had purchased. Julius Caesar IV had cost a bloody fortune. He pulled farther off the road and leapt the fence to check on him. The good news was his bull was still alive. The bad news—his gashed leg looked infected. Jake sighed and pulled out his cell phone to ring Gavin Finley, the local vet. Another damn bill he didn't have the money to pay.

"He's slashed his leg on something and can't get up. He seemed fine yesterday. An hour? Thanks." Jake gave directions and decided to take the dogs home before returning. He drove slowly, cursing when he noticed several other cattle were loose. Luckily, it didn't take long to round them up and return them to the paddock. A bit farther along the road, he saw the fence was down.

"Fuck." That was three strikes. Surely nothing else could

go wrong today. Sighing, he mentally rescheduled his day yet again. He'd have time to do a makeshift repair, stop at home to get more fencing supplies, drop off the dogs and make it back to meet with Gavin.

Despite the day's setbacks anticipation buzzed inside at seeing Hari again. After stopping to collect the mail from his box, he parked beside Hari's rental car, locked up the dogs, checked their water and strode inside.

"Hari?"

Silence greeted him.

Jake's shoulders slumped as he realized how much he'd counted on seeing the man, touching him and gaining comfort from his presence. He wandered into the kitchen with the mail and scanned the envelopes, wincing at the number. Apart from a bank statement, they were all bills—one for repairs on the tractor, another for the essential fencing materials and the next rates installment. Hell. With a bad taste in his mouth, he tossed them aside, knowing exactly what sort of picture the bank statement would paint. A bad one.

He wasn't only sinking. The debt was way over his head and drowning him. Something had to change, but hell if he knew how to turn the downward spiral into positive.

His phone rang. "Yeah."

"It's Kiran. Gavin and I are on our way now."

"Right. See you there."

Gavin and Kiran were waiting for him when he arrived.

"Sorry to keep you waiting."

"We've just arrived," Gavin said.

"My bull is down here. Can you take a look at the cows

in the next paddock for me while you're here? They've lost condition and I can't work out why." What was one more bill in the sum of things? He needed to sell these particular heifers to help settle some of his debts, and they wouldn't fetch a good price until their weight picked up again.

"Kiran will take a look at the cows," Gavin said. "I'll check on the bull with you."

"They're quiet," Jake said. "You'll be able to walk right up to them without a problem."

Kiran nodded and jogged away from them.

"What do you think?" Jake said while Gavin checked over the bull.

"Nasty cut." Gavin pulled out his bag and grabbed supplies, working while he chatted.

"Do you think he'll be all right? I'm kicking myself I didn't check him at close quarters. I've seen him from a distance and knew he had plenty of feed and water, so I didn't worry too much."

"I'm more worried about him being down," Gavin said. "We'll try to get him back on his feet before we leave."

Jake nodded, mentally working logistics if they couldn't move the bull. It was another four hours before he finished. Fixing the fence so the cattle didn't get out again had taken a good hour plus much cursing. They hadn't managed to get the bull on its feet, which worried him, but at least it was eating the hay he'd taken it. He'd check it again after dinner. The heifers had worms, according to Kiran, after he'd recently drenched them. Guess the cheap drench hadn't been such a good idea.

The first thing he was gonna do when he arrived home

was clean off the worst of the dirt and soak in the tub. Then, who knew? He thought he'd play things by ear.

AMBAR DIDN'T EVEN THINK about refusing to shift when Hari ordered, calling her human form to mind immediately.

"God, you're beautiful." His hot gaze skimmed her body leisurely as if he wanted to commit every dip and hollow to memory.

Trepidation danced in her mind, but her body wasn't having any of it, reacting with heat and desire. She wanted Hari, and this time she wouldn't run even if this was a mistake. Ambar hesitated, knowing one thing for sure. If she fled again, she'd regret it for the rest of her life.

"I'm going to fuck you now."

Fuck her. She winced inwardly. Talk about a lack of romance. A streak of disappointment hit her on hearing his emotionless statement. His words were hard with fact and brutal truth.

"Ambar?"

"Yes." She quivered on hearing the new, husky note in his voice, suddenly wanting him so much she could ignore her unease...for the moment. The big picture—a connection with Hari would mean she couldn't continue ticking off items on her life list. Her entire life would change and, as far as she was concerned, not for the better. The small part of her that wanted romance she'd worry about later and analyze her need when she was alone. This

124

was sex and simply two felines scratching an itch.

"Come." He clasped her hand and led her to a rock-free area where the tussock grew in soft clumps. "I've fantasized about you sucking me off. We'll start there first." Hari placed his hands on her shoulders, encouraging her to kneel in front of him.

"A little presumptuous, aren't you? I'm not a toy for you to play with."

"I don't play games." Hari met her gaze with an unwavering one. "I want you to touch me, take me in your mouth. Please." They stared at each other for an instant longer. It felt as if she'd known Hari for months rather than mere days, and it was this sense of familiarity that made her decide to trust him.

She sank to her knees and stared up at him, peeking through the long locks of her hair. Impatiently, she brushed them from her face, tucking the strands behind her ear.

"I like your hair loose like that. The shine reminds me of sari silks." He ran his fingers through the length, sweeping it away from her face and fisting the strands in his hands. It didn't hurt and wouldn't unless she attempted to move.

"Are you always like this?" she blurted.

He scowled down at her, his golden-brown eyes darkening. "Like what?"

"Demanding obedience. Expecting your partner to submit."

"I thought you'd find it easier if I ordered you."

Ambar considered his words and silently agreed. "And if I don't want easy?"

"You want to own your actions?" He sounded surprised yet approving.

"I know exactly what I'm doing. I'm not sure it's right, but I'm not gonna pretend I don't want you inside me now."

"Good girl. Would you like to suck me off?"

"Did Jake suck you off?" The careless note in Ambar's voice did nothing to conceal the lingering jealousy still simmering inside her. The image of the two men looking so cozy together on the couch kept circling her mind, slow and determined like a tiger stalking prey.

"No." Hari paused. "But I'd like him to in the future. Is that a problem?"

Ambar averted her gaze to study her hands. They'd clenched when she thought of Jake and Hari together. The green-eyed monster stalked her mind again. "Hell if I know. I don't know what to do or feel when I think about the two of you together." But she didn't want to stand aside. She knew that much, but it was tugging her in two directions.

"Jealous?"

The man was too perceptive for his own good. He'd better stop prodding—if he knew what was good for him. "Yes, I resent the idea of you and Jake. Is that wrong?" She lifted her head to look him in the eye. She'd considered Jake hers, thought Jake was enamored with her. Learning about Hari and Jake, actually seeing them together had bit at her pride. She glared, not hiding any of her roiling emotions or her uncertainty.

Hari smiled then, his dark brows rising. "You don't

think I felt jealousy when I had to listen to you and Jake the other night and again in the morning?"

"Is that what this is about? Going after something that isn't yours? A game? A chance for revenge?"

"That's the second time you've accused me of game playing." Hari drew back, releasing her hair, his top lip curling upward in distaste. "If you believe that, you're not the woman I thought you were."

"Oh please! You really believe the three of us can work together? Have a relationship, I mean." People would stare, ask questions. Speculate. She'd heard them discussing Leticia, Gavin, and Charlie. She didn't know if she was strong enough to deal with that sort of public interest and gossip.

"I wouldn't be here if I didn't. I wanted you from the moment I first saw your photo. That feeling solidified when I saw you at the store."

"And Jake?"

"We hit it off when we met in the café. I've never had the same reaction to a man before. He smells good. Gets me hot."

Ambar made a scoffing sound. "You like him because of his smell?"

"Come up here." Hari lifted her to her feet with easy strength. He wrapped his arms around her, drawing her against his naked body. Her mind lurched instantly to sex, and she rubbed against him, a rumbling purr erupting before she even formed a thought. Being naked and with Hari felt natural and right. And she sort of understood what he meant when he mentioned Jake's scent. She really

127

liked Jake's smell. Her brows furrowed. Hari's scent did it for her too, curse his striped hide.

"Last chance, love. If you want to leave, you need to go now."

He was placing responsibility in her hands. Instead of answering, she drew his head down and kissed him. Although she'd intended to go slow, need escalated into desperation almost from the first touch. Hari took over the kiss, holding her head firmly while he ate at her lips. Sweet yet demanding, he increased the assault on her mouth while his hands skimmed with purpose and skill, mapping her curves and seeking out sensitive spots.

"That feels so good." Pleasure suffused Ambar when he slid his hands down her back in a long, luxurious stroke. The slide of a masculine thigh between her legs and the firm kneading of her bottom had her nerve-endings singing in delight. Then Jake slipped into the mental picture, setting her heart pounding. It was difficult not to compare the two men. Jake acted more playful while Hari demanded and conquered.

She let out a disappointed groan when Hari pulled away. Her fingers curled into his biceps, trying to hold him in place. It didn't work. He was stronger and they both knew it.

"You're beautiful." His breath caressed her face as he glanced down at her breasts.

"So are you."

"I have scars."

"I don't notice them now." It was nothing less than the truth because his personality grabbed the focus once the initial shock of his scar ended.

He ran the back of his hand over her collarbone and halted on the upper slope of her breast. She shivered and silently willed him to continue, to cup her breast and pinch her nipple.

"Take me," she said.

"Good idea." Hari lifted her with ease, despite her height and sturdy build. He made her feel small and dainty. Feminine. He placed her on the grassy area and followed her down, holding her in place with his muscular chest.

"Offer me your breast." His husky voice lured her to obey.

She cupped one breast, feeling the weight of her flesh, the softness of her skin. Licking her lips, she watched him. He maintained an enigmatic expression, but the glitter of his eyes gave him away. As much as he wanted her, he didn't intend to hurry. This was going to be a feast rather than a quick, dirty roll in the grass.

"I feel as if I'm betraying Jake," she burst out.

"I keep telling you—it doesn't have to be either me or Jake. You don't have to choose. You could have both of us if you play your cards right."

"But what will people say? What will they think?"

"Does it matter? Your brother isn't exactly traditional. My family isn't here and neither is Jake's."

"That's true." And just like that, her lingering reservations faded, turmoil stilled. For now.

Holding eye contact, she lifted her breast for him. The peak pulled tight and her stomach muscles trembled as she strained toward him. His mouth closed around the tip, delicately at first with a slight tug. The pull became hard suction that sped straight to her pussy.

"Hari." His name was a plea for more, and they both knew it.

He lifted his head to laugh softly and pinched her other breast, the shooting pain adding another layer to his touch. "I don't have any condoms. Is that going to be a problem?"

"Gavin gave me a birth control shot." With felines, pregnancy was the only issue when it came to sex, something Ambar appreciated. They were lucky compared to humans who had to watch out for all sorts of nasties.

"Good." He lowered his head again, his mouth hot and wet. With lazy strokes of his tongue, he tormented her until sensual tension grew, coiling like a spring about to burst inside her. His loving felt different from Jake's, and if she closed her eyes, she'd know it was Hari making love to her. Each touch felt good in a different way.

She parted her thighs, silently requesting he touch her more intimately. She craved his fingers trailing over her folds, pumping into her pussy, needed it now that he'd awakened her hunger.

Despite her urgency, the frantic tilt of her hips, he kept the pace slow, touching her everywhere but where she wanted it most. She could feel the moistness of her labia, the liquid roll of desire preparing her for his possession, but still he dallied, taking a nibble here, a lick there.

"I knew your skin would feel soft." Hari dragged callused fingers over one hip, and her stomach hollowed. He nuzzled the delicate crease where leg and torso met, running his tongue downward.

She almost cried when he stopped short of his goal. "Keep going." Her hands gripped his shoulders in alarm. "Please, don't stop."

"There's no hurry. No one requires our presence."

"I require your presence," she snapped. "Here." She slid a finger down her body, over her mound and into the hot, needy flesh between her legs. A groan escaped when she grazed her swollen clitoris. "That feels good. It would feel even better if you did it for me."

"Stop." Hari grabbed her hand and lifted it to his mouth. He paused and studied the glossy juices shining on her forefinger before taking it into his mouth. Her pussy pulsed when she felt the drag of his tongue cleaning her finger. The suction of his mouth seemed naughty. A gasp escaped at the sheer sexiness of it.

"Put your hands above your head."

Another order. Ambar hesitated, wanting to touch and explore his body. The palms of her hands literally itched at the thought of stroking his hard chest and the contrasting silkiness of his cock. Her mouth watered.

"You don't follow orders well."

"Not since my parents died," she confessed.

"Following my instructions now doesn't mean I'll expect you to obey me all the time. I like your independence. Your audaciousness. I don't want a traditional woman, someone who will cling or expect me to do everything for them."

Ambar didn't know how to react to his declaration. Did he really think they had a future? She tried to read him, to weigh his response before slowly raising her arms above her head to await his next move.

Straddling her hips, he took his time, his hot gaze traveling leisurely across her face, lingering at the base of her neck and smiling when he finally reached her breasts. A prickle of sensation licked her pussy, just from having him look at her. Oh he was good. A quick breath lifted her breasts, the pregnant pause while she waited for him to touch almost unbearable. Begging words banked up in her mind, the bite of her teeth on her bottom lip the only thing keeping her silent.

Then he touched her.

Just a graze of contact, a barely there stroke she sensed instead of physically felt. A sizzle burned her skin when he repeated the caress, a brush of his knuckles across the curve of a breast. She couldn't hold back the inhalation of shock, the jerk of her hips. She parted her legs farther, shamelessly exposing her sex to the cool air.

"Am I doing better now?" Her gaze arrowed in on his throat and cruised down to the place where shoulder and neck met. In her mind's eye she saw herself leaning over, licking that delicate area until it shone and the blood pulsed beneath his skin.

"Hell," Hari cursed softly.

She felt his thighs tense, muscles straining while he fought for control. Then she visualized her teeth sinking into the pad of skin and imagined the taste of blood. Ambar shuddered, a low moan coming from deep in her chest. What the hell? First Jake and now Hari. If she wasn't careful she'd end up with a mate. She gripped his arms, attempting to push him away.

"Ambar?"

She blinked, gaze connecting with his as she primly closed her legs.

"What's wrong, love?"

"I want to bite you. God, what is wrong with me? I wanted to bite Jake too. It was so close the other morning. I nipped him but didn't break the surface."

Hari growled and she risked a glance before looking away.

He captured her chin with his fingers, forcing her to focus on him. "I want that. I want to mate with you. I want to mate with Jake. But if you think I'm not confused about it, think again."

"But don't you see? I don't want to mate with anyone. When my parents were alive, I had to follow their orders. They intended to hand me over to a man, giving me to him so I had to follow his orders. I had no choice. As much as I loved my parents, respected their opinions, I don't intend to obey anyone. I like my freedom, and I'm not willing to give it up. I am not a slave to my hormones, dammit."

"If I promise not to expect anything from you except pleasure, would that work?"

"You're a male. You're just saying that. Don't you understand? I don't want to stay in Middlemarch forever. There are things I want to do, places I'd like to visit." Yes, she could imagine wandering along a tropical beach, splashing in the warm turquoise sea.

"I'm not stopping you from doing anything," Hari said, a sharp note in his tone. "All I'm asking is to share some

133

mutual pleasure."

She stared, trying to weigh his response and decipher his expression. "Okay, but a warning. Don't try to force me because you won't like the result."

He nodded immediately. "I accept. Put your hands back over your head."

She frowned but acquiesced, noting the way her breasts shifted when she raised her arms.

"Spread your legs again for me."

She did as he requested, part of her amused at the constant orders. Jake really was so different. It struck her as weird, comparing two men while she was naked, planning on having sex with one of them.

Hari moved over her, fitted his cock to her entrance and slid home in one seamless thrust. Her sheath pulsed around him, the hard throb and unexpectedness of his abrupt move feeling so good she wanted to purr.

"Okay?"

"Very."

Hari pulled back and thrust smoothly until he filled her.

Ambar did purr this time, shifting her arms to hold him close.

He stopped moving. "Hands back above your head."

"But I want to touch you."

"I can't guarantee my control if you touch me."

"So I'm never allowed to touch you?"

"Are you going to let me make love to you again?"

"It would be sex," Ambar said sweetly. She clenched the muscles of her vagina, subtly taunting him because he wouldn't let her touch.

"Lie to yourself if you want, Ambar, but you know as well as me this is more than mere sex."

Ambar opened her mouth to snap at him, but he drove into her again, the angle of his thrust clipping in the perfect spot. Instead of a complaint, her throat rumbled with a satisfied feline mew.

He nuzzled her neck, licking across the mating site, hands skimming her arms, fingers pinching one nipple. The nip of pain jolted her, then smoothed out with a burst of pleasure when he slickly stroked into her body. In and out. In and out. The pleasure bloomed as he played her body like a musical maestro.

"Hari, please."

"Please what?" His warm breath teased her ear, detonated another explosion in her pussy.

"Please make me come."

"Fuck you or make love to you?"

"Both. Either. I don't care."

Face hardening a fraction, he increased the pace, snapping his hips with relentless surges that jolted her entire body. He ceased his tender touches, and she missed them. Subtly, he was showing her the difference. Ambar didn't care. Maybe she would later, but now all she wanted was to come. Never before had she felt so tightly wound, like a spring ready to explode.

Sweat beaded on their bodies, the liquid sounds of fucking loud. Hari surrounded her yet something was missing. She watched him and his expression softened, the harsh line of his scar relaxing.

"That's it, love." He dipped his head to kiss her, the

135

fevered meeting of lips the catalyst she needed to relax. Hari surged into her again and the pleasure started to unfurl. Another smooth thrust pushed her over, and with a cry, she shattered. She was vaguely aware of Hari coming, or at least he stopped his thrusting and rested his weight on her for an instant.

"Can I move my arms?"

"Go ahead."

Ambar stroked a hand across his damp back, savoring the feel of his body surrounding hers. She threaded her fingers through his black hair, taking pleasure in exploring and petting him.

He withdrew and moved away from her. Ambar made a grab for him and yanked his body back against hers, needing the contact and wanting to kiss him. Their lips met, lingered. She closed her eyes to focus on her surroundings. She heard the rapid beat of Hari's heart and the soft purrs of satisfaction that came from him even though she sensed he preferred to keep them hidden.

The cry of a bird flying somewhere overhead and the rustle of the breeze through the dried grasses added to her well-being. A sense of peace fell over her, and she knew this was right. Of course that didn't mean she needed to accept Hari or the future he offered. She'd meant it when she'd told Hari she wanted to travel and explore the world.

She frowned as she considered Jake. He was tied to his farm and wouldn't travel any time soon. Besides, she thought he had money problems after buying out his parents. Not that he'd ever mentioned anything. It was more of an impression she'd gained when she noticed he didn't go out as much and tended to stay at home if possible.

"What are you thinking about?"

"Jake. I think he has money problems." She half expected him to show jealousy, but he surprised her.

"I'm sure he does. That won't be a problem. I can help him."

"You have money?"

Laughing, he pressed a quick kiss to her lips. "Is that such a surprise?"

"You don't act like you have money."

"You can come with me when I return my rental car and splash out on a new vehicle. Would that convince you?"

"Are you going to Dunedin?"

"Yes."

"I'd love to. I haven't been to the city for ages. I wouldn't mind a new dress to wear to the Middlemarch Singles' Ball."

"Shopping doesn't scare me," Hari said in a dry tone. "I have lots of cousins. Female ones."

Ambar sat up and clicked her fingers. "Damn, my cunning plan didn't work."

"If you want to send me packing, love, you'll have to try a lot harder than that. You're not the only one who wants to bite."

Ambar scrambled away from him in alarm. "If you mark me, I'll never forgive you."

Hari rolled to his feet with pure feline grace. "I will never mark you without your permission."

Ambar surveyed him uncertainly, trying to gauge his

sincerity. "I'd make a formidable enemy," she said finally.

Hari grinned and stretched with unconcern. "I'm sure you would, but I have no intention of upsetting you. I suggest we take this back to the house, after another quick run." He extended his hand and waited, showing more patience than typified a human male.

Ambar's stomach roiled at his words, but in a good way. Her nipples, already pert and stiff, prickled with a wave of heat. Giving in to the urge she couldn't explain, she took the hand he offered, softening in a purely feminine way. "All right."

It was a step into an uncertain future and they both knew it.

Hari released her hand unwillingly and stepped back to call his tiger form. Ambar was unsure of the situation. He recognized her hesitation, but that wouldn't stop him from claiming his mates. Intuition told him all he needed to do was get the three of them together and let nature take its course. Ambar had already admitted she'd wanted to mark Jake and instinct had urged her to do the same to him.

The pain-pleasure of the shift forced a growl from him as bones lengthened and muscles reshaped. He fell to all fours and embraced the change, the enhanced senses and the scent of his mate. He barked a command at her, and when she ignored him, he crowded her, nipping her flank.

Ambar snarled a warning and lashed him in the face with her tail. Hari grinned. It would take more than that to cow him. He admired the swish of her tail while she padded away and thought about mating with her in tiger form. Maybe farther into their relationship. She needed to trust him first.

With a feline smirk, he zipped up behind her and sped past, enjoying the whistle of wind rippling over his fur and whiskers. He heard the thud of paws behind him and increased his speed. God, he loved Middlemarch. He didn't think he'd ever leave.

Back at the barn, they shifted and retrieved their clothes, dressing rapidly. They were both silent during the drive back to Jake's house. Hari had no idea of Ambar's thoughts, but he was busy planning his courtship of Jake and Ambar. This was their future and he intended to prove it to them.

Hari pulled up outside Jake's house, a little disappointed when he didn't see Jake's vehicle.

Ambar sighed heavily.

"Something wrong?"

"I can smell you. It's as if I had a cold and now I can smell everything again. You want me."

He turned to her with a grin, knowing it would come across as predatory. "Never doubt it, love."

She sighed again, an unhappy sound that made him frown. "Let's go," she said in a sharp voice.

Hari hesitated then held his silence. Patience. Ambar would come to accept this new arrangement. Besides, he was very good at compromise.

CHAPTER EIGHT

"Jake?" Hari called when they entered the house. There was no reply.

"He's been here. I can smell him." An appreciative smile curled her lips as she pulled Jake's scent across her receptors. Her nose twitched and her eyes glowed as a purr escaped. "I don't know why but he smells better than he ever has before. The mail is on the counter."

Hari wanted to stare at her and soak in her scent, yet the urge to touch governed most of all. "It's because you're actually embracing the idea of Jake as a mate." And him. Hari liked that part most of all, but he wasn't stupid enough to tell her and risk more of her skittish behavior. She didn't think they'd manage to work around their problems. Early days. She didn't know or trust him yet, but he looked after those he cared about.

Ambar and Jake.

Trying to focus on something other than Ambar and

the tantalizing scent wafting from her body, Hari scanned the mail rapidly and saw they were mostly bills. If Jake had money problems, he'd offer financial help, hopefully without upsetting any pride. It would be a way of showing the other man how serious he was about him, about them. He glanced at Ambar and reached for her hand. "Let's go and play."

"Oh, is play the new word for fucking?"

"We can do that as well." Instead of going to his room, he led her to Jake's.

She planted her feet and jerked him to a stop. "We can't do it in there. That's Jake's room. It's plain wrong to have sex in Jake's bed. It's bad enough now because I feel as if I've cheated on him. This would be like rubbing his nose in it."

"My bed is a single." Hari was determined to make love to Ambar in Jake's bed. He wanted Jake's scent to surround them. There were other reasons too, more complicated, that he didn't want to explain to Ambar. He was working to plan and she didn't need to know he was managing and finessing both her and Jake.

Ambar balked again just inside the doorway. Hari tugged her into his arms and started his seduction. He kissed her softly on the lips and trailed kisses and nibbles down her throat, taking care to stay away from the marking site so he didn't spook her.

He let his hands wander her body, learning and memorizing her ample curves. When she started purring, he led her to the bed and pushed her down. He dealt swiftly with her clothes and his own before joining her.

Jake's scent lingered on the sheets adding a new element to their togetherness. He inhaled, the combined scents driving his lust. Blood filled his cock, excitement like a throb in his veins.

Their three scents entwined in his mind.

Perfect.

He couldn't wait for Jake to join them. His canines lengthened, the need to mark his territory a siren song whispering through his mind.

"Do you smell Jake?" His husky voice rippled with anticipation.

"Yes, I smell him."

"Are you at least curious about how hot it will be with the three of us together?" He knew it would be good. Just thinking about the three of them together and touching each other, made his cock steel-hard.

"I don't want to be." But her words belied the tinge of excitement flashing in her eyes, the scent of arousal that came from her when she fidgeted beneath the weight of his chest.

Hari wanted to stoke the fire he saw banked in her gaze. Their mouths fused while his hands mapped her breasts. The soft globes overflowed his hands, her nipples pulling tight under his ministrations. She felt strong and robust beneath him, and he found that sexy as hell. It was great not having to temper his strength as he'd done with his human lovers. Like him, Ambar would heal rapidly in the case of an injury.

She arched beneath him when he gave her a sensual bite and the faint play of teeth.

"We need to get to the good stuff," she said.

Hari hid his smile at her bossy demand. He loved seeing her like this, the way she bit her bottom lip to hold back her groan of pleasure. "I thought women liked foreplay. Most of you can't get enough of it."

"Humph."

Hari smiled against her breast, licking around her nipple in a slow circle with his tongue. Her hands tunneled into his hair, tugging and making his smile widen. She was still trying to boss him around, this time in actions rather than words. He nipped the underside of her breast and she gave a shudder of pleasure, her purr rumbling through him. God, she was right. He needed her now.

Moving on, he shifted his body and laved the joint where leg and torso met before parting Ambar's legs and lifting her to his mouth. This time he didn't tease but worked hard to push her into orgasm. The taste of her juices struck his taste buds, and he didn't think he'd ever sampled anything so appetizing. It was time to move on to the main course.

"Use your fingers. Fill me," she pleaded.

Hari lifted his head briefly to grin at her. "It would be my pleasure, love." Then he went back to his feast, licking and using the rasp of his tongue to good effect. Although at first he'd intended to rush her, he slowed to savor the experience, taking great pleasure in keeping her on a knife-edge of an explosion.

"Hari, stop teasing." Her hands clasped his head and she forcibly held him in place.

He laughed, the burst of warm air against her clit

143

bringing a feminine growl. She tugged his hair again, the sting of his scalp sending a burst of lust to his cock. Perhaps she was right. With one easy move, he lifted her, turning her onto her stomach.

"Up on all fours," he ordered, unsurprised to find his canines had lengthened farther.

Almost primed for a protest or at least a show of unwillingness, Ambar's obedience took him by surprise. She was beautiful the way she presented for him, legs parted to display her pussy, her long dark hair a silky ripple over her shoulders. Grinning, he leaned over and nipped one butt cheek.

"Ouch!" She winced and glared over her shoulder. "Was that necessary?"

Hari nodded even though she wouldn't see. "I could do this instead." He skimmed a finger through her folds, collecting some of her natural lubricant and spread it across her rosette, pushing slightly against the resistance.

A tremble went through her, and Hari paused. "Do you want me to stop?"

"Don't stop." A glance over her shoulder reinforced her demand.

"I have no intention of stopping if you're enjoying it." Hari pushed his finger a fraction deeper and twisted it while gliding the fingers of his other hand over her clit. She shivered, but he wanted to know she enjoyed the way he was touching her. He wanted verbalization. "Does that feel good?"

"Yes." She pushed back against his finger, driving it deeper. Her scent deepened, swirling around him, pushing him to move faster, to mount her.

"When Jake and I fuck you together, one of us will fill your pussy and the other will fill you here."

Ambar snorted. "Is that meant to be a threat?"

"Of course not. The three of us together will be all about pleasure."

"And are you going to get fucked in the arse?"

Hari paused to consider it. His stomach muscles clenched at the thrill that filled him when he thought of Jake. "Maybe." Hell, who was he trying to kid? He wanted everything with both Jake and Ambar. Everything.

He withdrew his fingers and fitted his cock to her pussy. Slowly, he pushed inside, savoring the tight clasp of her sheath, the subtle flex when he rested fully seated.

"I thought you were going to fuck me." She wriggled, pulling away then slamming her hips back to impale herself again.

Her actions inflamed him, pushed past his restraint. He started to thrust and withdraw, pulling from her heat and surging back inside with a loud grunt.

"Hari, touch my clit. I can't balance and touch... I need you to touch me."

He swirled his fingers across her clit, teasing the swollen bud while continuing to piston his hips and pump his cock into her warmth. Her throaty moan spread straight to his balls, and he exploded into climax, his control past breaking point. He curled over her body, breathing hard. Sweat ran in rivulets down his chest, sticking them together but still he rested against her, loathe to separate their bodies.

Reaching for her breasts, he tweaked a nipple, pinching harder when she wriggled her butt against his groin, her entire body trembling. Still semi-hard, he lazily stroked into her and rubbed his fingers against her slippery clit.

"Harder, Hari," she implored then shuddered. "That feels good."

Hari smiled and nuzzled her neck, lightly grazing his teeth over the tendons, heightening her pleasure with the edge of pain. He felt a quick flutter around his cock before she groaned again and collapsed forward on the mattress.

After separating their bodies, Hari dragged her into his arms and relaxed. With Jake's scent swirling around them, he was content for the moment. He played with a lock of her hair, winding it around his finger.

A foreign sound dragged his attention to the doorway.

"Jake." He jackknifed upright and smiled. "I didn't know you were home."

"That's obvious," Jake snapped. "I thought..." A tic sprang to life near his right eye. "Did you have to do it in my bed? Make sure you're gone by the time I get back. Both of you." He turned to leave, his face pale and unhappy.

"Wait! You don't understand." Hari wasn't sure how to start. God, there was so much they needed to discuss. He glanced at Ambar but she remained silent, letting him do the talking for once. The one time he could have used her input, she buttoned her lips.

"Jake, we need to talk." Hari sprang up but Ambar grabbed him.

"Leave him. I knew it was a bad idea to do this in here.

146

What the hell were you thinking?"

"That Jake would be secure enough to come and join us?" Hari rubbed his hands over his face. "Fuck. I've screwed this up." He winced when he heard the door slam and shrieking tires indicating Jake's abrupt departure.

"I knew this was a bad idea."

"Yet you allowed me to fuck you. Twice so far," Hari snapped. Sniping at each other wasn't helping. He needed to do something. "Where would Jake go?"

"I'm not sure. Maybe to the pub or he might go to a friend's place."

"Who are his friends?"

"Joe and Sly Mitchell. Jonno Campbell."

"Humans or shifters. Are Joe and Sly related to Saber Mitchell?"

"They're Saber's brothers. Most of Jake's friends are shifters."

"He doesn't know?"

"He's never said anything. The shifters here are careful about revealing themselves to humans. Disclosure is only to a mate."

"I'd better go after him. Explain a few things. Make him understand we want him."

Ambar scowled. "Good luck with that. He found us in his bed. I knew it was a bad idea."

"So you've said." Hari quelled any further I-told-you-so quips with a fierce glare. "I told you I'll fix this." But maybe he should give Jake a little time—an hour or so to process what he'd seen—before he tried to talk with him. And if that didn't work, he'd seduce him all over and keep him in bed until Jake conceded.

JAKE DROVE TO THE pub, his mind screaming about betrayal. What made it worse was he'd found them in his bed. *His bloody bed*.

The pub was busy when he stomped inside, but he couldn't see any of his friends. Probably for the best since he didn't want to talk to anyone.

"Jake, I haven't seen you in here for a few weeks. Is Ambar with you?" The elderly barmaid was a friend of his mother's. Anything he said would go straight to his parents.

A vision of Ambar and Hari filled his mind. He bit down on a smart-ass retort about women. "Just stopped by for a quick drink." Maybe he should have stopped at the Mitchell place instead of coming here. "I'll take a beer and a whisky."

He suppressed a cringe when he handed over a twenty-dollar note. He didn't even have enough money for a decent drinking spree. Failure—it beat his mind in a frenzied cacophony. Jake tried to concentrate on the barmaid's chatter, but all he could think about was seeing Jake and Ambar going at it in his bed. When another customer walked up to the bar, he grabbed his drinks and headed for a table in the corner where no one would bother him.

Dropping heavily onto a chair, he sighed. His thoughts drifted to Hari. After this morning and the previous night he'd thought...hell! He didn't know what he'd thought.

What sort of game was Hari playing with him anyway? Had he wanted Ambar all the time and decided to play him? The thought had nausea tap-dancing in his gut.

Jake could have sworn Hari had been sincere. Hari's touch certainly hadn't indicated game playing or diffidence. Jake ignored his beer to down his whiskey in one gulp. The dry, peaty taste burned the back of his throat as he swallowed. He stared at his empty glass with regret. A pity he couldn't afford a bottle of whiskey. He'd tie one on and forget the pain of betrayal.

The image of them together had seared to his retinas. It replayed through his mind. He blinked and it started again. Hari and Ambar. Hari and Ambar with their limbs entwined, and the scent of sex heavy on the air.

In his bed.

"Fuck!"

Someone clapped him over the shoulder, and he whirled with a scowl.

"How's it hanging?" Sly Mitchell grinned at him and slumped onto the seat next to him.

His twin brother Joe arrived soon after, carrying three beers. He set them on the table. "Long time no see. Ambar here?"

"No." Jake couldn't look at them. He'd kissed another man and enjoyed it. He'd wanted more. He was sure his guilt and confusion about Hari would show on his face.

"Woman trouble?" Sly asked, his joking tone absent for once.

"Trouble full stop," Jake said, admitting the truth out

loud. His life was a bloody mess. He'd been able to ignore his financial problems because of Ambar and Hari. But now he knew it was time for honesty—at least to himself. He couldn't keep the farm going for much longer. "Nothing I can't handle." He barely winced at the lie.

Jake glanced up, caught Sly sniffing him and shoved him on the shoulder. "Quit that. I had a shower today. What the hell is up with you guys? You should have grown out of that childish behavior years ago."

Joe smirked, flashing a dimple that all the women seemed to like. "Funny, Saber said the same thing only this morning." He shot his brother a quick look, brows arching as if he asked a silent question.

"And quit with the spooky twin-communication thing." Jake didn't try to hide his crankiness. Ever since he'd met the twins at primary school, they'd practically communicated without words, or at least that's the way it seemed. It was fine when they were concentrating on someone else, but he wasn't about to let them dissect him. Even if they did keep it private.

"All right," Sly said. "Who's the guy?"

Shock struck like a lightning bolt. How could they know? A spurt of panic cramped his stomach. "What guy?"

"You might as well tell us," Joe said. "We can smell him on you. Only close contact leaves a scent like that."

Sly nodded, a sly expression distorting his face. "Yeah, mystery man with a hint of Ambar."

Jake picked up his bottle of beer, attempting to ignore his friends' amusement. If they weren't careful he was going to rearrange their pretty faces. A kink in their noses would go a long way to making him feel better. "I should have run when I saw Kaylee Girven punching you on the school grounds during our lunch break. Or at least stood back and let her give you a good whooping. I should have cheered instead of helping you."

"So why didn't you run?" Joe asked. "She'd already given Sly a bloody nose."

"Hey, it was a lucky shot."

"It didn't look that way to me," Jake said. "Kaylee had you both whipped. If I hadn't come along she would have broken your arm."

Joe snorted. "Have you been taking lessons from Emily? That's the sort of thing she'd say."

Sly narrowed his eyes. "We were talking about you, not the past. We're not stupid. Who's the man and what's going on with Ambar? If you don't want her, then maybe Joe and I will take her off your hands."

"She's not a possession." Jake grumpily slurped his beer. How could they know? It was that smell thing again. If he didn't know them so well it would freak him out. "Hari has just moved to Middlemarch. He's living with me."

"You're living with a guy?" Joe asked, his dark brows shooting upward in surprise.

"It's not like that...it..." Hell, it was like that. Just the thought of touching Hari and having that touch returned made him hot. Joe and Sly weren't stupid. One look and he knew they'd picked up the subtext, the things he hadn't said in his stuttering protest.

Sly leaned back in his seat, stretching his arms above his

head with feline grace. "Is this guy from India?"

"England, but he's of Indian descent. Apparently, his great-grandparents lived in New Delhi."

"Interesting," Joe said, his gaze shifting to the door. "Shift over. We have a friend coming to join us."

Jake scooted his chair over with a distinct lack of interest in the new arrival. Socializing was the last thing he wanted to do. Wallowing alone—now that sounded better, but part of him was glad Joe and Sly had turned up. They had a way of cutting through the bullshit. Maybe they could help him get his head straight. Why he was suddenly interested in Hari when he had a beautiful woman in his bed? Not that it mattered much now because it seemed as if Ambar and Hari had other ideas, and they didn't include him.

Sly stood. "We haven't met. I'm Sly Mitchell, and this is my brother Joe."

"Hari Daya."

"What the fuck are you doing here?" Jake half stood, but Joe pushed him back on his chair. Hari was wearing one of his shirts. Damn, wasn't using his bed enough? The man had to take his clothes as well?

Sly and Joe did their communication thing and this time they included Hari. It was the weirdest thing. Their nostrils flared, and they stared at each other before Hari nodded and took possession of the spare seat beside Jake.

"We need to talk." Hari didn't waste time with chitchat.

"About you fucking Ambar in my bed?" Jake snarled.

"If we'd wanted to sneak around, don't you think we would have gone to Ambar's place? Or found some place private?"

Jake opened his mouth to speak and snapped it shut again. Hari was right. Shit, he didn't understand any of this. He caught the three men watching each other. Joe reached over and touched Jake's arm. Hari let out a low growl and moved closer to Jake.

Sly and Joe chortled.

"Saber is right," Jake snapped. "You two are out-of-control."

Joe grinned at Hari. "Come on. We'll buy drinks at the bar. Jake, you want a beer or a whisky?"

"Both." Jake sensed Hari's hesitation despite him refusing to meet Hari's gaze.

"We've known Jake since we were five-year-olds at school. Sly won't do anything to upset him," Joe said, taking Hari's arm.

Jake scowled, his gaze fastening on the spot where Joe touched Hari. Damn if he didn't want to smack his friend. A low growl of protest erupted from him, and Joe laughed, lifting his hands in the air in a gesture of surrender. At least he'd taken his hands off Hari.

"This just gets more interesting by the minute," Sly said, watching the pair walk to the bar.

"I'm not gay," Jake blurted.

"That's a label," Sly said, his grin fading. "Joe and I don't do labels. Do you think less of Gavin and Charlie because they fuck each other? Rohan and Kiran?"

"Of course not!" In fact, he counted all the men as friends. They never made him feel uncomfortable, and it was obvious they were happy in their relationships. Then he recalled that Gavin and Charlie also lived with Leticia. His mouth dropped open, his mind working at warp speed for once. Nah! He shook his head sharply to clear the vision of Hari and Ambar from his mind.

"So why are you getting so bent out of shape about Hari? You want each other."

Fuck, was it that obvious? Jake risked a glance at his friend and saw that for once Sly was serious. "We only met a few days ago."

"Sometimes one look is all it takes." Sly's tone gave him away.

"You too?"

"Joe and I met a woman a couple of years ago. We knew she was the one, but she wasn't ready. Hell, I don't think we were ready either. It's been hard waiting."

Jake fiddled with one of the empty bottles in front of him. The twins had always shared lovers. After growing up with them, it hadn't bothered him seeming entirely natural rather than kinky. "Sounds serious."

"Not discussing," Sly said.

Jake didn't want to talk either. A sense of uneasiness settled in his gut. He kept seeing flashes of Hari and Ambar together. He shuffled on his seat as his mind played tricks on him, planting him between the two. Hands smoothed over his naked body, teasing and sensual. Feminine hands. Masculine hands. They both felt great, stroking pleasure across his nerve-endings.

"Earth to Jake." Sly clicked his fingers in front of Jake's face, making him start.

Heat collected in his face. That had never happened

before. The minute he and Hari were in the same room he started to think about sex. He groaned inwardly. It had to stop. It wasn't normal, dammit.

Joe and Hari returned, setting drinks on the table. The heat in Jake's face moved down, across his chest and sank to his balls. He fidgeted, only stilling when Hari sat beside him. Their legs touched as Hari moved his chair closer, and the agitation inside him settled to a low burn. Every breath he took seemed to smell like Hari—musky and full of fresh green scents with a faint spice.

Joe and Sly started asking Hari questions, leaving Jake to sip his whisky in quiet contemplation. He stared at the tan skin revealed in the V of the shirt Hari wore. His shirt. The reminder brought a surge of satisfaction in him. The urge to lick had Jake leaning closer, so focused on his goal he didn't realize the conversation had halted.

Jake blinked slowly, trying to break the weird connection. When he opened his eyes again, Hari smiled, slow and seductive. The heat in his cheeks intensified. They were in the bloody pub. It felt way too personal, exposing himself to his friends and neighbors this way, yet he couldn't seem to control his actions. Something deep inside compelled him to respond to Hari.

"You're toast," Sly taunted softly.

"Don't tease my mate," Hari said, his husky voice sending needy ripples all the way to Jake's balls. Jake shivered, lost in Hari's compelling brown gaze.

Joe lifted his bottle of beer in a salute. "He'll make a good mate."

"Of course I'm a good mate," Jake snapped. "I've put up

with the pair of you since we were kids." He turned back to watch Hari even though he worried about making a fool of himself.

"You haven't told him," Sly said.

Both twins had lost their edge of teasing, their faces completely serious again. Jake couldn't remember the last time that had happened, and it worried him, made him nervous.

Agitation pierced him without warning. "What are you talking about?" He wasn't in the mood to be the butt of their jokes.

Hari took his hand, holding it firmly when Jake would have pulled away. Hari's touch soothed him even as he met the incredulous looks of some of the locals who had known him since he was a baby. No doubt, he'd get a call from his enraged father once he heard, demanding that Jake explain himself. He might have problems with the rationalization because he had no idea what he was doing, so he could hardly justify his actions.

"Ignore them," Joe said, aiming a scowl at the nearest table. "They don't understand."

Hell, he didn't comprehend the driving need he had to touch Hari, so how could anyone else?

"Take him home," Sly said.

Joe nodded. "Talk to him."

Hari frowned at both twins. "It's too soon."

"I'm right here," Jake said, starting to get pissed. He picked up his whisky and downed it, relishing the burn as it slid down his throat.

"He deserves to know what he's getting into," Sly

persisted.

"Jake can take it," Joe added.

Jake knew he could take it, but it would be better if they stopped talking about him as if he weren't present. He grabbed Joe's whisky and drank that while the three men continued to argue.

When he reached for Sly's whisky, Sly grasped his forearm.

"No more," he ordered.

Joe smirked, his green eyes alight with devilment. "Yeah, you won't be able to get it up."

"Hands off my mate," Hari snarled.

Fury whipped through Jake, the frustrations of his day exploding into anger. Joe's slur against his manhood did the rest. He stood abruptly, toppling his chair as he let rip with a punch. His fist clipped Joe's jaw. Hari snarled, leaping to his feet when Sly grabbed Jake's fist to prevent another punch.

The action, the release of his turmoil into punches felt great. Jake let loose with another one, and suddenly the four of them were trading punches, he and Hari against Joe and Sly.

Joe let out a whoop and smacked Jake's jaw. A warning growl rumbled from Hari seconds before he struck Sly. The table went flying, no opposition to Sly's weight. Bottles and glasses smashed. Glass crunched underfoot. The barmaid shrieked orders to stop. They ignored her.

Jake charged Joe. They fell in a tangle of limbs. He aimed a fist at Joe's face. Joe struck back, a hard punch to his stomach. The air bled from Jake's lungs. He tottered and fell, his flailing arm catching a neighboring table. A curse sounded. More glasses smashed. Jake gasped hoarsely, sucking frantically for air. The three men and one woman at the table shouted. One cursed again, and another grabbed Jake and threw a punch. Then it was all on. Jake roared and punched back. Joe stopped one of the other men from adding his fists. A brawl developed from there with grunts, the crash of breaking glass and tumbling furniture filling the air.

Jake couldn't have said how long it went on. Perversely, he enjoyed the outlet for his frustrations, satisfaction filling him with every punch he landed.

Things started to get ugly when someone tossed a bottle. Charlie and Laura, the local cops, arrived. Their presence and sharp commands started to restore order.

"Fuck, Saber's here," Jake said. "Someone tattled."

Joe and Sly stopped fighting. Hari blocked a blow from a dark-haired guy who tried to take advantage of their distraction before stopping too.

"I think we're in trouble," Jake offered, watching Saber storm across the pub. The locals made way for him, parting like the proverbial Red Sea.

"You got that right," Sly said, warily eyeing his big brother.

CHAPTER NINE

SABER STOMPED OVER TO them, his face tight with anger. "Joe. Sly. Jake. Outside now." His nostrils flared as he took in Hari. "You with them?"

Hari nodded, his manner wary yet respectful.

"Outside," Saber barked.

Jake grabbed Hari by the hand and dragged him after Sly and Joe. He liked and respected the older man who had treated him like another Mitchell from the moment the twins had taken him home from school for a visit. It was Saber who had given them the sex talk when they were teens and who'd lectured them about correct behavior.

When he thought back, Saber had been more of a parent to him than his own. His father and mother only saw each other. Jake's arrival had been a shock to them after being childless for so long.

"What the hell were you thinking?" Saber demanded when they halted outside the front of the pub.

Jake swallowed. Saber and Emily were going through a bad patch after the loss of their baby, and the last thing Saber needed was for the cops to haul him out in the middle of the night.

"I'm sorry," Jake said. "It was my fault. I started the whole thing."

"You weren't the only one throwing punches," Saber snapped, scowling at them all in turn.

"I'll pay for the damages," Jake said, cringing inwardly. He didn't have enough money to pay the next mortgage installment, let alone for repairs to the pub.

"We'll all pay for the damages," Sly said.

Laura Campbell, one of the cops, stormed over to them. Her eyes narrowed as she scanned their faces. "Witnesses say the four of you started this brawl."

"We're sorry," Joe said.

"You dragged me from a nice, warm bed." Laura scowled. "Jonno wasn't happy and neither am I."

Sly's face lit up in a grin. "Did we interrupt your sex life?"

Laura's eyes narrowed farther to catlike slits. "At least my husband has the sense not to start pub brawls. Unlike his best friends."

Joe's grin echoed Sly's. "Must be your calming influence."

"Lock them up, Laura," Saber said. "A night in the cells will do them good. I'll come and pick them up in the morning. Tell Betty to send the bill for the damages to me."

"Saber—" Joe started.

"I'll be sleeping in," Saber said to Laura. "Don't expect me too early."

She gave a clipped nod. "You know the way, boys. Start walking."

"Laura," Sly said in a wheedling tone.

"Move it or else you'll be facing charges as well." Laura's no-nonsense tone told them exactly how pissed she was with their hijinks.

Half an hour later they found themselves locked in the same holding cell.

Hari watched Laura turn the key.

"I know none of you are a danger to yourselves so you can keep your phones. Ring me only if there's an emergency. I intend to sleep in too." Without a backward glance, she strode from sight.

"Laura has a thing for jail cells," Sly said. "She locked up Jonno when they first met because she thought he was a jewel thief."

"We could have slept in a comfy bed if you hadn't decided to thump me," Joe said with an eye roll in Jake's direction.

"Leave Jake alone." Hari growled, his feline agitated and plain cranky. There was nothing he'd have liked better—Jake in a soft bed. Irritation pulsed through him, aching like a sore tooth. Not even touching Jake comforted him. His gums ached fiercely and his canines pushed through. He looked up to find Joe and Sly regarding him closely. They sensed his edginess.

"Shift. Show him now," Joe said softly after glancing at Jake.

Jake glowered at them all. "I'm getting tired of the way you guys talk about me."

161

Hari tensed, the shift to tiger progressing despite his efforts to halt the change. "He's not ready."

"He can't run when he's locked up," Sly said. "It's the perfect time."

Hari's skin tingled. He wanted Jake so much, the desire bone deep and even more compelling than his need for Ambar. He questioned his sanity. Perhaps it was something to do with the fact Jake was a human or that they hadn't explored their relationship to its full extent. Yet.

"What the fuck are you talking about?" Jake demanded. "Tell me before I punch you all again."

Still uncertain, Hari scanned Sly's and Joe's faces. They both nodded encouragement, and since the change had already started, he whipped off his clothes.

"Whoa!" Jake backed up until the bars of the cell halted his retreat. He stared wild-eyed at the three of them. "I am not doing anything kinky with those two watching."

"So you admit you have the hots for him," Sly teased.

Joe just smirked, and Hari noticed neither of Jake's friends were perturbed about his choice of partner. With their silent approval, he backed up and let the change take him, praying that if Jake freaked Joe and Sly would look after him.

Hari embraced the pain-pleasure of the shift, the layers of arousal adding another dimension. For a fleeting moment he thought about running free across the paddocks with Ambar and he wished Jake could share the sheer pleasure of a run with them. It would never happen.

Apprehensive, he checked Jake's reaction. The other

162

man hadn't moved. His face was pale and his mouth gaped in shock or astonishment. Hari wasn't sure which. Jake never made a sound, and Hari had never wanted him more.

Fully shifted, Hari sat on his haunches and waited.

"Fuck," Jake whispered finally. "That's freaky." Hari saw the moment Jake registered Joe and Sly's lack of surprise. "You knew. How did you know?"

Hari grunted, a low sound of command.

Without another word, Sly and Joe whipped off their clothes and shifted, leaving Jake the only human in a cell full of feline shifters.

"You...all of you..." Jake trailed off, and sank onto one of the two narrow cots in the cell.

Hari edged closer to Jake, trying his best to look reassuring. It was a bit difficult with his large frame. As a tiger, he was bigger than the two Mitchell brothers in their black leopard forms.

"Why didn't I know?"

Hari didn't like the way Jake was staring at Joe and Sly. He sidled close enough to touch Jake and rubbed his head against Jake's leg. The physical contact soothed him and he let out a purr. Jake froze, and for one horrid moment, Hari thought he'd reject him. A few taut seconds passed where none of them seemed to breathe then Jake cautiously rubbed his hand over the top of Hari's head. He'd never had anyone pet him in tiger form before, apart from Ambar, and the fingers running through his fur sent a ripple of need skipping across his skin. His purr this time was low and sensual, and he crowded even closer, seeking more caresses.

Jake stroked him, almost without volition while he frowned at the twins. Hari grinned inwardly. Maybe this had been a good idea after all. The only thing that could make it better would be if he and Jake were alone, preferably with Ambar present.

Ambar. Heck, she'd be worried. He'd promised to ring her when he'd found Jake. Things had happened so quick, it had slipped his mind.

He backed away from Jake and shifted, bending to grab his cell. He punched in the number Ambar had given him earlier and waited for her to pick up. When he noticed Jake's expression, he moved closer, hoping to reassure him.

"Amber, it's Hari. Yeah, I found Jake." He paused while she fired questions at him. "No, that's what I'm ringing to tell you. We won't be home tonight." Home. Even thinking the word felt so right. "No, we are not having hot monkey sex."

"Not in front of us," Joe said wryly.

Hari watched the twins dress rapidly and noted they were careful not to approach Jake again. They sensed how possessive Hari was about their friend and didn't want any further trouble. Wise men. He was starting to like them and Middlemarch more all the time.

"Hell, no," Sly added his contribution, although his mouth bore a toothy smirk,

Hari told Ambar where they were and chuckled. "Ambar wants to know if she should break us out of jail."

"I'd like to say yes, but Saber is furious with us," Joe said, exchanging a glance with his brother. "He told them he'd pay for the damages, which means he has something totally devious in mind for a punishment."

"Sure, see you tomorrow morning. No!" He broke off to glower. "You will not do any touching, not without Jake and me there to see. If we have to suffer so do you." Hari hung up and checked Jake for his reaction. He went so long without saying a word Hari started to worry. "Are you okay?"

"Why didn't you tell me?" Jake glanced at each of them before returning his attention to Hari.

"I—"

"I think he's talking to us," Sly said dryly.

"Saber told us not to tell anyone," Joe said simply. "From the moment we were old enough to talk, our uncle who reared us emphasized the need for secrecy. When Uncle Herbert died and Saber took charge, the rules were the same."

Sly paced as much as a cell containing four adult men allowed him. "And to impress on us the need for secrecy, he took us to the zoo. We couldn't communicate with the animals, but it was easy to see that some of them didn't want to be there."

"Saber told us if we talked out of place we would end up in a worse place than the zoo, that there were plenty of so-called scientists out there who would have no conscience about keeping us contained and conducting experiments." Joe glowered as he said the words.

Hari remained silent, pleased Jake was listening and didn't avoid his touch. Running into the twins might not be so bad, even if his jaw ached like a bitch.

"What about the stories in the newspapers? The

sightings of the mystery black cats?" Jake asked.

Sly chortled, and Joe thumped him on the shoulder.

"Saber was really angry that time," Joe said. "It was Leo's fault. We came across these tourists and we had a bet to see who could make them scream first."

"Felix and Leo are our older brothers," Sly explained to Hari, taking over the explanations. "They're younger than Saber and older than us. We all shifted and took turns running past."

Jake shook his head, a grin playing on his lips. "Who made them scream?"

"Felix," Sly said in disgust.

"It backfired when they blabbed to reporters and stories started appearing in the newspapers," Joe said.

Sly snorted. "Yeah, that's when Saber and the other members of the council decided they needed to marry us off."

Hari listened, fascinated by the closeness of the brothers. An only child, he'd never gelled with his closest cousins. They were too different, which was another reason he'd had no problems relocating to New Zealand. "What happened next?"

"Saber married first," Jake said.

"Yeah." Joe did a high-five with his brother. "Saber got caught in his own trap. Meeting Emily was the best thing that happened to all of us. She turned us into a real family."

Sly nodded, a frown forming. "I wish we could do something for her and Saber now."

"Why?" Hari asked.

Sly lost his joking edge, his eyes losing their teasing glint.

"Emily was attacked by a madman who was after Kiran. She lost their baby and it's taking her a long time to get over it."

"I've never seen Saber so worried," Joe agreed.

"Hell, we've fucked up again," Sly said with a groan.

"You think? I'd rather have Saber angry at us than the iceman he's been lately," Joe said. "Maybe he needs to concentrate on something else, which is why I'm not going to complain about whatever punishment he thinks up for us."

"True." Sly nodded. "I never thought I'd say this, but I kinda wish Emily would get back to her matchmaking. I miss her evil smiles and twinkling eyes."

Both twins fell silent.

"Are there others like you living in Middlemarch?" Jake asked.

"Quite a few. Jonno Campbell. Gavin Finley. Duncan and Lana are shifters. Saul and Lucas. Leticia." Joe counted them out on his fingers.

"Rohan, Ambar and Kiran," Hari added.

"Ambar? All this time...fuck," Jake said. "I must be dense as a brick not to notice."

Hari reached for his hand, registering the calluses on his fingers and palm, the differences in their skin color. He and Ambar were golden brown, neither of them very dark, while Jake was pale in places the sun didn't see. Hari thought about licking that pale skin, running his tongue across the tan lines and sinking in his teeth. A soft growl rumbled through him.

"Hey, mind out of the gutter," Joe snapped.

"Put on your clothes," Sly said, after a furtive glance at Hari's groin.

Grinning, Hari released Jake's hand and stood to pull on his boxer-briefs and jeans. He was aware of the close attention Jake paid him, which made dressing a bit difficult.

"I wish I had a cold," Sly said wryly.

"Yeah, you two are letting off enough pheromones to pollute the entire town of Middlemarch."

"Not my fault," Hari said.

Jake stood and strode to the door of the cell. His hands clenched the bars and worry spurted through Hari. Before he could do anything, Jake whirled around.

"I don't understand any of this. Before Hari came, I'd never looked at another guy for sex. I had plenty of women and wasn't interested in changing my habits. Why have I changed so suddenly? Have you done something to me?"

"No." Hari shot a helpless look at Joe and Sly, silently imploring them to help. Luckily they seemed to catch the hint.

"Feline shifters have relationships just like humans," Joe said. "But there are some people who are perfect for us—both physically and mentally. They complete us."

"Mates," Hari said, spelling it out.

Jake's eyes widened. "What does that mean? What's different about a mate?"

"Having a mate means that you're not interested in anyone else. You physically can't have sex with another person when you're officially mated. Not while your mate is alive."

"Officially?"

"Shifters exchange bites. Here." Hari gestured at his neck—the fleshy part where shoulder and neck met. "The bites heal quickly, but during the bite, enzymes are exchanged that help bind a couple. They become mates."

"How do you know if someone has a mate?" Jake asked, fascinated despite himself. An entire world he'd never known about and it had been right under his nose.

"The bite leaves a slightly raised scar that's very sensitive to the touch. The mates start to smell different to other shifters as well." Sly took over the telling.

"Is that why you guys are always doing that weird sniffing thing all the time?"

Joe laughed. "We're so used to having you around that we forget you're not a feline. We were more circumspect while we were at university."

"Anything else I should know?" Jake asked. "What about kids? How old are you before you can shift to big cats?"

"We're born human and start to shift around puberty—twelve or thirteen. Much like humans, it depends on the individual," Sly said. "Joe and I could shift at age thirteen."

"Interesting," Jake said. "What about you, Hari? When did you first shift?"

"When I turned eleven. I have lots of cousins and the two the same age as me were giving me a hard time. I lost my temper and shifted. It scared the bejeepers out of them." Hari laughed, although recalling the moment didn't exactly bring happy memories. His oldest cousin had shifted and sliced his face and shoulder with his claws. For some reason the wounds had never healed properly, leaving both face and shoulder scarred. His uncle called them a badge of honor. Hari had remained wary of that particular cousin ever since the clawing incident. He was fiercely glad he'd managed to sneak Ambar's picture before his cousin of the same age had seen it. Ambar belonged with him and Jake, not with his arrogant cousin.

Hari caught Jake's hand as he paced past and pulled him closer. He desperately needed Jake's touch, to know Jake felt something for him. The unusual insecurity didn't sit well with him or his feline. He yanked Jake down beside him.

"Stay," he barked when Jake would have scrambled to his feet.

Sly sniggered and Hari found a focus for his angst. His growl deepened, his top lip curling up to reveal his sharp canines.

Joe grabbed Sly's shoulder and shook him. "Quit mucking around. He's close to the edge because they haven't mated yet. Stop pushing him."

Hari gripped Jake's shoulder, breathed in his scent and closed his eyes, trying to wrest back control. His chest rose and fell, and he was aware of Jake's quiet breaths, the taut way he was holding his body.

"Please," he whispered into Jake's ear. "Please let me hold you." Hari opened his eyes and sent a silent plea to Jake. Jake's blue eyes darkened. He remained tense for long moments before relaxing, his head lowering in a clipped nod. "We might as well try to sleep," he said in a low voice.

"Lie down." A faint tide of color swept into his cheeks and he sent an uncertain glance toward the twins.

"Ignore them." Hari tugged Jake down beside him on the narrow cot, sighing softly as their bodies touched.

"As long as you don't forget we're here," Sly said.

"Not much chance of that with the way you keep yammering," Hari retorted.

The cot was small for one large man, and it was crowded with both of them. Jake fidgeted, the nearness of the other man having a predictable reaction on his body. Hari's cock lengthened until it pushed painfully against his fly. Jake moved again, turning to face him.

Hari was vaguely aware of Sly and Joe talking quietly while sitting on the other cot bed. Thankfully, they'd given up needling or watching them.

Jake's warm breath whispered over his chin, and Hari couldn't help himself. He leaned in, angling his head to capture Jake's lips with his. Jake made a surprised sound and froze when their lips touched. Hari knew he was worried about the twins' presence, but if they knew what was good for them they'd remain silent. All he wanted was a kiss or two then he hoped to go to sleep with Jake in his arms. He'd leave everything else to a time when they had the luxury of privacy.

Hari kept the kiss soft and gentle, coaxing Jake into returning it. He wanted acquiescence and participation, just a hint that Jake really did want him in return. There he was, second-guessing again. Hari couldn't remember a moment when he'd felt more off-balance. Silently seeking reassurance, he deepened the kiss, wanting to taste Jake, make them both shake with need.

Jake moaned and pressed closer, the needy sound sinking straight to Hari's balls. God, he might not have experience making love to another man, but he sure as hell hungered for him. As much as he'd enjoyed making love with Ambar, he knew the act would be no less explosive between him and Jake.

Their bodies aligned. He could feel the eager press of Jake's cock and couldn't prevent the jerk of his hips.

"Hari," Jake said with a groan, burrowing even closer. Heat suffused Hari, a shiver of need. He pushed their groins together, despite knowing they needed to call a halt. This time, he stifled Jake's groan with his mouth, drinking in the other man's reaction. A deep shudder went through Jake, and damn if Hari didn't feel the same wonder.

"Hey, I thought you two were going to sleep," Joe said.

"We are sleeping," Jake said, abbreviating it with a growl, the warmth of his breath tickling Hari's cheek.

It made Hari smile. "Going to sleep now."

"Pleased to hear it," Sly said, and it was easy to hear the laughter in his voice.

Hari eased Jake's head onto his shoulder, happier than he'd been in a long time. He didn't even care that the cot was lumpy.

AFTER A SLEEPLESS NIGHT spent in Jake's very empty bed, Ambar was up early to drive to the police station. Agitation and confusion warred inside her during the journey into town. The insidious need, the yearning curling through her veins really pissed her off. She'd been happy before with Jake. The casual friendship with no expectations had worked for her.

Now that Hari had come along, everything had changed.

A bolt of sheer lust emphasized her uneasy thoughts. He was the catalyst that had sent her tidy life and her future plans careening off course. Moodily, she tapped her forefingers on the steering wheel while she waited for a cattle truck to rattle past. She turned onto the main road, stopping briefly at Storm in a Teacup for a coffee and a blueberry muffin to go.

When she pulled up outside the police station, it was still early. She parked and slurped her coffee, desperate for the jolt of caffeine to kick-start her system.

Her cell phone rang, and she fumbled through her handbag to find it.

"Yeah?"

"Is that how you answer your phone?" Rohan demanded.

"Yes, Mother," Ambar said. "I did it on purpose because I knew it was you. Do you need something?"

"We had several orders come in late yesterday afternoon, and I need them packed for delivery this morning. I didn't have time to do them. I had a bit of a rush during the afternoon."

"And I bet you and Kiran wanted to make use of the Ambar-free house." Ambar smirked as she checked her watch. "I can be there around nine. Is that okay?"

"Can't you get to the store earlier?"

"No, I'm at the police station, waiting for Jake and Hari." Ambar paused, bracing herself for the inevitable questions.

"What's wrong? Do you need me?"

Rohan in big-brother mode. He was a sight to behold and a force to reckon with. The way he instantly offered his support made her warm inside.

"There's no problem, or at least I don't think there's one. Hari and Jake were in a fight at the pub last night. Laura was so pissed at them she locked them in a cell overnight. I'm waiting to take them home."

A chuckle floated down the line. "I look forward to hearing details."

Ambar snorted. "Why do you think I wanted to pick them up? Evidently Laura locked up the two Mitchell twins as well."

"I wish I'd been a fly on the wall last night." Rohan sobered. "Are things okay between you all now?"

Ambar didn't try to pretend or avoid the topic. Hari had sounded fine when he rang her. "I think so." Ambar scowled at her coffee. "Hell, what do I know? I've no idea. I'll let you know when I get to work."

"See you there," Rohan said, hanging up before she could say anything else.

Ambar pulled out her muffin and took a bite. She couldn't help but worry, despite telling Rohan things were okay. No matter how much she liked Hari and Jake, she still didn't want a mate. She'd always planned on taking time to see a little of the world. The last thing she wanted was a marriage trap, not at her age. Her mother had never done anything without her father's approval. They'd spent their entire lives in the Auckland region, running their business, looking after their children and socializing with other tiger shifters when time allowed. The thought of repeating such an insulated life made her teeth ache.

Maybe she should talk to some of the other shifter women. Leticia might be a good start, although her case was a bit different because she suffered from feline AIDS. Isabella might work because she always seemed so confident and together.

The sound of determined footsteps penetrated her thoughts, and her head jerked up. Laura. A masculine voice hailed Laura, and Ambar spied Charlie, the other Middlemarch cop. She climbed out of her car.

"Hi, Laura. Charlie."

"Problem?" Laura asked.

Ambar grimaced. "I've come to pick up Jake and Hari."

An evil grin surfaced on Charlie's face. "I don't know about the two of you, but I need a coffee before I deal with those four."

"Good idea," Laura said. "You coming with us, Ambar?"

"I can't stay for too long. I need to go into work."

"Half an hour won't make much of a difference," Charlie said, taking her firmly by the arm and directing her away from the police station.

Ambar could have pulled away, but instead she laughed. "I'll get them to drop me at the store and they can take my car home. Can you tell me what happened?"

Laura's brows rose. "Apart from the fact Saber is furious and the owner of the pub is baying for their blood?"

"Um, yes."

"Witnesses said that Jake started it and threw a punch at Joe. No one knows for sure what the argument was about, but I'd say it might have something to do with Hari?" Charlie looked at Laura for verification and she nodded.

Ambar had to beat her guilt down. "Probably, Jake was furious when he left the house."

"Oh good. Gossip with our coffee," Laura said cheerfully. "Do I get to tell Jonno?"

Exactly half an hour later they entered the police station.

"About bloody time," a masculine voice shouted.

Ambar knew it wasn't Jake or Hari.

"It's punishment, not a holiday camp," Laura shouted back.

"Jonno should take charge of you more often," the voice returned.

Laura cackled. "He tries." She turned to Charlie. "As much as I like them in the cell, I guess we'd better let them out."

"I'll do it." Charlie grabbed a set of keys from his pocket and disappeared out the back.

"Do you like being mated to a shifter?" Ambar asked. "Do you ever feel trapped?"

Laura glanced at her in surprise. "Jonno is fairly easygoing. We have a good partnership. It's true I'd intended to return to the city and wanted promotion, but I'm happy here. I've never felt trapped, not once I got over the shock of being a shifter's mate."

Ambar spoke quickly, aware the men would arrive soon. "I like it here in Middlemarch, but I've always wanted to travel, to see some of the world. My mother lived in Auckland her entire life. She never left, never traveled or even went on a plane ride. I don't want my mother's life."

Laura's face softened. "That's understandable. You need to talk to...which one? Jake or Hari?"

"Both."

A chuckle escaped Laura. "You should see your face. Being a mate is no different from marriage to a human. It takes compromise and communication. All you need to do is talk to them, tell them how you feel and what you want."

"That's easier said than done." Ambar stopped talking and turned to face the doorway she presumed led to the cells. How did she reiterate she wanted to stand on her own two feet and exert her independence? Quite frankly, she didn't see how she could learn what she wanted from life if she stayed with the two men.

"Ambar!" Joe Mitchell grabbed her and snuck a kiss. Ambar heard a low growl but didn't know who it came from because Joe immediately handed her over to his brother. Sly stole a kiss and used a little tongue.

Ambar wrenched away and hit him on the shoulder. "Yuck! No wonder you're both still single."

Jake came up behind her and placed a hand on her shoulder, and she was aware of Hari standing silently on her other side.

"Just as well you hit him," Jake said. "I didn't want to spend more time in the cell."

Laura glared at the twins. "Jeez, you two know better.

177

What the hell were you thinking?"

"Aw, Laura," Sly said, or at least Ambar thought it was Sly. The pair was difficult to tell apart. Jake didn't seem to have any trouble, but they'd grown up together. "You know there's a shortage of single women around here. We had to see if there was a connection."

"You knew Ambar was taken," Hari snapped, his English accent crisp and businesslike.

Ambar sighed. *Taken*. They considered her unavailable already. What chance did she have for independence when everyone thought she belonged to a man—men—already?

"I have to go to the store," she said. "You can take my car back to the farm." She handed Jake the keys and jerked from their touch with two brisk steps.

"Wait, Ambar," Hari said.

She stopped automatically, realized she'd obeyed without thinking and muttered a curse under her breath. It was starting already, the conditioning to respond and obey. "I promised Rohan I'd be there. I have to go."

"We'll pay for the damages," Hari said. "Is there anything else?"

"Saber has already taken care of the damages. The four of you are doing community service." Although Laura's face remained sober, there was a touch of glee in her voice. "Twenty hours each. I'll let you know what you need to do next week. Some of the school buildings require painting, and I believe the town gardens all require weeding."

Joe groaned out loud, but that was the only protest any of the men offered. In an odd way, Ambar was proud of them.

"You're free to go," Charlie said.

Jake and Hari ushered Ambar from the police station, and the twins followed them. Outside, they paused and all of them, even Jake, heard the unrestrained hilarity coming from inside the police station.

"I guess we deserve that," Joe said.

"I thought Saber might come and pick us up," Sly said. "He said he'd be here."

"Hari and Jake can give you a ride home. I'll walk to the store." She turned away, glad of the mindless work awaiting her at the store because it would stop her thinking too hard about her problems.

"Ambar, wait." Jake grasped her hand and pulled her around to face him. He stared into her eyes, the frisson of heat beneath her clothes weakening her knees. "Hari and the twins explained a few things to me during the night. I think I understand a little better now."

"You understand what?"

Jake scanned their vicinity before turning his attention back to her. "About felines and mates."

"Oh." Well, she hadn't expected Hari to do the big confession when he went after Jake. She paused a beat, but Jake treated her much as usual instead of acting freaked, she nodded slowly, cataloguing his scent. It was a familiar aroma, now overlaid with Hari's musky spice. Doubly enticing. She bit her inner lip to prevent herself from walking into his embrace. "We'll talk either tonight or tomorrow, okay? I really have to go."

Hari and the twins must have done a good job because Jake didn't seem too perturbed about her tiger status or

Hari's.

"Okay." Jake hauled her into his arms and kissed her. Somehow the kiss was different this time. It was more possessive and impossibly sweet. Accepting. She opened for him, inviting deeper contact. His touch roared through her, her feline basking under the attention. Jake felt so good, hard and solid. He was dependable and still had that hint of easygoing bad boy who had attracted her in the first place.

"My turn," Hari growled.

Jake surrendered her to Hari without a protest, but instead of stepping away, he pressed into her from behind. Hari took control of her mouth, his flavor bursting across her tongue and filling her with heady need. The feel of Jake behind her, sandwiching her body closer to Hari's brought a needy moan. She was vaguely aware of the hoots and cheers coming from the twins then both men stepped back. She swayed, her balance challenged while her senses danced in turmoil.

Two men.

Holy Hannah, double trouble for sure.

Jake and Hari exchanged a grin, and she realized how happy Jake looked. She hadn't seen him looking that way for a long time.

"We'll see you later," Hari said.

"Maybe not until tomorrow. We're really busy at the store."

Hari skewered her with a piercing gaze before finally nodding. "How about tomorrow night? Jake probably has stuff he needs to do on the farm. Do you need your car tomorrow?"

"No."

"We'll come and pick you up." Jake edged closer to Hari, seeming to need the touch of the other man.

Ambar nodded. "Tomorrow around six." She strode away without looking back, ignoring the frustrated rumble from her feline. Jake wasn't the only one who craved Hari's touch. Heck, she wanted Jake to touch her too.

Was. Not. Gonna. Happen.

Not today anyway.

She increased her pace in an attempt to outrun her thoughts. Her mind played tricks on her though, repeating the thoughts in a loop so she couldn't escape them. Her mind centered on one thing. What hope did she have of independence when she turned into a mass of trembling lust whenever she encountered Hari and Jake?

CHAPTER TEN

"I DON'T THINK AMBAR wanted to spend time with us," Jake said.

"Work was a convenient excuse," Hari agreed.

"Should we worry?"

Hari smirked. "I don't think so. Not when she kissed us like that."

Jake pulled up outside his house. "I need to feed the dogs and the chickens."

"I'll do the chickens for you. Anything else that needs doing urgently today?"

"I need to shift the heifers, but that can wait until this afternoon. They'll have enough feed until then. I have to check on the bull though."

"What's wrong with it?"

"Cut its leg. I'll do that as soon as I've fed the dogs. What are we going to do the rest of the time?" Jake licked his lips, excitement surging through him. He had a fair idea of what they'd be doing, but he wanted Hari to verbalize his thoughts. The last thing he wanted to do was presume. That would be embarrassing.

"We'll be getting to know each other better," Hari said in a husky voice. "There might be a little sleep involved but it will be in the same bed. Together."

"I'll meet you in the shower after I've finished my chores." He glanced at Hari's groin, the other man's erection easing the lurking fear in his gut. His apprehension wasn't surprising given this was a step into the unknown.

For both of them, he reminded himself. That knowledge was the only thing keeping him from freaking, turning tail and running.

"Sounds like a plan." Hari leaned across to give him a swift kiss. "See you soon."

Fifteen minutes later, Jake heard running water when he walked in bare feet down the passage to the bathroom. His cock shot to alert, and he rubbed the heel of his hand roughly over the bulge. It did nothing to quell his anticipation. A zip of excitement tightened his balls and made his jeans uncomfortably tight.

He stepped inside the bathroom and saw Hari's silhouette through the glass door of the shower. He was lazily stroking his cock, his head bowed and his forearm pressed against the wall of the shower stall.

Hunger grabbed Jake. He whipped his T-shirt over his head and scrambled from the rest of his clothes, his stomach tight with longing.

Hari's head jerked up, his mouth curling up in a grin.

His hand worked faster, squeezing his cock, catching the underside of the flared head while his gaze never left Jake's. Jake couldn't look away from Hari pleasuring himself. Hari's face bore a strained grimace. His eyes glowed with gold while tension thrummed between them. Jake watched in fascination, feeling each stroke as if he were masturbating himself.

Jake opened the door and stepped inside, frowning when Hari's hand stilled.

"How's the bull?"

"He's up and eating, which is a relief. He looks fine. Don't stop." His voice emerged with clear hunger and strain. He shook his head. Nah, the jogging of his brains didn't make a difference. He still wanted to stay in the bathroom with Hari. He needed to watch. Participate. Hell, he'd given up trying to work out what was happening between the two of them. Ambar was easy. The woman wore sexy like a second skin, so it was no secret as to why he wanted her in his bed. But this desire for Hari stumped him.

At least Sly and Joe hadn't given him too much of a hard time. They were feline shifters. Fuck, his mind boggled every time he thought about it. All this time and he'd never had a fuckin' clue.

Enthralled, he followed the slow stroke of Hari's hand with his eyes, saw the glossy sheen on the blood-filled crown and ran his tongue along his bottom lip. With shock, he realized he wanted to taste, even more than he wanted to touch himself.

Before he could transform the thought into action,

Hari groaned, the tendons in his neck, the muscles in his shoulders tensing as his orgasm burst over him.

Jake shifted his body, angling it so he pressed against Hari's back. His cock slid across Hari's arse, the friction squeezing a moan of pleasure from Jake. Damn, that had felt good. "I thought you were going to wait for me."

Hari chuckled. "Too impatient."

"It gets better if you wait." Jake suppressed his grin, the teasing reminding him of times spent with Ambar.

"So I'll make you wait." Hari turned to face him, his eyes glittering with a hint of amusement. "I could withhold your pleasure."

Jake snorted. "You're not the boss of me."

Hari reached for a bar of soap and rubbed it between his hands to create lather. He ran his hands lazily over Jake's chest, dragging his thumb across a nipple. A shiver streaked down Jake's spine.

"Again. Do it again."

"You're not the boss of me either," Hari said with a smirk, but he did as Jake requested, pinching a fraction this time.

Jake leaned against the wall of the shower cubicle, letting his eyes drift shut while he concentrated on the pleasure. Hari played his body like an instrument. He pinched, tugged lightly on Jake's chest hair until his skin tingled and desire sang through his nerve-endings. Hari kissed him but only briefly before his touch disappeared. Jake's eyes snapped open. "Why did you stop?"

"I have something else in mind. Close your eyes again." Hari put the soap aside.

185

"What are you going to do?"

Hari grinned. "Do you trust me?"

Surprisingly, he did, even though they hadn't known each other for long. "Yeah. Yeah, I trust you."

"Hands at your sides. Eyes closed. I'll stop the minute you tell me to, but I'm not intending to do anything kinky. Okay?"

Jake nodded. Hari didn't move.

"What?"

"Give me verbal permission. I don't want you to scream rape."

Jake snorted. "Yeah right, like that's gonna happen. Yes, I trust you. Yes, you can touch me." He studied Hari's face, realized he was staring like a teenager with a crush and snapped his eyes shut.

The water hit his chest, which meant Hari had stepped away from him. There wasn't much room inside the shower. What the hell was he doing? Jake's skin tingled all over, his cock drawing impossibly tight while he wondered what Hari intended to do to him. Nothing like a little anticipation to get things going.

He thought he felt a touch on his hip. The nip of teeth confirmed it. That wasn't so bad. Then he felt the brush of a finger over the head of his cock. All the muscles in his stomach tensed, wanting more yet feeling apprehension too. What would he do next?

Fingers curled around his cock, and the air bled from Jake's lungs.

"You'd better breathe." Hari's voice held amusement. "I want you standing on your own two feet."

Jake sucked in a breath until he felt the warm heat of a mouth around the tip of his cock. Damn, that felt good. Even knowing another man had his mouth on his privates didn't spoil Jake's pleasure in the moment. His heart thumped erratically while he waited for Hari's next move. He didn't have to wait long for the rasp of a tongue over the head of his dick. The faint suction from Hari's mouth felt amazing while the teasing swipe across his sweet spot made him quiver with need. The experiences piled on top of each other, one after another. Exhilaration grew as Jake slid toward climax. His legs started to tremble, the tension in his balls almost unbearable.

Hari broke his rhythm, releasing his cock. "I don't know if I can swallow, man. This is a bit weird. In a good way," he added hastily.

"Fuck." Jake opened his eyes and looked down to meet Hari's golden gaze. "I hadn't even thought about that."

Hari rasped his tongue over the head of Jake's cock, collecting the drops of pre-cum before lifting his head. "That tastes all right."

A laugh spluttered from Jake when he took in the indecision on Hari's face. "We're both stumbling along here. Just do what you want. I'm gonna get off either way."

After that Jake fought to breathe. The pressure in his balls swelled even more with each lap of Hari's tongue and the strong, unrelenting suction.

"Don't stop. Hari, don't stop!" Jake slid the fingers of one hand through Hari's wet hair while the other gripped his shoulder. Hari moaned and Jake felt the vibration along the length of his shaft. Unable to help, he jerked his hips forward, driving his cock deeper. He glanced down and saw the hunger in Hari's gaze, the pleasure he took in giving, and Jake exploded. Hari swallowed automatically then drew back, extending Jake's orgasm with the pump of his hand. Finally Jake collapsed against the wall of the shower to bolster his weak knees.

"Hari, come up here." Jake wanted to kiss him in the worst way. When Hari stood, Jake pushed his tongue past Hari's lips and slid their tongues together, tasting himself in the kiss. He ran his tongue over Hari's front teeth and drew back with a jolt. "Your teeth have grown."

"Feline trick. Sometimes it's difficult to control the urge to change when I'm excited or angry."

Jake arched a brow. "And are you? Excited?"

The water picked that moment to run cold.

"Let's take this to the bedroom." The gleam in Hari's eyes promised more, and Jake was fine with that. Jake grabbed the soap and rubbed the bar across his chest. He cleansed his body, wincing at the cold water. Jake stepped from the shower and reached for a towel. He dried his body with brisk, economical moves before getting another towel for Hari. The shower shut off. Jake leaned against the vanity unit and watched Hari.

Muscle rippled across Hari's chest and shoulders when he reached for a towel. The solid slab of muscle shouldn't have turned him on, but it did. Their similarities fascinated him as much as Ambar's differences and softness had always attracted him.

"Stop staring at me like that."

Jake enjoyed studying him. It was a novel experience,

openly watching another man. "I like looking at you." It was nothing less than the truth and it still had the power to shock him.

Hari grinned and held out his hand. "Let's spend an hour or two in bed."

Jake took his hand and grinned back. "I wish Ambar was here with us."

Hari kept walking and didn't reply until they reached Jake's bedroom. Hari sat on the edge of the rumpled bed and tugged Jake down beside him. "I'm not sure that Ambar is ready for both of us. She told me she didn't want a mate."

"What does that mean?"

"Nothing, if we play our cards right. You want this? With both of us?"

Jake didn't have to think about it. "Yes." He'd felt a surge of jealousy when he'd seen Hari and Ambar together, but when he thought about the three of them, it felt right. "How do we persuade her to change her mind? When we first started going out she was very clear about not wanting anything permanent. It suited me so I didn't argue."

"Things change," Hari said. "I came out here from England because of her photo. She's even better in person. You know about her parents trying to arrange a marriage for her, right? That's how I came to see her photo."

"Yes, she told me about escaping an arranged marriage. We could go and get her later this evening."

"Good idea, but meantime..." He turned and pounced on Jake, shoving him back against the pillows. Heat sizzled over Jake's chest when Hari pinched his nipple. Their mouths met, hungry and urgent, desire flaring anew. Their bodies strained together, cocks rubbing, hips pumping. They clutched each other, hands and mouths exploring, bodies learning each other as they fell into pleasure. Together.

AMBAR FOUND IT DIFFICULT to concentrate, and the day seemed to drag despite the huge number of orders she packed. After making a second mistake, she took to double-checking each order. At least business was good.

Finally, at six she and Rohan closed shop and walked home.

"Are you going out tonight?"

Ambar shook her head. "I think I'll have a shower before I start cooking dinner."

"I can cook if you want."

"No, it's my turn. I don't mind. I won't be long." Ambar marched to her bedroom, closing the door behind her. Once inside, tears flooded her eyes and she swiped at them angrily. This was stupid. She knew both Hari and Jake found her desirable and wanted her physically. She didn't intend to stay in Middlemarch forever, so why was she so pissed with them for spending time together? Why did she feel so left out?

Cursing under her breath, she moved closer to the bed and stripped off her clothes. They landed on the bed in a heap. Without giving them a second look, Ambar thrust her arms into her robe and headed for the bathroom.

Her mood deteriorated even further during dinner.

"What's wrong?" Kiran demanded, having arrived home just before seven. "You've got a face like a sour apple."

She pulled a face. "Men trouble."

"I thought you guys had sorted that out," Rohan said.

Ambar tossed her cutlery down so hard her fork clattered to the floor. She bent to retrieve it and placed it more carefully this time. "I'm jealous, okay? And I don't want to talk about it."

"You're making it our problem because we have to watch you sulking," Kiran pointed out.

"Jake and Hari are alone."

"So?" Kiran said. "They live in the same house."

"I doubt they're playing house," Rohan said dryly.

"The mattress mumbo?" Kiran's lips quivered as if he wanted to chuckle.

Ambar shot him a glare. "I don't want to talk about sex."

"You were quite happy to talk about sex when it came to us," Kiran said.

Rohan swallowed the last of his lamb chop. "Payback is a bitch."

"I don't want payback," Ambar wailed. She gulped, irritated to find herself close to tears again. She blinked rapidly and jumped to her feet.

"What do you want?" Kiran asked.

"That's the problem. I don't know what I want."

A car pulled up outside.

Rohan smiled. "That sounds like your car, Ambar."

It was her car. She recognized the distinctive throaty

roar her little car made when the driver changed gears. Anticipation skipped through her. Was it Jake or Hari?

"I'll get the door," Kiran said, darting away from the table before she could argue.

She heard the door open and the low rumble of masculine voices. Suddenly nervous, she sank back on her chair.

"Do you think it will be Hari or Jake?" Rohan asked.

"If you stopped yammering I might be able to tell you," Ambar snapped at her brother.

They both turned to face the door. Ambar's nostrils flared, drawing in their combined scent. She gasped, jealousy thumping her in the stomach even when she'd prepared for it, had known they'd spend the day lovemaking. Happiness blazed on their faces, and Hari touched Jake's shoulder with easy intimacy. They were a couple.

"Ambar," Rohan said with a sly glance in her direction. "They look well-rested."

Ambar kicked him under the table, fiercely wishing she wore her pointy-toed boots instead of bare feet.

"Would you like a beer?" Kiran asked.

"Have you eaten?" Rohan asked, with a smirk in her direction. He'd noticed the way Jake leaned into Hari. The wretch had probably noticed the dark bruise on Jake's neck too. Ambar wanted to lick it in the worst way but forced herself to remain seated. Her jaw ached with the wide smile she forced on her mouth.

"We've come for Ambar," Jake said.

"Does Ambar want to go with you?" Rohan asked,

standing so she couldn't kick him again. Her brother was no slouch in the brain department.

Kiran walked past on his way to the fridge, pausing to squeeze her shoulder in silent reassurance.

"That's entirely up to Ambar," Hari said. "We needed to return her car anyway."

A problem. If she went with them she was making a commitment of sorts, even if she stated otherwise. The pause grew uncomfortable. She was aware of Rohan's amusement, the hum of the fridge as Kiran opened it and the faint rattle of beer bottles.

Ambar worried her bottom lip, weighing her options. If she did nothing, she'd regret it. She knew herself well enough to know that, and the jealousy would drive her to madness. Imagining Jake and Hari together today had been bad enough. But if she went with them, wasn't she taking a step past the point of no return? A shard of pain and the faint coppery taste of blood made her quit the lip gnawing.

"Ambar?" Hari's husky voice served as a prod for a decision and she came to a resolution. No matter what, she'd stick to it.

Ambar stood and pushed her chair back under the table before she focused on Jake and Hari. "Just for tonight."

She stared at Hari until he acknowledged her words with a curt nod. He thought he could change her mind. That was obvious, but it wouldn't happen. She intended to keep her freedom. She would travel soon. There would be no clipped wings for her.

CHAPTER ELEVEN

AMBAR INSISTED ON TAKING her car so she could make her escape whenever she wanted. Hari and Jake drove back together in Jake's vehicle. She pulled up outside Jake's house, her stomach a tangle of nerves. Mistake or not, she wasn't about to back out now.

A deep inhalation did nothing to settle her trepidation. A sharp knock on her window made her head jerk up.

Jake and Hari.

Both men stood watching her.

A united front. Waiting.

She grimaced at the pain stabbing her heart. There went that damn jealousy again. It was a bit like being a new kid on the playground, unsure of the rules or social structure.

Hari opened the car door and stood back, still waiting.

"You're not usually so shy," Jake said.

"Yeah, well. Things are a bit different now."

"Not really," Hari said.

"My boyfriend and his roomie spent the afternoon having sex. What's not different about that?" *And didn't that sound like jealousy? Rats!*

"This is probably the time when I should mention the secrets you've kept from me," Jake said, shifting the topic of conversation. "I'm not sulking."

"Are you coming inside?" Hari looked as if he was suppressing a smile.

Ambar's mouth struggled with a grin. They were right. She was acting like a child who'd had her party spoiled. "I drove out here, didn't I?"

Jake led the way inside and Hari walked behind her.

"Trying to stop me from fleeing?" she asked sweetly.

"Just appreciating the sway of your arse," he countered.

Jake turned, giving an approving nod. "She does move well."

"Stop discussing me as if I'm not here."

"This doesn't bode well for tonight." Hari exaggerated his plumy English vowels especially for her.

"Knock it off," Ambar said, beginning to wish she'd said no and stayed at home.

"I think we need a drink." Jake stood aside to usher Ambar to the lounge.

"I'll get drinks," Hari volunteered. "I bought some whisky yesterday. Is that okay?"

"That's fine," Ambar said in a faint voice as she dropped onto a dark brown leather couch. They were organizing her, treating her like something fragile or a wild creature about to flee. Her mouth twisted in a quick grimace. It appeared they knew her well.

Hari came back with a bottle of whisky and three glasses. He opened the screw top, poured the liquor in all three glasses and handed Ambar and Jake a drink each.

"To the three of us." Hari lifted his glass in a toast.

"The three of us," Jake echoed.

Ambar stared at them, hesitating yet again. "Are you sure this is a good idea?" Good idea, huh! It had the potential to blow up in their faces. Besides, Middlemarch was a small town and one where she and Jake held close ties. If things backfired between them, they couldn't avoid each other.

Jake and Hari grinned at each other, communicating silently. They both crossed the threadbare carpet to reach her side. One sat either side of her, the warmth of their thighs heating her body, making her crave more despite her brain trying to overrule her physical desires and make her see sense. A shiver stole down her spine, her nipples tightening against the fabric of her bra. *Danger, Ambar. Danger.*

Hari set his glass on the nearby coffee table and took hers from nerveless fingers. A murmur of protest escaped her at his highhandedness. It didn't make a difference to the outcome. Jake's glass clicked when he placed it on the wooden surface. Like a choreographed ballet, they touched her. Hands skimmed her jeans-clad knees, smoothed her back. Tremors sped across her skin as they petted her. Her breath caught in her throat.

They were so close. Too close and impossible to ignore.

Their scent twined all the way to her lungs, filling her senses until dizziness assailed her from their presence. Their touch didn't feel weird, it didn't feel kinky. No. She felt as if they belonged together.

And that scared her most of all because they didn't have a future. Not if she intended to keep to her plans. But was this so bad? The traitorous voice in her head said no. It urged her to greedily soak up the experience, to hoard the good feelings. Their time together would be something to think about later when she explored the world.

Alone, the little voice declared.

She frowned, her scowl deepening when she realized her clothes were askew, her shirt gaping open because one of the men had adroitly unfastened buttons while she argued with herself.

"Lean forward," Jake urged.

"Why?"

"Don't argue. Just do it," Hari said. "Let us make you feel good."

Good? Already she melted like her favorite white chocolate on a sunny day. "I don't think—"

Jake cut off her protest with his mouth. If he had tried to conquer and exert his strength, she might have won her mental argument, called a halt and gone home. But no, he was smarter than that. He persuaded her with his lips. Cajoled. He sipped and stroked her mouth in a gentle manner that made her heart pound. While he tasted, the pads of his fingers massaged her scalp. Jake seduced her, and she let him, relaxing and letting the feelings and emotions flow through her. The sensations fell, layer upon layer, until she sizzled with urgency. Like a hot plate ready to cook, she thought with a flare of disgust before a second pair of lips nuzzled her ear. A second tongue explored the whorls of her ear and the delicate skin behind it. A moan broke free then, along with the last of her doubtable restraint.

She surrendered—that's what she did.

Ambar relaxed into their care. The soft murmur of approval against her lips told her Jake knew he'd won her over. The fight had ended. All they needed to do was reel her in like a fish.

"Let me take off your shirt." Hari's whispered suggestion sounded good to her.

Jake took her right hand and tugged her to her feet while Hari removed her shirt and unhooked her bra, sliding it down her arms and tossing it aside. The rest of her clothes and footwear disappeared and soon she stood in front of them, naked. Her nipples pulled even tighter in the cool air, the swirl of nervousness in her stomach making her fidget.

"It's hard to know where to touch first," Jake said in a thick voice. His eyes glowed with both excitement and desire, and when he reached out to delicately touch one pouting nipple, his hand trembled.

The small show of nerves boosted Ambar's confidence. Her attention turned to Hari, searching for anything in his face that might bring alarm. His gentle smile, his inherent approval helped her shed the last of her inhibitions.

Ambar cupped her breasts, offering herself to the two men.

"I think we should move this to the bedroom," Hari said.

"Good idea." Jake scooped Ambar off her feet and

carried her rapidly down the passage to his bedroom. They'd changed the bed linens for fresh ones. She'd scarcely processed the thought when she found herself flat on the mattress, jammed between two hard male bodies. A blip of excitement shot to her sex.

A quick glance at Hari told her he knew. The golden flecks in his eyes glittered and his mouth curled with satisfaction.

"She wants this, Jake," he said. "I can smell how excited she is at the thought of two of us loving her."

"I'm starting to wish I was feline. I'm going to have to investigate at closer quarters before I can smell her excitement."

Sudden heat suffused her face. Jake saw it—curse him—because he shot her a boyish grin, the one she'd never managed to resist. "Guys, I'm right here. You're embarrassing me."

"You can smell us right back," Jake said, caressing one breast. He leaned over and kissed Hari, taking his own sweet time.

At first, astonishment filled Ambar then she started to get hot watching the two men interact together. Their kiss was slow and tender with none of the roughness she'd envisaged. They angled their heads to achieve the perfect fit, the affection morphing into need and desire. Jake moaned and the masculine sound rippled through Ambar. She stirred uneasily, aware of how wet she was and how much the physical exchange made her hot and bothered rather than uncomfortable. It made her curious.

Who knew she'd harbored voyeuristic tendencies?

SHELLEY MUNRO

Both men were breathing hard when they came up for air. They grinned, entirely comfortable with kissing each other and doing it in her presence. The very air hummed with undercurrents and sexual desire.

"I'm starting to feel like an outsider." At her protest they both turned to her.

"We wanted you to witness we're serious about each other," Hari said. "We're not ignoring you. Both of us want you."

Jake dropped a kiss on her forehead. "Never doubt it, sweetheart. We intend to show you exactly how much we need you." He lowered his head to her breast, taking a teasing swipe around the areola with the tip of his tongue.

On her other breast, Hari mirrored Jake's actions. It felt the same but different. Teeth nipped gently, before they licked and sucked on her breasts, both men knowing exactly what she liked. The dual sensations amazed her. Ambar ran her fingers through Jake's brown locks and Hari's short black hair while they sucked and teased her. Magical sensations writhed across her skin. Ambar wanted to plead for them to go faster, to give her more. Contrarily she hated to end the teasing and pleasure. Heck, she could smell her excitement now, and she started to think she might actually climax from their attention to her breasts alone.

As if they sensed how close she was, they backed off a little, easing her down. They moved toward her feet, pausing to nibble and lick all the curves and hollows. When they reached her hips, she started to shiver, so close to coming her clit throbbed with a gnawing ache.

"Part your legs as wide as you can," Hari said.

"Yeah. We both want to taste."

Ambar swallowed and silently obeyed them. Tomorrow her muscles might ache but the pain would come with wonderful sensual memories.

Instead of diving in for the main course, they continued to dally, licking along the joint where leg and torso met. Hot, wet tongues left a damp trail, the contrasting cool air after their licks bringing another prickling sensation to her body. Ambar bit down on her inner lip, determined not to give voice to her pleas for them to hurry. Her eyes slid shut and her other senses ruled.

The cadence of her breathing became increasingly louder. Her imagination danced ahead, almost feeling Hari's raspy tongue sliding down her slit, the softer texture of Jake's tongue as he circled the swollen bundle of nerves aching so incessantly for their attention.

The duvet cover crinkled under her restless body. They moved. Ambar almost let out a cry of protest until she heard the whine of a zipper and the fall of cloth on the floor. The masculine figures in her mind lost their clothes. Still her eyes remained shut, her entire body tingling.

The mattress depressed a fraction, telling her Jake and Hari had returned to her side. This time they didn't tease. They went straight to business. Someone's fingers parted her folds.

"Look how wet she is for us," Jake said.

"She's beautiful." Satisfaction coated Hari's voice. Ambar felt a spurt of indignation until the rasp of a tongue snared her attention. She waited anxiously, breath held, for another slow pass of that tongue. Instead, she felt a second tongue. She gasped, the air rushing from her body on a moan. That felt incredible. The first shimmers of her orgasm twirled down her legs, ending at her toes. Her heart thumped in hard beats, her body tense as she waited, balanced on the cusp of pain and pleasure.

Although the temptation to open her eyes to see what they were doing drifted through her mind, she kept them firmly closed. Somehow, she thought it was better not to see.

This time, lips pressed against her swollen folds. They met above her clit and pulsed together. Tongues flickered out and stroked. Her flesh. Each other. The result was the same. Ambar jerked her hips upward into the pressure of their tongues.

Pleasure exploded, speeding through her sensitive nerve-endings. Ambar gripped the duvet cover with both hands, her body straining to experience every possible ounce of pleasure. Gradually, the tension left her limbs and she relaxed into the mattress. Her eyes flickered open and the first thing she saw was both men grinning at her. Her juices covered their lips and chins. Both sets of eyes glowed. They were beautiful.

Jake crawled up the bed and kissed her, the spicy flavor of her arousal filling her mouth. Then Hari joined them.

"We want to take you together. Are you okay with that?"

Her brows rose in consternation, the tautness returning to her body. "You've discussed this?"

"Of course we have," Jake said. "The last thing we want to do is hurt you."

They cared enough to worry about her safety. Some of the stiffness eased from her at the knowledge. "I guess we can try. What were you thinking?" The idea of taking two men into her body at once...holy heck...her parents truly would spin in their graves. Not only was she sinning without marriage, she intended to do it with two men at once.

Hari kissed her on the lips. "Thank you, love."

"What for?"

"For trusting us," Jake said. "Scoot over a little. Toss me a condom, Hari."

"You don't need one," Hari said. "Neither of us can catch or spread diseases."

"What about pregnancy?"

Ambar took over the explanations. "Gavin gives us contraceptive shots. Pregnancy isn't a problem."

Jake frowned. "So why did we use condoms before?"

"You would have asked questions," Hari said. "We try to fit in and act like humans as much as possible."

"Fair enough." Jake rolled over on his back and grinned at them. "When you guys have kids, they don't come in litters, right?"

"No, thank goodness," Ambar retorted. "And before you ask, we don't go into heat either."

"What about the twins?"

"Most shifters have single offspring like humans," Hari said. "Although it isn't uncommon to have twins."

Ambar snorted. "The world should lament the fact. Joe and Sly are a handful."

"You're cute when you get feisty." Jake stroked his

203

cock, his rhythmic moves attracting her attention. His eyes sparkled with devilment. "Come over here and climb aboard."

Ambar groaned, especially when he waggled his eyebrows, but she obeyed his instructions. Only because it was what she wanted too, she told herself, straddling his thighs. A glistening bead of pre-cum tempted her, and she leaned over to lap it up with her tongue.

"I never thought about it before, but your tongue is rougher than mine. Hari's too."

"It's the feline genes." Ambar wondered briefly about how Jake had experienced Hari's tongue before shoving it aside. This jealousy had to stop. They were here together. Jake and Hari had driven to collect her, and together they'd seduced her. She had to remember that.

The sound of a nightstand drawer opening snared her attention.

"Focus on me," Jake said. "We're not going to do anything that you and I haven't done before. Look at me."

Ambar shivered, seeing the swirl of passion in his blue eyes. Excitement filled his entire face.

"Take me inside you. I want to feel the tight clasp of your pussy squeezing my cock."

Ooh, she wanted that too. Ambar swallowed and lifted her body a fraction before guiding Jake to her entrance. She sank down slowly, savoring the stretch like a favorite treat.

"Damn, that feels good without a condom." Jake's eyelids slid to half-mast, his low, husky voice dragging an answering response from her. Her pussy fluttered, grabbing at his cock.

Ambar continued to push down, taking his rigid flesh into her body. It soothed the renewed ache of awareness yet made it worse as well.

"I never thought I'd get off on watching the two of you together," Hari said from behind her. "Watching Jake's cock disappear into you is the sexiest thing I've seen in a long time."

Ambar jerked at the throaty sound of his voice, his accent more pronounced than normal. While she'd concentrated on Jake, she'd put his presence from her mind. Now he was there again, center stage.

"You should be on this end," Jake said with a chuckle. "No, don't move. We want to wait for Hari. Lean forward and let me take most of your weight."

Ambar hesitated until Hari placed a hand on her back, silently encouraging her to follow Jake's instructions. There was no doubt in her mind who was calling the shots here. Somehow, Hari had managed to seduce them both, and she couldn't find it in herself to feel sorrow. Anger, she might experience that later, but right now Hari was doing a good job. She closed her eyes again, finding it easier to release the lingering reservations that crept in to question her judgment when she couldn't see.

Jake pressed his lips to hers, igniting a fire in her with the slow surge and retreat of his tongue. She shivered, recalling the way it had felt with both of them touching her pussy, licking and teasing her. Her sheath clenched around Jake's cock as she imagined the two men shuttling in and out of her body, loving her together. No matter how much her brain disliked the idea of submitting to the pair of them, her body had no problem.

A hand stroked over her back. Another cupped her arse, a glide of fingers trailed across her buttocks. She tensed for a moment before a groan from Jake made her eyes flick open. Arousal shone in his face.

"If you don't stop tightening your pussy, I'll lose control." His warm breath whispered past her ear. "Hari, move things along."

The throaty chuckle from behind her sent another jolt of heat through her sensitized nerve-endings. Her pussy fluttered at the merest suggestion of more. She'd never last.

Hari seemed to take Jake's warning to heart and quit his teasing strokes and touches. Ambar drifted, her eyes closed again as she relaxed and gave responsibility over to the two men.

The wheeze of a plastic bottle cut through the air. Lube. A trace of worry accompanied the clenching of her sex this time. Anal sex had hurt last time with Jake. They'd gone slow, but she hadn't liked it as much as Jake had, which was why they didn't do it very often.

A thought occurred. "Did the two of you…?" she trailed off in a delicate manner.

"We tried almost everything except full penetration," Jake said gruffly.

"Did you like it?"

The finger tracing her rosette stilled, and she sensed the two men looked at each other.

"I liked it," Jake said without hesitation. Part of Ambar was impressed. Jake was very masculine, the last man she'd consider curious about sex with another man. "There's something about Hari that appeals to me. I couldn't do it with another man, but with Hari it's different."

The finger wriggled again, this time slipping inside her, pushing in and angling the careful strokes down so he caressed Jake's shaft at the same time. There was a slight burn and she must have frowned because Jake distracted her with another kiss. It was slow, but not tentative. Jake ate at her mouth, distracting her with a nip of teeth followed by the soothing slide of his tongue. Ambar floated, whimsically imagining Jake's cock as the only thing anchoring her to the bed.

Belatedly, she became aware of more than one finger piercing her. Hari stretched her carefully yet with insistence. After a while, it didn't feel so bad. Jake kept kissing her, distracting her, allowing her to relax.

Soon, she felt Hari shift his weight behind her. The men must have communicated silently again because Jake started to kiss and nibble at her throat between kisses on her mouth. Ambar kept her eyes closed, enjoying the way it amplified her senses, distancing her from the act even as it made her feel more connected.

"Damn," Jake whispered, tearing his mouth from hers. "I can feel you against my cock."

"Yeah." It sounded as if Hari was gritting his teeth.

Ambar breathed carefully through a jolt of pain. It eased almost immediately and she realized the more she relaxed, the easier this would be for all of them.

As if he read her mind, Jake pinched her nipple, kissing her at the same time. The pain ran from her breast down to her pussy, starting up an ache that made her want to move. She jerked her hips back and pushed onto Hari's cock. He exhaled loudly in her ear. Like a chain reaction, her pussy tightened around Jake's cock and both men groaned.

"Just a bit more, love, then we can start moving." Hari swept aside her hair. "Kiss her right there."

Seconds later, Jake's lips latched on to the spot where one day she might wear a mating mark. The air hissed from her lungs as a mini climax rocked across her nerves.

"That's it, love." Hari stilled, his cock feeling huge. Her anus no longer burned, but a sense of extreme fullness took its place. "Now, Jake."

Jake sucked her marking spot again as Hari withdrew. He pushed inside her again, and Jake moved his hips, forcing her upward. They settled into a rhythm that immediately had her gasping. Pleasure simmered at the edges of her pussy like a slow burn. Ambar wanted to grasp the sensation, clutch it to her heart and make the bliss last forever. Heat, so hot. She'd never experienced the like before, the ecstasy.

A groan escaped at their next stroke, her body on erotic overload at the fullness. Jake and Hari increased the pace, forcing her onward, pushing her higher. The pleasure ballooned, suffusing her body until a final nudge against her clit pushed her over the edge. She toppled headfirst into her climax, the colors she saw behind her closed eyes as bright and colorful as a fireworks spectacular. She was vaguely aware of the two men continuing, groaning, urgently pursuing their pleasure. Gradually they stilled.

Hari pulled away and lifted her off Jake before settling

her back on the bed. Long moments later a warm cloth drifted across her lower body. Sleepily, she cuddled up to Jake. Hari settled on her other side, wrapping an arm around her waist. She fell asleep with a smile on her face.

CHAPTER TWELVE

"Hari?"

"Yeah?" Hari smiled across Ambar at Jake.

"I want you to do that to me. Soon."

Hari thought about Jake's request for a few seconds, surprised at the conclusion he came to. "I want you to do it to me too."

Jake sighed. "Good."

"We have to be careful not to close out Ambar," Hari warned.

"Are you kidding? Both of us making love to her at the same time was the hottest thing I've ever experienced. No wonder Sly and Joe like to share their women. I thought they were nuts, but that felt fuckin' amazing."

Hari smiled. "Yeah, it was." He'd do some research on the internet. Maybe he'd buy some toys the three of them could use together. He'd never felt so loose and limber after sex. Jake was right. The three of them together had been incredible. "Are you tired?"

"Nah."

"You wanna come over to this side of the bed and fool around a bit more?"

In lieu of answering, Jake moved away from a sleeping Ambar and slid off the bed. He padded around to Hari's side of the bed, his cock swaying in a tantalizing manner. Hari licked his lips, wanting to taste Jake this time. He lifted away from Ambar, smiling at the whistling sound she made in her sleep. She'd probably deny snoring but she wasn't far away.

"On the bed," he said to Jake.

"You like giving orders."

"Do you mind?"

Jake snorted. "As long as you don't think you can order me around outside the bedroom. My father used to order me around, which is why we butted heads so much."

"Is that why he left?"

"No, it was mainly his health. My mother and father are so self-involved it's embarrassing. I always felt as if I was a third wheel. My arrival came as a surprise because they'd given up trying to have children. They'd done all the tests and decided they didn't need a child to complete their lives."

Hari frowned, remembering his own parents. They'd loved him, made him feel treasured. "Did they mistreat you?"

"No, of course not. I had everything I needed growing up, but I still felt as if I was in the way. They'd always planned on moving to Dunedin and traveling as the fancy

211

took them. Dad had the health scare and the next thing I knew they'd decided to move."

"Is that when you bought the farm?"

"It was either buy the farm from my father or look for a new job. Farming is the only thing I know."

It wasn't difficult for Hari to read between the lines. The purchase of the farm had placed financial hardship on Jake, and he felt anger toward Jake's parents. Luckily, he had enough money for the three of them. Website design paid well and if his game sold, as he thought it would, he'd never need to worry about money again. None of them would.

Hari leaned over Jake. He stared at his lover's lips as he closed the distance between them. Who knew how much he'd enjoy kissing this man? He took his time, tasting Jake's lips and savoring the contrast between his hard teeth and soft palate. Loving Jake had a rough edge to it that Hari enjoyed. His grip on Jake's head tightened while his fingertips curled into one muscular biceps. He didn't have to be careful, and Jake's soft moan proved he enjoyed Hari's contact. One glance at Jake's cock signaled how much his lover enjoyed a particular stroke or nip of fingers. He pinched one of Jake's nipples, the needy sound a double-edged knife. A bolt of arousal struck Hari's balls and had his cock stretching to full length. He ground his shaft against Jake's leg, the friction of hair and skin almost perfect.

Ambar stirred, her eyes fluttering open. "Hey, are you starting without me?"

Hari smiled, noting the interest in her sleepy

golden-brown eyes. "Why don't you join in?"

Ambar slid one of her hands across her breasts, cupping the tawny mound. She rolled over a fraction, offering it to Jake. Hari watched as Jake's mouth closed around Ambar's nipple, saw Jake's cheeks hollow when he sucked hard.

Ambar's throaty groan acted like the brush of a hand across Hari's cock. All the rest of the blood in his body seemed to shoot south. His hips jerked, driving his shaft against Jake's leg again. He must have made a sound because Ambar grinned at him.

"Patience," she said. "Your turn will come soon."

With anticipation simmering through his veins, Hari moved down the bed and started to torture Jake. He gripped Jake's cock, noting the rapid leak from the slit on top. Curious to taste again, he bent his head and lapped at the clear liquid. It didn't taste too bad. Hari sealed his mouth around Jake's cock, testing with each lash of his tongue. Gradually, he increased the suction and fondled Jake's tight balls, giving experimental tugs. He could hear Jake moan as he sucked on Ambar's breasts and kissed her.

Jake obviously liked what he was doing and was ready for more. Hari took Jake's cock deeper while he played with his balls. His finger drifted downward while his mind busily thought ahead. Why not? He pulled away from Jake for a moment to grab the lube. Seconds later, his mouth covered the tip of Jake's shaft again, and he brushed his fingers across Jake's hole. The other man trembled violently. Gratified by the reaction, he decided to push further. He tongued across Jake's cock and slipped his finger carefully inside Jake.

Jake's hips surged upward, driving his cock deeper. Hari lifted his head a fraction and teased the sensitive underside. At the same time, he angled his finger and slid it deeper. A shudder shook Jake and he groaned. That must be the right place. Hari grinned around Jake's cock and stroked the spongy mass of Jake's prostate until Jake trembled with the sweet caress. His hips jerked upward, driving his cock deeper and taking Hari by surprise. Hari gagged a fraction before easing back enough for comfort. The next thing he knew Jake was coming, shooting semen into his mouth. He decided it really didn't taste too bad. He'd done it once before, so Hari swallowed a couple of times before drawing back. Semen shot over his chin and dripped down his chest.

"Sorry," Jake said, a faint trace of embarrassment coloring in his cheeks.

"No problem 'cause you're gonna lick it off," Hari said.

Jake hesitated, before chuckling. "Sounds fair enough." After shuffling over on the bed, he reached up, snagged Hari's wrist and yanked him closer. "Ambar, you want some cock?"

Together, Ambar and Jake arranged him on the mattress. Before he could blink, Ambar had straddled him and guided his cock to her pussy. She sank down with one hard push, the parting of her inner muscles feeling incredible. Hari relaxed, wordlessly giving the pair of them control over his body. Weird, it was the first time he'd actually trusted a lover enough without trying to call the shots. They made him feel secure and comfortable as if he was home.

Ambar taunted him with languorous rises and falls designed to drive him to the edge of control while Jake sipped at his lips, licked his chin clean and nuzzled his neck.

"Can I bite?" Jake whispered against his ear.

"If you want to, but mean it because once you've bitten me, I'm pretending you're feline. I want you, Jake. In my mind, we'll be mates. I'll mark you in return, and there will be no going back." Hari drew him closer, encouraging him with actions as well as words. He felt Ambar stiffen, hesitate before regaining her rhythm, so he knew she'd heard Jake's whisper and his reply.

A spurt of worry brought a frown, which he wiped clean the second he noticed the pucker between Jake's brows. The last thing he wanted was to discourage Jake. In the short time he'd known the other man, Hari had fallen hard. The idea of Jake wanting to mate with him was a powerful turn on and he'd treasure his lover.

"I'd like that very much, love." Hari snaked a hand behind Jake's neck, drew him closer, wanting to solidify his words with a kiss.

Taking his time, he coaxed Jake to participate, worked on driving out the concerns his frown at Ambar had caused. Soon Jake pressed for more, the kiss going deeper, a mating of mouths. The feline trembled under his skin, forcing Hari to fight to keep his canines and claws at bay. He wasn't very successful, but the appearance of sharp canine teeth didn't seem to faze Jake. He pulled away, the glow of passion darkening his blue eyes.

"You like the idea of me biting you. You can't control your feline."

"It's both of you," Hari said, wanting Ambar to know he wanted her as badly as he needed Jake.

"I can live with that," Jake said, reaching out to stroke Ambar's hip.

Jake's touch seemed to settle the agitation Hari had been feeling in Ambar. She'd become difficult for him to read. The last thing he wanted was for her to feel excluded. At least Jake's presence soothed her, his touch. Their combined touch.

"Ambar, make him come," Jake said.

"Aye, captain," Ambar said, her smart-ass remark making them both chuckle. And just like that Hari's worry faded. Ambar's pussy clamped him tight. Velvet heat surrounded his dick, the pulsing friction during the invasion and retreat of his cock making him wish their lovemaking would never end.

Jake took possession of his lips again, appearing to enjoy running his tongue over Hari's sharp teeth. Ambar groaned suddenly and fell forward. She kissed Hari's neck, moving slowly down his throat, nipping his marking spot. Then, without warning, she bit. Her teeth sank into the fleshy part at the base of his neck. The painful sensation roused nerve-endings he thought were already awake. Electricity leapt across his body, joining his pleasure spots into one big erogenous zone. A growl squeezed past his teeth, more catlike than anything he'd heard himself make while in human form. Jake jerked away in shock while Hari's hips bucked, his cock growing impossibly big. Hari groaned again, a burst of acute pleasure-pain in his balls signaling the point of no return. He came violently with Ambar's teeth sunk in his marking site, pain and pleasure warring for dominance while she lapped at the wound. The white-hot conflagration crashed over into the side of pleasure and his growl was like no sound he'd ever made before. The pulses went on and on, rippling through his cock, his balls, until only muted garbles issued from his throat. She pulled back a fraction, lapped at the bite mark she'd inflicted. Hari shuddered again, the pulse of pleasure more than he'd ever imagined.

Ambar climaxed again with a sexy moan, her pussy rippling hard and forcing another minute spurt from his cock. She fell forward against Hari's chest, her long black hair hiding her face from him as it pooled around them in silken strands.

"You okay?" Jake asked, his blue eyes wide with questions. He glanced from Hari to Ambar and back again, a frown drawing his dark brows together.

"I'm feeling great." Hari smiled, hoping to reassure Jake. They could talk later.

"You're bleeding," Jake said.

"Lick the blood off for me, love. Make the bleeding stop." Hari didn't like the way Ambar had stiffened against him. "Ambar?"

Ambar lifted her head, and one glimpse told Hari things were far from all right. She might have marked him, but she wasn't pleased about it.

"I...ah...have to go." Ambar scrambled off the bed, scooped up her clothes and fled the bedroom.

"Ambar?" Jake stared after her in surprise before turning back to Hari. "What's up with Ambar? Hell, she's leaving." The slam of the front door confirmed it.

Hari remained frozen on the bed, the ripples of pleasure still firing his blood. He swiped a hand over his face and turned to Jake. "Fuck, that's not the way I saw my marking going."

"And you're still bleeding," Jake said, moving closer to gently touch the oozing wound on his neck.

Hari winced, not in pain but in shock at the spike of pleasure that struck at his balls.

"Shit, I didn't mean to hurt you."

Hari rolled his eyes, wanting to smile, even though laughter was the last thing he felt like at the moment. He gestured at his erection. "Does this look as if I'm in pain? When you touch my mark it's like a bolt of electricity shooting straight to my groin."

Jake settled back on the mattress beside Hari and leaned over to take a closer look. He pressed gently, watching Hari's reaction the entire time. Hari shuddered, unable to hold back his response. A gasp shot from his throat and they both watched his cock twitch once before it lengthened farther.

Jake shot him a mischievous smile, one that Hari hadn't seen before, and it lightened his heart. He liked seeing Jake this way. Hari just wished that Ambar hadn't run off. They'd go and see her tomorrow—give her the night to straighten her thoughts. Despite his disappointment at Ambar's reaction, he couldn't find it in himself to be sorry about the mark he now wore. He felt connected and grounded in a way he hadn't before. For now, that was enough.

The touch of Jake's finger at his mark dragged his thoughts from Ambar and back to the present. With his mischievous grin still intact, Jake leaned against Hari's chest, sealed his mouth around the wound and gently cleaned it with his tongue.

Hari's response shouldn't have surprised him, but it did. He felt invincible and privileged, happier than he had for a long time. He'd be happier still if Ambar hadn't fled again. She really needed to get past the habit of running whenever something scared her. The swish of Jake's tongue, followed by the faint bite of teeth yanked a groan from deep in his chest.

"Fuck that feels good. I want you inside me," Hari said. "Please."

"Will you mark me?"

"Do you want me to?"

"Yeah, it would be a bit like a tattoo. I like the idea of belonging, having a family. The Mitchells are more of a family to me than my parents. But I'd like my own family with you and Ambar."

Hari had to blink rapidly so the flood of emotion that hit him didn't escape as tears. The thing was, he knew exactly what Jake meant about family. Since his parents had died he'd felt adrift, despite his aunt and uncle's presence in his life. When he was with Jake and Ambar, the loneliness disappeared.

"It's not something I can take back. You need to be very sure. The mark will only start to fade if one of us dies.

Divorce isn't an option."

"So you and Ambar are sort of married now?"

"I haven't marked Ambar yet. With felines, both parties have to mark each other before their mating is official. With you and me, all I need to do is bite you and it's done."

"So I can't bite you back after all?" Jake sounded disappointed.

"You can bite me any time," Hari purred, and Jake's eyes lit up.

"I intend to bite back—consider yourself warned. You really want me to fuck you?" Jake reached for the bottle of lube Hari had left sitting on the nightstand before Hari had a chance to answer.

"I want you any way I can have you. Always." Hari meant every word.

"I have mountains of debts, bills coming out my ears. I'm tied to the farm."

"I have enough money for the three of us."

Jake stiffened and speared him with a glare. "I'm not taking charity."

"I'm thinking more of a partnership. It would work both ways, Jake. I help out on the farm, and you help me get the last of the bugs out of my game."

"A partnership, huh?" The indignation seeped from Jake. "The farm does need a cash injection. I had to use all my savings and borrow more to pay off my parents. It will be profitable in the future, but right now I'm struggling to stay afloat."

"My game will be a winner once I get the final kinks worked out. Jake, we can do this together."

Jake nodded, more confident now. "What about Ambar?"

"She belongs with us, but something is still worrying her. We have time. Neither of us is going anywhere. What we do is court her. Let her take things at her pace. We need to show her we trust her and need her in our lives." Hari gestured at the livid mark on his upper shoulder near his neck. "This mark proves she wants this, but she's dragging her heels because she's frightened."

"Probably worried about losing her independence," Jake said. "When we first started going out together, she said she didn't want anything permanent. She wasn't interested in a relationship. From what she's told me about her parents, she didn't have much freedom while growing up."

"That's what I think too," Hari said. "I've tried to reassure her, but she's not thinking things through. She's clutching her gut reaction and running with it."

"So we give her space and woo her. I hope that means seduction because there's nothing better than fucking Ambar, except when it's the three of us together." The color in Jake's cheeks deepened, the show of embarrassment making Hari smile. The man looked damn cute despite his clear masculinity.

"Let's worry about Ambar tomorrow."

Jake nodded, skimming his fingers across the mark again. Now that Jake had licked it, the bleeding had stopped. It felt tender and so sensitive to touch.

Hari groaned as Jake carefully licked it again, his cock growing so hard he thought he might burst. "Now," he said.

"Have you ever done this before?"

"Nope, I told you that before. There's a first time for everything," Hari said.

"We'll go slow. I want you to like this." Jake grabbed the bottle he'd discarded and flipped the lid open, squeezing lube onto his fingers. "Probably on your hands and knees is best first."

A hard shudder went through Hari at the idea of Jake covering him from behind. The thought of Jake taking him, pushing inside and filling him made Hari's pulse race. Another tremble sped the length of his body. "I want you so bad." He laughed as he arranged himself in the middle of the mattress. "I never thought I'd say that about another man."

"Me neither." Jake skimmed his hands over the cheeks of his butt, stroking and massaging Hari's flesh until he parted it. He blew a stream of warm air across his hole before stroking the nerve-rich area.

Despite the new experience, not a shred of fear hit Hari. Instead anticipation danced across his skin, his new mark throbbing in time with each brush of Jake's fingers. The first finger felt a bit weird, a streak of pain taking him unawares. Balancing on one hand, he pressed a finger against his mark and a tide of pleasure replaced the nagging ache at his entrance.

"Does that hurt?"

"A little." Hari didn't intend to lie because this wasn't feeling like his idea of pleasure.

"Do you want me to stop? Ambar says it gets better as

long as I go slow."

"No, keep going. I think."

Jake smiled as he added another finger, slippery with lube, and scissored them, gently stretching Hari. He pushed deeper and brushed a sensitive spot.

Hari let out a low moan at the zap of unexpected pleasure, the charge streaking from his balls and down his cock. It almost felt as good as when Jake sucked on his mark. "Hell." His breath hissed out. "Didn't expect that."

"I told you it would get better." Jake continued his slow, careful preparation, occasionally pegging Hari's sweet spot. When he finally removed his fingers, Hari felt empty and needy.

Jake reached for the lube and rubbed some along his length.

Hari laughed suddenly, looking over his shoulder at his lover. "I don't know why, but I'm nervous."

"A tiger like you?"

"Don't start on kitty jokes. I've heard them all from my family and cousins."

"I wouldn't dare," Jake said, and his tone told Hari the opposite. The knowledge warmed Hari's heart. Jake wasn't frightened or nervous despite Hari's obvious strength. Not that he would ever use his strength against Jake. That wasn't his way.

A hand stroked his back, a fleeting slide of skin against skin then he felt nothing. Hari's breath caught, anticipation warring with worry. He wanted this, wanted Jake, but he'd never considered being in this position.

"Stop thinking so hard." Jake nipped him on the arse to

emphasize the order.

"I'm not."

"I can hear you," Jake said with a catlike growl that made Hari smile. Before Hari could reply, he felt pressure, a sliver of pain then Jake's fingers curled around his shoulder and stroked over the mark Ambar had left. Erotic promise twisted in him, his nostrils flaring and drawing in their combined scents. Jake pushed deeper, invading his body while caressing Hari's mark over and over. It seemed the man learned quickly when it came to pleasure.

"How does that feel?" Jake asked.

"Different."

Jake chuckled, his warm breath blowing across Hari's neck. "I'll see if I can make things better for you." Invading and retreating, he set up an easy rhythm, taking his cue from Hari's body. Hari's ribs expanded with an inhalation, his breath hitching when Jake angled his next stroke a little differently. The air hissed from his lungs, his balls lifting. He clenched his butt muscles as fire exploded in his groin, a cry of pleasure surging from his throat. Damn, Jake was good. Every stroke touched the sensitive spots in him, a mixture of pleasure and pain combining to make something spectacular.

"Jake," he whispered, not sure exactly what he was asking for, but wanting it all the same.

"Want more?" Jake's hips snapped into a rapid surge and retreat. His hand left Hari's mark to curl around his cock instead. Hard pressure both inside and out. Hari groaned, lost in the swirl of pleasure. Heat flushed his skin, swelled his cock and squeezed his balls. He sucked in air, gasping, on overload.

The uneven pumping of Hari's heart almost drowned out the purring sound of approval that came from Jake. Hari wanted to smile, but Jake's next stroke slid across his sweet spot, and orgasm consumed him. A line of semen caught him on the chest, his channel clamping down on Jake's cock. Another spurt shot from his cock, his body shuddering, clenching as the tension in him snapped. He trembled while Jake took his pleasure, the strokes across his gland overburdening nerves already strung tight. Damn, Jake loving him felt good, and he wanted to do it again. Soon.

Jake stilled, curling over Hari's body, their skin sliding together in a sweaty kiss. Jake nuzzled at his neck, kissing a trail to Hari's mark. A hungry noise escaped Hari and Jake laughed.

"That good, huh?"

"Better," Hari said, and it was nothing less than the truth.

Chapter Thirteen

Ambar didn't remember much of the drive home. All she knew was the driving need to flee, panic nipping her heels.

She'd done it this time.

She'd marked Hari.

Marked him.

God, how could she have been so stupid?

Ambar let herself into the house and rushed down the passage to her bedroom, an ache stopping up her throat. In the living room, she heard the muted sound of voices and saw the faint glow of light under the closed door. Rohan and Kiran would have heard her come inside, smelled her familiar scent. Usually she joined them, but not tonight when her emotions seesawed back and forth.

She'd marked Hari.

How had everything gone so wrong?

Shaking her head did nothing to shift the frenzied

thoughts, the panic and fear. She'd attacked his neck, biting down. Her feline had taken over, instinct driving her to claim what she considered hers.

Hers.

Ambar sank onto her bed, her legs shaking so violently they wouldn't hold her any longer. If she'd stayed a moment longer, she would've bitten Jake too.

The knowledge brought tears to her eyes. She'd fought so hard to keep her freedom. If she gave in now and moved in with Jake and Hari, she'd lose herself. She'd become a wife, a mother.

A bitter laugh escaped. If she lived with and fucked two men all the time, it wouldn't take long to fall pregnant, and once children came she really would be trapped. Her dreams of travel and exploration would haunt her for the rest of her life. She'd end up miserable and so would everyone else.

A shiver racked her body at the thought. Suddenly freezing, Ambar kicked off her shoes, yanked back the covers and crawled under fully clothed. She closed her eyes, but sleep eluded her. Instead, she castigated herself, appalled at her lack of restraint. She thought of Hari and her stomach hurt. When she added Jake to the picture, tears squeezed from between her eyelids.

It was a long night.

At six the next morning, she dragged herself out of bed. Not even a shower shifted her sluggishness. It certainly did nothing to wash away the guilt rippling inside her in tsunami-type waves. At least Jake and Hari would have each other.

She couldn't commit herself to a permanent relationship. The last thing she wanted to do was end up like her mother, dependent on Hari and Jake for everything.

Ambar shuffled into the kitchen. She thought of the other Middlemarch women and how they seemed so happy. Like her mother, they didn't leave their mates, remaining at their sides. Ambar checked the time again and picked up the phone. She was so confused. Maybe Isabella could help her or at least talk her down from the panic threatening to overpower her.

Five minutes later, she was on her way to Storm in a Teacup since Isabella and Tomasine Mitchell were opening for breakfast. Ambar tapped on the rear door and Isabella—an attractive blonde with blue-violet eyes—let her inside.

"Hi, Ambar." Tomasine waved one floury hand, busy rolling pastry. Tomasine—a petite black leopard shifter—was mated to Felix Mitchell while Isabella and Leo, the third Mitchell brother, were mates.

"I hope you don't mind, but if I don't talk to someone I'm going to burst," Ambar said to both women.

"No problem." Isabella grinned, managing to look feminine yet strong and sexy at the same time. Ambar had heard rumors about Isabella being an assassin. She found them difficult to believe, although she knew Isabella helped Charlie and Laura at times with police work. "You're going to help me set up this morning. I figure the least I can do is listen."

Ambar accepted a basket of jam and breakfast spreads

and followed Isabella in to the dining area.

Isabella started setting the tables, ready for opening in half an hour. Ambar followed, working on automatic pilot as she set out the condiments. "I marked Hari last night."

"Hari? The guy I've seen with Jake?"

"Yeah." Tears stung at Ambar's eyes but she refused to let them fall. "I don't want a mate. I want to travel and do some of the things I've always dreamed about."

"Hmmm. Did he bite you back?"

Ambar sniffed. "No, I didn't give him a chance. I left Jake and Hari and went home."

Isabella issued a small choked sound, and Ambar frowned at her. "Sorry," Isabella said. "But two of them? You don't do things by halves, do you?"

"I don't want either of them," Ambar said, a twist of anguish grabbing her chest, making it difficult for her to breathe through the lie. "I feel as if my foot is caught in a trap."

"Leo marked me early in our relationship before he really knew me," Isabella said. "I know he was worried about it, but everything turned out all right. Sometimes all we need is a chance to get used to the changes." She moved to the next table and Ambar followed her. "Sometimes hormones and our shifters propel us forward before the trust builds. Hari hasn't been in Middlemarch for long."

"No, it's all happened at speed." Hari had stormed over her and Jake like an unexpected tornado, taking them both unawares.

"I'm sure Jake and Hari feel just as stunned by the suddenness of your relationship as you do."

229

"But they're not trapped," Ambar said.

"Why? Why aren't they committed to you as much as you are to them?"

Isabella's question made her stop to think. In a way, they were forced into being with her, especially Hari now that she'd marked him. "But I'm the one who will have to give up my dreams."

"Why? How do you know if you haven't discussed your dreams with your men?"

Her men. A shudder hit her on hearing Isabella's casual reference. "How did you know I haven't said anything to them?"

Isabella laughed. "I know what it's like at the start. You can't get enough of each other. I expect it's even more difficult with three of you in the relationship. Talking gets pushed aside in favor of sex."

A startled laugh escaped Ambar. Well, that was true. The second she saw either Jake or Hari she wanted them physically. When she was with both of them at the same time, it was impossible to think with clarity. "So what do I do?"

Isabella finished setting the last table and turned to Ambar. "If it were me, I'd think about taking some time out. Why don't you pick one of the things you've always wanted to do and go for it?"

"You're saying I should walk away?"

"No, I'm suggesting you take some time away from your two men and think about what you really want. Is there a place you'd like to visit for a week? Time away from Middlemarch will help you see things more clearly. At the very least you'll find out if you actually miss Jake and Hari."

"You're telling me to keep running."

"But if you intend to return in a week it's hardly running." Isabella winked at her. "If you leave and never come back, that would qualify as running. Leaving Hari marked and alone would qualify as running. Think about things. Maybe make a list of pros and cons, and when you come back to Middlemarch, go and see your men and tell them what you want to do."

"I like the idea, but I can't leave Rohan alone with the store. We've been busy lately."

"That's no problem. Tell Rohan to give me a call." Isabella headed back to the kitchen, and Ambar followed. "I think I have a way to get Emily back at work again," she said to Tomasine. "Ambar needs to go away for a week, but doesn't want to leave Rohan short-handed at the store. I said I'd help."

"*Ooh*, sneaky," Tomasine said with approval. "No matter how bad she's feeling Emily would never turn her back on someone needing help." She turned to Ambar. "We thought Emily was doing well, coming to the café for a few hours each day, but suddenly she did a U-turn and tells everyone she is heading to Storm in a Teacup but she goes off to spend time on her own. It's not healthy."

"I don't know. Rohan might not—"

Tomasine waved a hand, dismissing Ambar's protest. "You'd be doing us a favor."

"Exactly," Isabella said, beaming at Ambar. "You have to go now."

231

Since they were ready to open for breakfast, Ambar left and drove back to her home, deep in thought. What Isabella said made a lot of sense. She wandered into the kitchen.

"What's wrong? You look like something the cat dragged in." Kiran stood, grabbed a mug and poured her a coffee, fixing it the way she liked. He shunted the mug across the counter. "Sit. Tell me what's wrong."

"I marked Hari."

A smile blazed across Kiran's face. "Congratulations."

Ambar yanked out a chair and collapsed on it. "You don't understand. I didn't mean to do it."

Kiran frowned, and she could tell he didn't comprehend her misery. She'd have to explain. Heck, maybe talking about her problems again would help her come to a final decision. Sometimes talking with Kiran was easier than communicating with her brother.

"I don't want a mate." Jake's image popped into her mind. "Mates," she corrected automatically. That instant correction made her stomach jump with nerves. She really did want them both. *Crap.*

"So you ran away again."

The trace of disappointment in his voice made her defensive. "It's not like that."

Kiran took a seat opposite her. "Explain it to me."

"I'm frightened I'll lose my independence and end up like my mother with nothing. Hari and Jake will become my world, and I'll never have a chance to do all the things I've dreamed about—the things on my bucket list." Ambar swallowed. "I want to travel. See the world. I want to go to concerts and to the movies. Eat different food. Run as a tiger in India. Africa. I want to taste what freedom is really like."

"Have you told Hari and Jake that?"

"You don't understand." She threw up her hands. "How could you? They'll expect me to have children, to stay at home and make a home for them."

"How do you know if you haven't talked to them?"

"It's just the way it is, the way my parents and their friends did things."

"The Mitchells aren't like that."

"They are. They never leave Middlemarch." But Isabella's words echoed through her mind. The mating trapped the men just as much as the women. Guilt filled her because she'd marked Hari. Lord, what had she done?

"None of the women seem unhappy," Kiran said. "Why don't you ask them?"

"I did. I talked with Isabella this morning."

"And?" Kiran waited before speaking again. "I know one thing—you can't keep running away. It's childish. If you want us to treat you as an adult you have to act like one."

Ambar raised her chin to glare at him even as she acknowledged he spoke the truth. Her behavior had been infantile recently, and she was better than that.

Rohan joined them in the kitchen, coming to an abrupt halt. "You've been crying. What the hell did they do to you?"

Ambar took a deep breath. "Rohan, we need to talk." She waited until he'd poured a coffee and topped up their mugs before starting to speak. She explained everything she was feeling, her confusion, her doubts and her dreams. When she finally finished talking her throat ached.

"Why didn't you say something before? Did you even want to go into partnership with me in a store?"

"Of course I did. After our parents died, we were both a little lost. I needed you. Moving here was a good idea and buying the store. I don't regret any of that, but the need for something more sort of crept up on me after we'd settled. I thought I'd have more time."

"You didn't count on Hari and Jake."

"I was okay with Jake. I didn't have a problem until Hari arrived. He seduced me." Her nose wrinkled in disgust. "He seduced both of us."

"Seduced," Rohan mused, tugging a rueful grin of recognition from her. "That's the point. He's never coerced you, so you obviously feel something for him—enough to bestow a mark."

"I know," Ambar said, abject misery filling her. This situation was her fault. She was the one who'd taken this step, and she couldn't blame anyone except herself for the outcome.

"What are you going to do?" Kiran asked.

Rohan remained silent but she could tell he had a lot he wanted to say.

"If it's okay with you Rohan, I'd like to take some time off to go away to think about things." She saw Kiran open his mouth to protest about her fleeing her responsibilities and decisions and hurried to placate him. "No, I'm not intending to run away. I've done enough of that recently.

234

It's time to act with more maturity. I've put things in motion, and I need to deal with marking Hari, but I'd like some time to come to terms with everything. Work out a plan for my future."

"Having a mate isn't a life sentence," Rohan snapped. "Kiran and I have separate lives."

"You're men," Ambar said. "You have different expectations. People don't expect you to have children."

"I suppose I can get someone to cover for you," Rohan said finally. "How long do you intend to be away?"

"Isabella said she would fill in for me."

Both men studied her with expectation, and she suspected they thought she didn't intend to return. No, that would be cruel on her part. Her gaze fell on the previous day's newspaper and an advertisement for a resort hotel in Samoa.

"I'm going to Samoa for ten days," she announced. "I'll book my flights this morning."

Samoa was hot and humid, the air sucking from her lungs when she exited the flight from New Zealand. Not even the sense of suffocation she'd undergone on the plane and the knowledge she'd face the return journey in ten days could dull her pleasure in the new experience.

Three hours later, she walked barefoot on the white sand, carrying her leather sandals while she explored the confines of the resort. Everywhere she looked tropical trees and flowers bloomed in brilliant splashes of red, pink, and green. Other tourists lazed around a pool, a loud game of water polo brought a smile to her face.

Her first overseas holiday and already she felt calmer and more centered. She found an empty lounger facing the lagoon and dragged it out of the direct sun, placing it under the shade of a thatched roof. Her sarong drifted to the sand, and after arranging the tilt of the lounger to her satisfaction, she lay back and relaxed, letting her mind drift over Jake, Hari and what she wanted for her future.

The gentle swish of the waves, interspersed by the laughter of children who paddled on the water's edge, lulled her and she fell asleep with a smile on her face.

"AMBAR IS WHERE?" JAKE demanded, his brows shooting toward his hairline. This shock, added to a call from his bank manager, did nothing to soothe his agitation. He shifted his weight from foot to foot, his skin feeling tight. Twitchy. Yeah, that's what he felt—damn twitchy.

Hari slipped an arm around his waist and hauled him close, the skin-to-skin contact going a long way to soothe his irritation.

"She's gone to Samoa for ten days," Rohan said.

"Our woman needs a few smacks on the arse," Jake snapped. "What the hell is she thinking? She never used to act like an irresponsible tease."

Rohan growled, a sharp sound holding distinct warning. Jake didn't give a shit and growled back, baring his teeth. Let the man snap and snarl as much as he liked. His mate hadn't run off to Samoa.

"Quit it," Kiran said. "Both of you."

Hari chuckled, breaking the taut atmosphere in the kitchen. "I don't suppose we could get a beer?"

Ten minutes later they all sat around the kitchen table with a drink each.

"Why is Ambar in Samoa?" Hari asked.

"She said she needed to think," Rohan said.

Jake scowled. "Couldn't she do her thinking here?"

"She's frightened," Kiran said. "She has this idea that being mated to the pair of you will curtail her freedom. When it was just Jake, she didn't have a problem, but since your arrival, Hari, everything has happened quickly. She feels as if her feet have been yanked from under her."

"Crap," Jake said, tapping his fingers on the tabletop. "We're not cavemen."

Hari grasped Jake's hand, stilling his busy fingers. "She's our mate. Why would we treat her like a possession? We don't intend to restrict her freedom, dammit."

Rohan sighed. "You need to talk to her."

"A bit difficult when we're here and she's in the middle of the Pacific," Jake said, not trying to hide his sarcasm.

Kiran and Rohan exchanged a glance before Kiran turned back to them. "You could give her a few days then go and join her. We know where she's staying."

"Will that work?" Hari asked.

Rohan shrugged. "It's as good a plan as any."

Back at the farm, Jake paced the kitchen. Night was falling, the sky lit in a stunning array of pinks and reds he might have lingered to watch another time. Not tonight.

"Hari, I can't afford to go to Samoa. I got a call from the bank manager this afternoon. If I don't bring the overdraft back in line and catch up on my mortgage payments they're going to foreclose." His throat hurt just saying the words. Despite his hard work, he'd end up with nothing.

"How much money are we talking about? Give me specifics so we can do a budget."

Silently, Jake handed Hari the latest bank statements. They were still in their envelopes, unopened because he'd hoped the ostrich approach might work miracles. Nothing doing, as the bank manager had informed him in no uncertain terms today. He had until the end of the month to put things right.

Jake pressed a hand to his stomach, his heart pounding while he waited for Hari's reaction.

"No problem," Hari said. "It will put a dent in my reserves, but between us we can work on getting them back. Hang tight while I get my laptop."

Speechless, Jake blinked. Hari returned in minutes and powered it up. His tan fingers moved rapidly over the keyboard, connecting to the internet. Another series of swift commands and Hari settled back on his chair with a grin. "All done. Your overdraft is cleared, and I've transferred enough to cover the missed payments."

"Just like that?"

"You're my mate. We're a team." His smile faded. "Can you get someone to look after the farm for a week?"

Jake's brow wrinkled before clearing. "Sly and Joe would probably do it. They're still at loose ends while they decide where they want to live. I don't think they've settled on a farm to purchase yet."

"Ring them. Find out."

Was it simply that easy?

Jake rang Sly, chatted for a few moments before hanging up, excitement exiting in a wide grin. "Done deal. They can be here when we need them."

"Good," Hari said. "Let's go to bed."

"It's still early."

"I didn't say anything about sleeping."

Jake chuckled and stood, accepting Hari's outstretched hand. "I do like the way you think."

"We need to think up a plan to woo Ambar," Hari reminded him.

"We'll have the entire plane journey to work out a sneaky strategy. Ambar won't know what's hit her once we claim her."

AMBAR AMBLED TO THE swimming pool, pausing at the poolside shower to wash the white sand from her feet. The days had slid together and she hadn't looked at a clock since leaving New Zealand. She'd come to a decision about her mates though. In the end, it hadn't been difficult because she'd pined for Jake and Hari even more than she'd missed her brother and Kiran.

She'd made a list as Isabella had suggested, going for total honesty since no one would see it apart from her. The big disadvantage was the possible restrictions on her freedom. She considered her friends who were in relationships and had officially mated, acknowledging they all seemed incredibly happy. Somehow, she would work things out too. When she returned to Middlemarch, she needed to discuss the future with Jake and Hari and lay out all her fears. She'd discuss things calmly without panicking.

Ambar scanned the pool area. Due to a camera crew preparing to film a tropical version of a popular reality show, there were lots of people her age staying at the resort. She'd made friends quickly, although without Jake and Hari it felt as if a part of her were missing. The anger and confusion that had hovered like a storm cloud when she left New Zealand had cleared, a few days helping her to see things at a distance.

She had feelings for both men. Whenever she'd considered her future, she'd hoped to have a mate. She just wished it had happened when she was older.

"Ambar! Over here." Anna, one of the girls she'd met on the first day of her holiday hailed her. "We saved you a lounger."

Ambar smiled and waved, heading in her direction. She dropped her orange straw basket on the ground and shrugged out of her coverall to reveal her lime green bikini.

"Ambar, are you sure you don't want to go out with me tonight?" Sam, a cameraman from Texas leaned close, his face full of expectation.

"I told you. I have someone in my life." She waved her left hand at him to flash the gold ring she'd inherited from her mother. Normally it resided on her right hand, but instinct had made her transfer the ring to her left soon after her arrival. Another telling action, she realized. She thought of herself as taken.

"I'm not sure I believe you," he drawled as his gaze did a smooth trip from her head to toes and back again.

"If Sam can ask you out, then I want to throw my hat in the ring too," Gary, one of the soundmen said.

Anna waved a languid hand at her. "Leave her alone, boys. She's already told you she's not available."

"Tell us about your man," another woman said.

Ambar blushed, thinking the relationship she'd become embroiled with was hardly traditional. "It's too hot for a chat. I'm going for a swim. Anyone up for a game of volleyball?" She indicated the volleyball net strung over a portion of the pool.

"I'm knackered after trudging halfway around the island scouting for film locations," Anna said in her English accent. "I'm staying right here."

A punch of longing hit Ambar, the accent reminding her of Hari. Did she miss them? Yes. Did she want to give up her dreams? Definitely not.

A dilemma, that's for sure. Hopefully they could reach some sort of compromise.

"I'm in for some volleyball," Sam said. "I'm on your team, Ambar."

Ambar jumped into the pool, the water slipping over her skin in a cool kiss. Like most tigers, she loved the water and felt perfectly at home in it. With a whoop Sam and several of the others, both male and female leapt into the water. They were soon embroiled in a hard-fought volleyball match, shouts and victory cheers filling the air.

Ambar watched the ball sail over the net and called it. She jumped from the water, doing a perfect spike over the net.

"Woohoo!" Sam shouted, pumping his fist in the air. With each successive point they scored, the man became more exuberant. He hugged her, copping a feel at the same time. The first time she ignored it. The second time she started to get pissed.

"Knock it off, Sam."

He shot her an innocent look, as if he didn't know what she was complaining about and moved away.

Ambar held her breath and counted swiftly to ten. The next time he touched her she intended to deck him.

JAKE AND HARI ARRIVED at midday and, after checking into their room and changing into their swim gear, they made their way to the pool, hoping to find Ambar. Hari grinned when he caught her scent. "I've found her."

They followed the trail, ending up near the pool.

"There she is," Jake said, grabbing Hari by the shoulder. He laughed softly. "Hell, I can't believe I'm so nervous."

"I've missed her," Hari said. "It's not the same without her around." He'd felt the separation even more than Jake because of the mark Ambar had placed on his shoulder. The few days without her had been like a nagging ache in his soul.

Jake's hold on his shoulder became a caress. "I know you have. I've missed her too." He watched her leap into the air, her lime green bikini displaying her feminine curves to perfection. "She is so beautiful. Sexy. I can't believe she's ours."

"Yeah," Hari whispered. "Let's go claim our mate."

Continuing to watch Ambar, they both stepped forward only to come to an abrupt halt. Hari growled low and mean, deep in his throat.

Jake gnashed his teeth. "If that guy doesn't stop touching her I'm gonna thump him."

"You'd have to beat me to it," Hari snapped.

They took a collective step closer to the edge of the pool, an unearthly howl of pain stopping them in their tracks.

"She hit him," Jake said, not bothering to hide his satisfaction.

"There's blood. She didn't hold back. That's our girl."

As they watched, Ambar swam to the wall of the pool and hauled herself out.

"Serves him right," a woman said when Ambar joined her. "Good job."

Fury pumped through Ambar as she picked up her beach towel and dabbed at the droplets of water clinging to her skin. She breathed in deeply, freezing at the familiar scent that hit her. Jake? Hari?

Nah, it couldn't be.

It was her fevered imagination—that's all. She was homesick, missing her family and friends. She turned just to make sure and her mouth dropped open in surprise.

"Oh, they're fine," Anna said beside her. "I call dibs on

243

one of them."

"Jake. Hari," she breathed. They'd come for her. Almost as the thought formed, she moved, throwing herself at them. Hari reached her first and hauled her into his arms, kissing her as if they'd been apart for months instead of mere days.

"My turn," Jake said and he gently disengaged Hari to kiss Ambar as well. Their familiar scents wound through her senses, their lingering touches filling her heart with gladness and pleasure.

They were here. They'd come for her.

It was in that moment she realized she'd unconsciously set them a test to see how much she meant to them. Her two men had seemed just as happy without her, but their arrival meant they wanted her in their lives as well. Her gaze drifted to their necks, noting they bore identical marks. They were committed to each other and now they'd come to claim her.

"Come and meet my friends," she said, taking their hands and drawing them over to where she'd been sitting. "Anna, this is Jake and Hari."

"So you really do have someone," Anna said. "Which one is yours?"

"Both of us," Jake said, without taking his gaze off Ambar.

Anna's brows rose sharply. "Both?"

"That's right," Hari said, slipping his arm around Jake's shoulders, silently staking a claim on him too.

"I've missed you both," Ambar said, nerves suddenly making an appearance. "I shouldn't have left like I did."

She glanced at Anna and saw the others she'd met this week were watching with avid curiosity. A couple of them whispered to each other.

Hari must have noted their interest. "We can talk later."

"We're here for the rest of the week," Jake said.

"Who is looking after the farm?"

Jake leaned into Hari, at ease despite the audience. "Joe and Sly Mitchell are taking care of things for us."

Us. His natural use of the word told her far more than words and backed up the story the mark told. He'd fully accepted Hari and his shifter status. And now they'd come for her.

A shudder went through her, sapping the strength from her knees. Fickle things. For an instant she thought she might fall, but Jake curled an arm around her waist, bolstering her faltering stance. His touch filled her with need.

She cleared her throat. "What do you want to do now? Do you want to go to my room?"

"Don't go," Anna said. "We want to witness the next step."

Ambar stared at Jake before letting her gaze drift to Hari. "I'll let you know if we ever decide to get into voyeurism."

Someone out of view made a shocked sound.

Anna continued to grin. "Well done, woman. With men as fine as this, I don't blame you."

"Let's go," Hari said in a firm voice.

Ambar grabbed her belongings and found herself between the two men and walking to the opposite end of the resort to where her room was located. It didn't seem to matter. Nothing mattered.

Jake and Hari had flown all the way to Samoa to find her. The idea kept repeating through her mind. It was a thought tinged with relief and excitement. If she could get past the next step and suggest they put off children and maybe travel or at least do non-traditional things, they might have a chance.

They crossed a large grassy expanse before taking a path around the corner of the end block of rooms. Jake and Hari led her up two flights of stairs before stopping in front of a locked door. Hari retrieved a keycard, and Ambar found herself in a room similar to hers but on a larger scale. Fresh pink hibiscus flowers and greenery decorated the desk in a welcome arrangement.

She shivered as the cool, conditioned air hit her heated skin. It would be all too easy to fall into their arms. Before she succumbed, Ambar took three hurried steps toward the balcony overlooking the turquoise lagoon. From here she could see the waves breaking on the coral reef farther out. Two small boats bobbed on the water, their passengers snorkeling along the reef.

Turning her back on the view, her gaze zoomed in on Hari and Jake. They eyed her like hungry dogs after a bone. A bit disturbing yet flattering too.

"Wait," she blurted, holding up a hand to enforce her order.

Both men froze, and she hurried to reassure them when she saw their wary expressions.

"I want you both, but if I don't tell you this up-front we're never going to have an honest relationship."

"What?" Jake growled.

Hari remained tense, his face watchful.

"I watched my parents and the way they ran their marriage. I lived with their rules, and if they were alive now I'd be living with whichever male my father chose for me. I loved my parents, but I hated their rules and the lack of freedom in their narrow world. I promised myself if I ever had a chance I would savor my independence." She paused to study their reactions. Neither one of them gave much away, although she noticed Jake had moved closer to Hari in order for physical contact.

A tight sensation formed around her chest and she had to battle to draw breath. They were here for her. She had to remember that.

Ambar swallowed and pushed out the next words. "I don't want to end up suffocated in a relationship like my mother. I've always thought about travel. I've never told anyone before how much I want it. It's a dream that kept me sane when my parents were alive. I love you both. I want to be with you, but I can't see how it would work. I don't want to fall into the same trap my mother did."

"What about your share in the store?" Jake asked.

"I thought I could take a month off now and then to fit in my travel and to do some of the things I've always dreamed of doing."

Hari frowned. "Like what? Give us specifics."

Heck, she'd known this would be difficult, that they wouldn't understand. Hari especially since she'd marked him. Guilt assailed her as her gaze slid over the raised skin of his mark. "I want to see the Taj Mahal at sunrise, the pyramids in Egypt and glide down the Nile in a felucca. I want to see Buckingham Palace and shop on Bond Street. Look for the Loch Ness monster. That sort of thing."

Hari's frown died away and he glanced at Jake. Something passed between the two of them, their silent communication making her feel left out. Her fault since she couldn't have it both ways.

"How often would you want to travel?" Jake asked.

"Probably once a year. Maybe I'd take a week somewhere in New Zealand or Australia if I can swing it. I expect Rohan will want time off too."

"So, you don't want to leave Middlemarch permanently?" Hari seemed relieved.

"No. I like it there. Middlemarch is home."

Hari exchanged another glance with Jake, and this time they grinned at each other.

"What's so funny?" she demanded.

"We can make this work," Jake said. "Tell her, Hari."

"I've invested in Jake's farm, and Jake is helping me with my game and web design. Once my game is fully tested, we're going to need to travel to market and display it at various trade shows. There will be lots of traveling involved. Worldwide travel. Jake and I talked. We can swing it so the three of us can go."

Ambar's heart started to beat faster. She realized her mouth had dropped open and snapped it shut. "Together?" she asked finally.

It had never occurred to her they could leave together or that she could fulfill her dreams with Jake and Hari at her side. The more she thought of experiencing new things with Jake and Hari, the better she liked the idea. It meant they could plan their trips together, study photos and reminisce about their holidays once they'd returned to Middlemarch.

"Yeah, together," Jake said with a nod of confirmation.

Jake and Hari crossed the room, each smiling at her, each making her breath catch and her heart beat faster.

"What do you think?" Hari asked.

"Yes." She didn't need to think about it. The solution was so easy now that she thought about it, so right and perfect for each of them.

Jake stared at her intently. "Are you sure?"

"Yes." Ambar threw herself into their welcoming arms. Mouths met. Noses bumped and laughter filled the room. They kicked footwear aside and clothing dropped to the floor. In a tangle of arms and legs, they fell on the bed, mouths snatching kisses wherever they could reach. She rolled, ending up with her back flat on the mattress and the two men leaning over her. "I've missed you both this week."

"That surprised you?" Hari ran his hand over her shoulder, his fingertips coming to rest on the curve of her breast.

Ambar couldn't suppress a shudder of sweet anticipation. "No, not really. Wanting you both has never been a problem, not since you walked into Middlemarch and started seducing Jake and me."

Jake chuckled. "He's good at seduction."

"You're not so bad yourself," Ambar said, her smile wry. "What chance did I have with the pair of you trying to seduce me?"

"No chance. We'll make a family and have children eventually. No, not straightaway," Hari said when she would have argued.

"We'll have children when we all agree it's time," Jake reassured her. "No pressure. We promise. If there's ever a time you want to do something, tell us. We want to know, have the opportunity to discuss the alternatives. We're partners as well as lovers. Agreed?"

"Agreed," Hari said.

"I'm so sorry I doubted you both." Ambar smiled with enthusiasm. "I agree." She kissed Jake, purring with approval when he stroked one breast.

"Make her hot. Make her whimper with need." Hari spread her legs as he gave instructions to Jake.

Each pinch and tug of Jake's fingers at her breasts swirled pleasure through her body, the sensations twisting until heat blossomed over every inch of her skin. They dominated her, their touches consuming her. The scrape of stubble against her thighs heightened her hunger, the hot stabs of Hari's tongue gathering the juices flowing from her pussy increasing it further.

Jake whispered against her neck. "I want to be inside you, Amber." He rolled until he stretched out on the mattress. "Ride me. Mark me. Make me yours so I belong with both of you." He cupped her cheek in a tender gesture, his eyes full of love.

"I love you, Jake." And she did. It felt so right saying it aloud.

"I love you too, sweetheart, very much."

Hari lifted his head. "We both love you, Ambar."

"And each other," Jake added, his voice husky as he smiled at Hari. He lifted Ambar, letting her guide his cock into place. She sank down, groaning softly as he impaled her. When she would have started moving, Jake held her hips in place. "Wait for Hari. Wait for both of us."

Ambar relaxed into his embrace, quivering a fraction when Hari started to stroke and prepare her. Jake wanted to wear her mark. She nuzzled Jake's neck, running her tongue back and forth over Hari's mark. Jake let out a strangled groan, a violent tremble racking his body.

"God, that really gets me going," he said. "I'm going to come if you don't stop. You'll see when Hari marks you. It's bloody amazing." He kissed her, the twin sensations of Jake's mouth and Hari's fingers doing a good job of keeping her on edge.

"You've always turned me on," she whispered.

"And Hari?"

"That's what I want to know," Hari said, pausing while he waited for her answer.

"Of course you do. I need both of you in my life. You've no idea how much I missed you both this week."

The wet pull of Jake's mouth at her nipple distracted her then Hari's hard flesh pressed into her. Her stomach went fluttery, the blood roaring through her ears as they possessed her and took what she freely offered. A needy cry escaped as Hari covered her back and his mouth latched on to her neck. Immediately lust lanced her body. She writhed between their hard male bodies, a strangled moan rippling from her throat as the erotic promise coalesced into a firestorm.

When Jake and Hari started to thrust in countermoves, it was heaven. Hot and perfect. They dominated her, consumed her, surrounding her with pleasure. Heat flushed her skin. The coiled power grew, spiraling into a sharp vibration in her pussy.

"Bite me," she whispered. "Please."

"Are you sure?" Hari asked.

"We don't need to do this today," Jake added. "We have time."

"No." When both her men froze, she realized they'd misunderstood. "I mean, I want to do it. I've done enough thinking this week. I want this and I'm ready. Please mark me."

They didn't give her another chance to say no. Jake took possession of her lips, bruising her mouth with his need. Hari withdrew and surged into her again, a rich rush of desire blooming inside her. This time he remained fully embedded and nuzzled her neck. The curl of heat in her exploded the second his teeth sank into her flesh. Sensual flames licked her sex while a slash of lava-hot pain quickly transformed to ecstasy.

"Hari." She tore her mouth from Jake's, sobbing out Hari's name. Her passage clamped down hard on Hari's cock while he climaxed, the subtle slide of Jake's cock bringing another layer of sensation to the orgasmic rush that hurled her into deep pleasure. On instinct, she lowered her head and licked across the mark Hari had bestowed on Jake. With ripples of pleasure still lighting her body, she bit down, tasting Jake's coppery blood as she licked it away. Jake shuddered, crying out as he came.

Hari lazily licked the spot where he'd bitten her. She did the same for Jake. It was like a connection slotting into place, and not a single regret pierced her satisfaction when they stilled in a sweaty tangle of limbs.

"Wow," Ambar said finally.

Jake's chuckle sounded knowing while Hari just looked smug when she glanced over her shoulder. Hari pulled out and disappeared momentarily. She heard the rush of running water. Soon he returned with two damp cloths for them. Once they cleaned up, they rested in a loose embrace, all three touching each other. United. Ambar didn't know about her men, but she needed the contact.

"I'm sorry I caused so much trouble," she said.

Jake squeezed her upper arm. "You needed to think."

"You needed our reassurance," Hari added.

"I don't know," Ambar said, fully relaxed for the first time in weeks. All the turmoil had left her mind and happiness filled her, making everything around her appear brighter. "Everything happened pretty quickly."

"I knew exactly what I wanted," Hari said smugly.

"No you didn't." Jake winked at her and she had to fight to keep a smile at bay.

"Jake's right. You arrived in Middlemarch to meet me."

"Ah, but I knew Jake was special from the moment I saw him," Hari said, reaching across her to kiss Jake on the mouth.

Ambar watched them with avid curiosity, squirming a little when they reminded her how hot it was watching them show their open desire and love for each other. It was so sexy, and they both belonged with her. She grinned. They belonged to her. Watching them kiss didn't make her feel left out any longer. Knowing they'd wanted her enough to locate her and come to claim her for their own made all the difference.

"Hey." She punched Hari lightly on the shoulder. "You came to Middlemarch with seduction in mind."

"He's good at it too." Jake winked, undisturbed by the fact he had a hard-on from kissing another man. She loved the confidence the two men displayed with each other and with her. That was sexy in itself.

Ambar laughed. "The seduction of Ambar and Jake or a romantic tangle?"

Jake caressed Hari's cheek, his hand rasping audibly over Hari's stubble. Then Jake reached over to kiss Amber. She tasted Jake's unique flavor along with a hint of Hari.

Hari grinned at them without apology. "What can I say? I knew what I wanted. Seduction was the way to go, tangle or not."

"And do you always get what you want?" Ambar asked.

"Not always," Hari said. "I got lucky this time."

Ambar smiled. She didn't think there was much luck involved in their relationship. Hari had seen them both, decided what he wanted and set out to seduce them to his way of thinking. And he'd been right. Already the connection between them had strengthened due to the mating marks, and with time, their feelings would only get stronger.

If this was seduction, bring it on because nothing had ever felt as right as being with Jake and Hari. Their future glowed with brightness, and she couldn't wait to step forward with her men and embrace it with love and laughter.

Bonus Chapter

Mitchell Farm, Middlemarch, New Zealand

Feline Shapeshifter Council Meeting.

Present: Sid Blackburn, Agnes Paisley, Valerie McClintock, Benjamin Urquart, London Allbright, Saber Mitchell

Saber boiled the kettle and made the tea, his mind on his mate, Emily. It had been six months...six months since they'd lost their baby, and his beloved wife was still pushing him away. These days they seemed to drift rather than live, and he wasn't sure what to do.

Aware of the ticking clock and the imminent arrival of the Feline council members for their meeting, he pulled out cups and saucers and placed them on the kitchen table.

In the past, Emily would have arranged everything ready for him—not that he expected her to wait on him—but now she wandered around in a daze.

At least she'd gone into the café to work for a few hours this week. It was a start. Now if only he could get her to talk, to curse or shout. To react instead of buttoning herself down and ignoring him and their marriage.

She wasn't the only one suffering.

He hurt, dammit. He'd lost a child, too, and now it felt as if he'd lost his mate.

A car pulled up outside the house, and Saber hurriedly grabbed a packet of shortbread, opened it and tipped the contents on a plate. He shoved aside the thought that before Emily would have arranged cakes or savories from the café for him. Guilt filled him at the disloyalty toward his mate.

A knock on the door had him squaring his shoulders and striding to answer the summons. "London."

She took half a step back. "Am I too early?"

"No, of course not. Come in. Have...did you see Emily?"

"She was at the café when I left to come here. Isabella and Tomasine persuaded her to start planning a Valentine's Day menu. She was busy beating on some bread dough."

Saber nodded. "Thank you for pulling so much extra time at the café. I know you have your own business to take care of."

"It's fine. Henry and Jacey have turned out to be good at computer graphics, so they're helping me a lot."

"If I can do anything to help in return, make sure you let me know," Saber said.

SHELLEY MUNRO

Another car pulled up and Ben, Agnes and Valerie climbed out.

"Go and pour yourself to a cup of tea. I've set up the table in the kitchen. You know the way."

London made her way into the kitchen and hovered by the long wooden table. From where she stood, she had a view of the lounge. The flowers in a vase on the coffee table were dead and a layer of dust covered the wooden surface. Elsewhere, she saw signs of neglect that had never been noticeable during her previous visits.

An ache sprang to life in her chest, sympathy engulfing her in a wave. She'd known Emily was struggling with the loss of their child, but she suspected Saber wasn't doing well either. She needed to help—somehow.

Agnes and Valerie hustled into the kitchen, handbags draped over their arms, followed by Ben and Sid. Saber trailed them, his expression set in a frown. London could tell his mind was elsewhere.

Valerie set a container on the tabletop and peeled off the lid. "My granddaughter is going through a cupcake stage. You all have to eat one so I can tell her the members of the Feline council enjoyed her baking."

Everyone took a seat around the table. London dispersed cups of tea while Valerie distributed cupcakes in lurid colors.

"They taste better than they look," Valerie promised. "You have to at least try them, so I can tell Edwina honestly that you ate her cupcakes."

London eyed her bright green cupcake and peeled away the paper casing. "I like a little adventure."

"That's the ticket, lass," Sid said with approval.

London noticed Saber never cracked a smile.

Ben winked, reminding London of a pixie with his piercing green gaze and his mischievous expression. "What's on the agenda today?"

Agnes pulled her notebook out of her brown leather handbag. "We need to start planning the next Middlemarch Singles Ball. I believe we decided that the Easter weekend would work best?"

London switched on her tablet and took notes about ticket prices, hire expenses for the marquee, parking and the Love train.

"This cupcake tastes better than it looks," Sid said, his gentle grin and gleaming eyes making London want to giggle. His cupcake was a garish purple color.

Ben pushed his bright red cupcake away and plucked a piece of shortbread off the plate in the center of the table. "We've held these dances a few times now. They don't offer much of a challenge. Are we having the same band as last time?" He crunched into his cookie.

Valerie tugged off her glasses, peered at the lenses and frowned. "They seemed popular with most age groups." She fumbled in her handbag, pulled out a tissue and cleaned her glasses. "What do you think, Saber?"

"Saber, lad," Sid said.

Saber jerked. His green eyes blinked, and it was obviously he hadn't heard a thing discussed.

The oldies exchanged telling glances, but didn't say a thing.

"We were wondering if we should book the same band

for the dance as last time," London said in a crisp voice. While she sympathized, this had to stop. Both Saber and Emily were mere shadows of themselves.

"Yes," Saber said. "They were excellent. We'll need to book them soon because they're very popular."

"Right," Agnes said and jotted in her notebook. "I'll take care of booking them. We've decided on the Saturday night?"

"Yes, I think so," Sid said.

"Well, unless anyone else has anything to add, I think we're done." Agnes picked up her handbag and stashed her notebook.

London hesitated, nervous anxiety suddenly leaping about in her gut. She'd been thinking about this for a while, had discussed the matter with Gerard, her mate, and his friend Henry. She'd even spoken with Pop, Henry's father, and his mate, Megan. They'd all agreed her concerns were real and viable, and she should bring them up with the council. Having their approval and actually doing it were miles and miles apart. Then, she glanced at Saber. The man she admired was drifting in his head again.

Right, she thought. Big girl panties.

"Before we end the meeting, I have something I'd like to discuss. Two things, actually."

Sid gave her a gentle smile, encouragement in his nod. "Go ahead, lass. The floor is yours."

She took a deep breath. "I think we need a bank in Middlemarch. We have several businesses that have large amounts of cash—the pub and the Patel store. We collect a lot of cash at our council events. We need to approach our local MP, maybe write to some of the banks and ask them if they would consider setting up a branch here in Middlemarch. If both of those fail, I suggest that we investigate setting up our own cooperative bank." London stopped speaking to take a breath. They were all staring at her, but she wasn't sure what they were thinking.

"Saber," Valerie said in a sharp voice. She applied her elbow to his ribs, and he let out an oomph of pain. "Wake up and pay attention. London has raised a valid point. Catch him up, Ben," she added in an exasperated tone.

"You just want to make sure I listened," Ben said.

Agnes gave a toothy grin and her brows rose. "Well, did you?"

Ben scowled but repeated the info to Saber.

"What are the benefits to us, apart from saving people from driving to the nearest bank in Dunedin?" Saber asked, looking more like his normal self.

"It will bring people to Middlemarch. The other nearby towns who don't have banks will come here to use ours. They'll spend money here at the café, the grocery store, the markets or buy petrol. They might attend one of Isabella's keep-fit classes or come to one of our functions because we have a bank. It would provide employment for someone. Our local businesses wouldn't need to secure as much cash. They could bank every day and reduce the chances of a robbery. Those are the main benefits. I can't think of any disadvantages. If we have to setup our own coop bank, the red tape might be a problem, but I'm sure we could work through that."

Saber nodded. "What do the rest of you think?"

"It is an excellent idea," Valerie said. "Would we offer loans?"

"My thought would be to offer basic banking services at first, get the bank running and maybe offer small loans once we've been running for a few years. Of course, if we can persuade one of the trading banks to open a branch here, we wouldn't need to worry about that side. They'd offer the services of a regular bank." London glanced down at her tablet, not that she needed to, but because she still felt like the new kid and didn't like to overstep.

Agnes patted London's hand. "I knew you'd be an asset to our community. That is an excellent idea."

"I agree," Saber said.

Ben and Sid both nodded approval.

"How do we get started?" Sid asked.

"I can draft a letter to our local member of parliament and to the main trading banks. I think there are five we could approach. Anyway, I'll draft letters ready for our next meeting and once you approve we can put the plan in action. I don't think there is any point researching a co-operative bank until we receive responses from the existing banks," London said.

"Does that work for everyone?" Saber glanced at each of them.

London saw everyone nodded, and she relaxed a little.

"Was there anything else?" Saber asked.

London's nerves ratcheted up again. "Um, yes." She gulped as she found herself under the spotlight again. *You wanted to jerk Saber from his thoughts.* Go on, her inner self prompted.

"Go on, lass," Sid said. "We won't bite."

"But you could," London blurted.

There was a moment of silence before the oldies chuckled. London peeked at Saber. Yep, even he appeared amused.

"Go ahead, London," Saber said. "We asked you to join the council because we value your opinion. The bank idea is excellent, and we will listen to everything you suggest."

London straightened, took a quick breath and started. "There is an element of the community who don't approve of human-feline mating and many of the things that are happening in Middlemarch. They have become quite vocal. Marsh's father spat at me last week, and Tomasine said Sylvie punched one of the feline boys at school. She got detention, but she was sticking up for Emily."

"Felix didn't say anything to me," Saber said.

"Tomasine told me as a Feline council member," London said. "Someone keyed my car, and I found a nasty note tucked under my windshield wiper. I talked to Laura and Charlie. They have experienced some of the same heckling and rudeness I have. They told me they tossed a group of felines in jail on Saturday night."

"I heard they were drunk and caused a brawl at the pub." Agnes scowled at Saber. "I also heard gossip about another fight at the pub."

Saber tensed. "My brothers have been dealt with."

"What else did you hear?" Sid asked hastily.

London bit back her amusement at the change of subject. "The brawl started because of the human-feline

263

thing. I asked around."

"Crap," Ben said.

Sid scratched his thin gray hair. "I hadn't heard any of this."

"Because those creating the disturbance don't want to attract council attention," London replied. "They're counting on us not fighting back. By us, I mean humans."

Agnes patted London's hand again. "You're a good girl. What do we do, Saber? We've already warned everyone at the Feline community meetings."

"You need to make sure the human partners attend the meetings along with the wolf, tiger and lion contingents," London said before Saber could reply. "You need to start taking a hard line and spell out the consequences. A little teasing is fine. I can deal with that, but pushing and shoving and threats are not acceptable. This is spilling over to the children and that's not right."

"I agree," Saber said. "But I'm mated to a human. Sid, I think you need to take the lead with this. The rest of you have feline mates. You need to lay out the rules and make the community believe the council will carry out the punishment."

"Which is?" London asked.

"In the past, we've banished any wrongdoers," Agnes said. "I agree with London. We shouldn't put up with this type of behavior."

"We should issue one official warning to any offenders," Ben suggested. "Give them one chance and send them packing if they reoffend."

Valerie tapped her fingers on the tabletop. "That works

for me."

"Aye," Sid said. "I hate to banish individuals or families, but we can't have this type of misbehavior. From what London said, it sounds as if things are escalating."

"We have a Feline meeting scheduled for next week," Saber said. "We can issue a warning then and spell out the consequences. I'll personally invite the human mates plus our other felines and wolves."

"Agreed," Agnes said.

They all glanced at London.

"Was there anything else?" Saber asked, more alert now.

"Um...one more," London said.

Ben chuckled. "Spit it out, lass."

"I think we should draw up a plan to deal with humans sighting a feline or wolf when they shouldn't. From what I hear, there have been two close calls in recent times. The feline community has managed damage control so far, but given modern methods of communication, there will come a time when the community can't conceal the truth. We need to plan for that so we can limit the damage."

"Ah, lass. You're intending to make us work hard," Sid said. There was a distinct twinkle in his green eyes.

Ben took a sip of his tea and pulled a face. "Cold tea. Hate cold tea." He set his cup in the saucer. "Girl has a point."

"I discussed this with Jacey Anderson not long ago," Saber said. "All we need is a video to go viral and we're in big trouble."

"We had a discussion the other night with Jacey and Megan," London said. "Megan suggested that we run a type of simulation, a bit like a civil defense dry run. It was also proposed that several families adopt big dogs that might look like a cat or a wolf at a brief glance. Henry has a way with dogs. He could train them easily enough."

"And if that doesn't work?" Valerie asked.

"We have a plan to deal with the damage," Saber said. "Depending on the circumstances, we deny or we come out and tell the world we're shifters. If we went with that option it would be best for other groups across the world to come out to the public too."

"It would also pay to have several shifters in high positions. Judges, members of parliament, business people, police and the like," London said. "We would need to be able to show the general public we are just like them and capable of being productive citizens."

Saber grinned. "Lucky for us, our prime minister is a vampire."

London spluttered. "But...but I've seen him out at events during the day."

"Really?" Valerie asked. "I didn't know that. No wonder he's so pale."

"But he goes out in the sunshine. I've seen photos of him in Hawaii, playing golf with the American president." London gaped at Saber. "You're pulling our legs."

"Nope." Saber leaned back in his chair. "Some of them have some sort of ring that allows them to walk during the day. As long as they wear the ring, which contains stones from a sacred rock, they can go out in the sunlight."

"He eats food. Drinks wine."

"You can't believe everything you see or hear," Saber

said.

London exhaled. "Obviously not."

"All in favor of London's suggestion for a damage control plan?" Saber prompted.

"Yes," Valerie said.

Agnes nodded.

"I agree," Ben said.

Aye," Sid declared.

"We'll move ahead then." Saber glanced at his watch. "Anything else?"

"No," London said. "I'd better go soon. I have an online party to organize."

"We'd better meet next week," Sid said. "Organize exactly what we're going to say at the shifter meeting."

London stood. "Let me know what time."

"We'll walk you out," Sid said.

Chairs scraped the floor as everyone moved. Plates and crockery clattered, and there was a general exodus.

London climbed into her car. Sid rapped on her window and she opened it. The oldies gathered around, all beaming at her.

"Good job, lass," Sid said.

Valerie reached through the window and squeezed her shoulder. "Well done."

"What did I do?"

Agnes made a scoffing sound. "Don't play innocent, miss."

Ben's eyes glittered with approval. "You jerked Saber out of his funk. You made him aware of a danger to Emily. You've given him enough to keep his mind busy, given him

267

a purpose. The boy has been drifting as much as Emily."

Sid sighed. "Yes, now all we have to do is work on Emily."

"Um, I might have demanded her presence at the café," London confessed.

"Perfect." Valerie inclined her head in approval.

"You're a good lass," Sid said. "Those felines who say otherwise need their heads seeing to."

Five minutes later, London drove toward town, a sense of satisfaction filling her. That hadn't been so bad. Jenny would have been proud of her. Since meeting Gerard she'd grown as a person. The council members valued her. Gerard loved her, and she had lots of friends who sought her company.

It was a good day, and she couldn't wait to report back to Gerard.

WOULD YOU LIKE TO read more books set in the *Middlemarch Shifters* world? Sign up for my (www.shelleymunro.com/newsletter) to learn about the upcoming additions to this series. What is up with Emily Mitchell? **My Blue Lady** is next and offers all the answers.

Shelley

ABOUT AUTHOR

USA Today bestselling author Shelley Munro lives in Auckland, the City of Sails, with her husband and a cheeky Jack Russell/mystery breed dog.

Typical New Zealanders, Shelley and her husband left home for their big OE soon after they married (translation of New Zealand speak - big overseas experience). A twelve-month-long adventure lengthened to six years of roaming the world. Enduring memories include being almost sat on by a mountain gorilla in Rwanda, lazing on white sandy beaches in India, whale watching in Alaska, searching for leprechauns in Ireland, and dealing with ghosts in an English pub.

While travel is still a big attraction, these days Shelley is most likely found in front of her computer following another love - that of writing stories of contemporary and paranormal romance and adventure. Other interests include watching rugby (strictly for research purposes), cycling, playing croquet and the ukelele, and curling up with an enjoyable book.

Visit Shelley at her Website
www.shelleymunro.com

Join Shelley's Newsletter
www.shelleymunro.com/newsletter

ALSO BY SHELLEY

Paranormal

Middlemarch Shifters
My Scarlet Woman
My Younger Lover
My Peeping Tom
My Assassin
My Estranged Lover
My Feline Protector
My Determined Suitor
My Cat Burglar
My Stray Cat
My Second Chance
My Plan B
My Cat Nap
My Romantic Tangle
My Blue Lady

271

My Twin Trouble
My Precious Gift

Middlemarch Gathering
My Highland Mate
My Highland Fling

Middlemarch Capture
Snared by Saber
Favored by Felix
Lost with Leo
Spellbound with Sly
Journey with Joe
Star-Crossed with Scarlett

Ingram Content Group UK Ltd.
Milton Keynes UK
UKHW011700130323
418485UK00004B/417

9 781991 063168